A Call From France

Published by ATLA (Europe)
IBAN 978 1475116656
IBAN (10) 1475116659

Cover illustration (Jasmina age 7) by CatherineBroughton.
All rights reserved.

A Call From France is a true story but for the sake of
diplomacy and for the protection of Debbie and the children,
some names of people and places have been changed. All
peripheral characters are fictitious, even though the events are
true, and any resemblance to person or persons is purely
coincidental.

A Call From France

A
CALL
FROM
FRANCE

based on a true story
by

Catherine Broughton

1

A Call From France

A Call From France

Other titles by the same author

French Sand
The Man With Green Fingers
Saying Nothing

A Call From France

About the author.

Catherine Broughton is British but was born in South Africa. Her father's work as a doctor of tropical disease took the family around the world for many years, to include all over Africa, the South Pacific, Spain and Switzerland. Catherine Broughton attended London University where she did a BA (Hons) degree in French, and she later did a History (Hons) degree with the OU. She has been married for thirty-five years and has three children and two grandchildren.

Catherine Broughton's childhood life of travel has given her a wanderlust that has never left her. She has travelled a great deal and her books reflect this. She now lives partly in Sussex, partly in France and partly in Belize.

A Call From France

A Call From France

For Euan, Debbie, Max, Bernie, Jasmina and
Mustafa,
with so much love.

A Call From France

A Call From France

A CALL FROM FRANCE

A Call From France

Debbie left her handbag on the table.

This was deliberate. *Grand'mere* sat in front of the fan, in her usual place by the kitchen window where she could watch the Paris suburb streets. She had removed the black scarf from her head and her grey hair rose in small wispy strands in the cool draught from the fan. Her forehead, where the scarf hid her face down as far as her eyes, and tightly up under her chin, was beaded in sweat and she turned her face to the rush of cool air.

She would not notice the handbag and, for now at any rate, the significance of it would be lost on her. It was almost the only thing Debbie owned. In it she had left one of Mustafa's dummies and Jasmina's wax crayons. There was also a small packet of tissues and a 20 centime coin. She had removed the four Euros, and they sat in her pocket, literally the only money she possessed. The handbag made a statement for her: "I'll be back soon".

She hitched Mustafa onto her hip and took Jasmina's hand.

"It is so hot," she said in French to Grand'mere, "I'd like to buy ice creams for the children ....?"

As she had hoped, the old lady reached over to a shelf at her side and pulled several coins out of a jar. Hesitating just a second, she then extracted a twenty Euro note.
"Get some coffee, *ma puce*," she replied in her habitual mix of Arabic and heavily-accented French, "and some fruit if it's not too much to carry."

Debbie tucked the money in to her pocket, aware of the cellotape around her middle making a faint scratchy sound as she did so. For a split second a small wave of regret passed through her. *Grand'mere* had always been kind to her. She looked at the wrinkled face and felt sad as she realized she would almost certainly never see it again.

"Leave *les enfants* with me if you like," now said the old lady, "it'll be quicker for you."

Debbie was ready for this.

"Oh, no – *merci* – they want to choose their own ice creams and I thought I'd take them to the swings for a while too."

This was a risk. Hussein didn't like her to go to the swings. *Grand'mere* could tell her no, to come straight back, but she didn't comment. Going to the swings gave her more time, at least half an hour more, before she was missed. Hussein and his father would not be back for several hours, though Fatima could arrive at any moment.

Trying to not rush, Debbie made her way down the concrete staircase out of the block of flats. The children's buggy lived in a lock-up in the entrance area. It was a dank corner at the foot of the stairs and always smelt of urine. She had already put a carrier bag of a few essentials in there – a couple of nappies, a change of clothes for the children – plausible things that nobody would question.

"*Allez, vite!*" she urged as the children scrambled in to place on the buggy. They were used to it. Jasmina got in first and hitched her legs right back, leaving just enough room for Mustafa to perch in front of her. She strapped them in quickly, sweat already pouring off her face, and set off at a brisk pace across the tarmac towards the road.

It was too early to smile. Far too early. If she got it wrong she would never see the children again.

Her route took her past the other council flats. Flies swarmed around the dustbins. She was tempted to glance back to see if *Grand'mere* was looking out of the window and, in case she was, Debbie forced herself to walk calmly, if briskly. She wanted to run. Everything in her screamed at her to run, but she knew she must not.

At the road she turned left towards the ice cream shop and the swings. She was pretty sure that *Grand'mere*, if she was watching, which she probably wasn't, would not be able to see this point in the road, but she couldn't take any chances. Fifty metres later she crossed over and took the first right and then right again, bringing her back on to the main road further up. Then she ran. Pushing the buggy in front of her, the children squealing in delight, she tried to pretend it was a game and to look like a carefree mum taking the kids for a ride. It was very hot, devastatingly hot, and the heat seeped up off the pavement and off the walls around her. She crossed the road at the traffic lights and then went down in to the underground pass and up the other side. She ran when she could, walked as quickly as she was able, and the children, totally unaware of what was happening to them, sat in contented silence as the streets of Paris unfolded around them. Sometimes they looked up at their mother and she grinned at them, but mostly they clung laughingly on to the sides of the buggy as Debbie headed for the better part of the city.

At the roundabout she hailed a taxi. She glanced nervously about as she got the children and the buggy in. She was already two or three miles from the flats, the furthest she'd been in almost three years. Nobody knew her in this part of town.

"Hotel Bois d'Amour," she told the driver.

17

"*B:en, Madame.*"

Fighting back a sudden panicky weepiness, Debbie permitted herself a small smile. She settled herself and the children on to the seat and sat back before she reached under her T-shirt, pulled at the cellotape and retrieved the passports.

***

South-west France, ten years earlier.

She was such a skinny little thing.

A bag of bones. All legs, pale skin, several freckles, big smile with teeth that looked as though they might grow goofy one day, strong little hands that would one day be elegant. Pretty blue eyes, a delightful way of tossing her hair as she spoke, a little laugh like a quiet gurgle. She was so thin that one of my brothers, a doctor, commented on it. We were at my parents' house in Somerset – it must have been just before we moved to France – and Hugh, my brother, was there ... she had got a hacking cough and he listened to her chest. Her rib

18

bones stuck out like in those pictures you see of third world children. Hugh's brow was creased in his concern that I should understand he was not criticising my ability to raise and feed my child.

"She's dreadfully thin," he said. That was all.

"She eats," I replied, grinning at him, "she eats a lot … she's just the skinny type."

When she was born I remember sitting on the bed – the pain killers distorted everything and I felt as though I was sitting at the foot of the bed – holding her, my tiny baby. I was frightened of dropping her. I had had a baby! I marvelled at her, little eyes shut tight, angry red marks where the forceps had dragged her … and her thumbs … her thumbs were just like mine, mini versions of mine. I was twenty-eight.

She had a ready wit, even when very little. She was sociable, laughed, joined in. She was quick-off-the-mark, alert. She remembered things. You didn't have to tell her twice. She was not brilliant at school, but not bad either. She held her own. She was cheerful, adaptable, energetic, willing, funny.

A Call From France

She was nine when we moved to France. Max was seven. Bernie was a baby.

We did things *en famille*, all five of us, and by the time we were living at Tulips, and she was eleven or twelve, Debbie could ski and ride, play the flute and sail, she was keen on tap-dancing, she had tried yoga and karate, she had travelled a fair bit, she was totally bi-lingual, she was brilliant at card games and card tricks and took part in the building and re-building of our home and our lives. Both needed plenty of re-building.

We cycled regularly in those days, usually on the Ile de Re near La Rochelle, and I can still picture her so clearly, long brown leggies going round and round, wearing her "fishy" shorts – navy with pictures of fish, a top to match, long auburn hair tangled in the wind, back straight, skinny arms forward on the handle bars, invariably calling something out to me. Her pale blue eyes would gleam with delight.

"Mummy! Look! Somewhere for a gin for you and ice-cream for us!"

A Call From France

They were special times, those week-ends on the Ile de Re. We were perfectly happy to sleep in our two little tents. People used to stare at us in disbelief. Surely those rich (I mean, they are rich, aren't they?) English people don't sleep in those little tents when they go away ? From a chateau to a tent. We loved it. The stress of life was left behind in the office while we biked along the *pistes cyclistes*, Bernie bundled into a kiddy seat behind Euan, Max , Debbie and me.

It never dawned on me that things would change so radically.

As soon as you get on to the Ile de Re, over that magnificent bridge by La Rochelle, you feel you are Somewhere Else. Abroad. The whole atmosphere changes. The smell of pine forests fills the air, the sound of birds, the huge presence of the sea. Ancient fortifications contemplate with silent majesty the mighty waters of the Atlantic. Biking along in the latticed shade of the trees there was a sensation of holiday, of well-being, of freedom, of huge pleasure .... as soon as we were over that bridge.

We haven't been there for a long time now. We could go, of course, but it doesn't seem worth while any more. We talk about it from time to time but there is too much water under too many bridges.

Tulips was a beautiful house, seven bedrooms, four bathrooms, pool, five acres of land. It was in the middle of nowhere. We paid 350,000ff (about £37,000 at that time) plus £10,000 for work on it and slogged our guts out restoring it. We both had an eye for that kind of thing and the babes seem to have inherited it.

Set at the top of a hill, Tulips was like a beacon in our minds eye. It was a point, a statue. We thought it symbolized something. Or was that only me ?
Of course, it wasn't really called Tulips. It's real name was *Manoir de la Meteraie*. Tulips was our special name for it and we never used it with anybody else, though Gran refers to it as Tulips, of course. I don't know why we named it so … perhaps there were tulips despite the snow, or was it a memory of a boat my father had had when I was a child and which was called Tulips?

22

A Call From France

When we left, four years later, an English woman who happened to be staying nearby said to me

"How can you bear to leave this idyllic place?"

"It's only idyllic if you're on holiday," I said.   I smiled at her as she sat drinking in the sunshine, eyes closed against the light. The peaceful countryside unfolded around her. Sometimes, depending on the light, the view gave the impression of an unreal world, bounded only by the horizon and the season.

"I'd love it," she said, "you don't know when you're well off my dear!"

"I've been very lonely here," I replied, "it is beautiful, but isolated."

She remained sitting on the grass, her big orange and yellow towel spread out underneath her and a half-empty bottle of coke at her side.

I wanted to tell her, but I said nothing.

A Call From France

You could see for miles in all directions, out over the silent landscape, the small trees, a red-roofed hamlet dotted here and there, the brown fields, almost as far as the sea. During late summer there was the distant hum of combine harvesters and tractors and we could see them, like insects on the landscape, droning back and forth. At night we could just pick out a light flashing on and off, far far away, and reckoned it was the lighthouse at Fouras, though we never investigated it. If you watched closely you could see a car go by, trundling along the road hidden behind the bushes, there at the bottom of the hill. In winter the scene was brown and grey, echoed in the brown and grey sky. Nothing moved. Sometimes it was frozen in its immobility. Then as spring came it turned a vibrant green. You could almost touch it. The yellow-green of spring filled the view and brought with it the sound of birds and new life and things on the move. By the end of summer everything had scorched brown, and the world became brittle and the heat was like a bedspread, layered over us, hanging there in the air. Then the view became orange-brown as autumn moved in. A slight wind would get up from the east, bringing the change in colour with it, inexorably, a little more each day, till

24

the silent oranges and browns had gone and the brown and grey was back again. I watched this silent scene slowly changing colour, like giant chameleon, four times round. Four years.

The sounds changed with it too. In winter the sound of the wind.

I stood by the back door and let my coat fly open as the cold dampness of the wind whipped in through my clothes and undid my plaited hair. I held my face up in to the wind and closed my eyes and stretched my arms out as if to embrace it.

"Wuthering Heights, eat your heart out!" I cried.

Then in spring the fluttering of the birds, zipping back and forth carrying twigs. The sound of the wind thinned. After that came the sound of cicadas all summer and frogs down in the pond and – most of all – the sss-ssss-ssss-ssss of the sprinkler systems belonging to the farms all around us. I rocked myself to sleep to the sound of the sprinklers.

A Call From France

To the east of us was the little town of Tonnay Boutonne with a handful of small shops, the inevitable stone church, a couple of doctors and a dentist and of course la Mairie. It also boasted a pretty river, the Boutonne, and a medieval arch.

"Ganelon," I told Debbie, "was the bad guy in the story of Roland and Charlemagne. He was a traitor. He was lord of Tonnay Boutonne and legend has it that his body is buried somewhere under that arch."

I had told her the story of Roland once. I was fond of telling her True Stories and she was fond of listening. Watching my face with those pale eyes, she was always interested. Girls are. Boys prefer anecdotes about ships and planes and tractors. Well, computer games these days.

"Apparently," I went on, " the ghost of Ganelon's lover haunts the archway to this day."

Her blue eyes looked up at the foreboding grey stone. I nudged her.

"But it's not a ghost," I told her, "it's me in my best nightie!"

"Oh, mummy!"

"It is called Tonnay Boutonne," I told her, "because the English used to live here. The area was called Aquitaine. It was united with England, so to speak. Tonnay Boutonne ... town on the Boutonne .... Do you see?"

"Yes, I see..." she said. Then, after a bit of reflection:

"Why was it part of England?"

"Because a great lady called Eleanor of Aquitaine married a king of England – Henry – and so all her land became part of England and vice-versa ... well, in a nutshell."

"In olden days?"

"Yes, hundreds of years ago."

Immediately to our west was the hamlet of Touvent, not pretty, not even a bit. The dogs barked menacingly at us and the people ignored us except when they burgled our house. They were small folk, true backwater French peasant stock in the good old-fashioned sense. They lived in a row of squat stone houses, perhaps ten of them, terraced, with fields full of stinging nettles to the back and yards full of chickens and dogs to the front. Both back and front of the buildings were adorned with grey shutters, the paint well peeled off, and invariably closed. We abandoned any attempt, despite valiant efforts, at friendliness within the first month of our arrival. Touvent means "all wind" and when that wind blew up off the Atlantic in the winter months and I understood why the place was named so, I wondered what had possessed us to buy Tulips. Sometimes the wind was so fierce I could barely open and close the back door. The rotating washing line, bought in England for just that spot, lasted only a few weeks that first winter, battered beyond recognition in the gales. It groaned like a dying animal, flailed about in its death-throes. But in

summer I can remember it being so hot, standing there by the back door fumbling with my keys , the

28

sun beating down onto my neck and head, that I had to go round to the side of the house to find the right key in the shade. Then in the heat, my fingers sweaty and swollen, trying to dig out the right key, it was difficult to recall how cold it could be in the winter.

The south-western side of the house faced the garden, an expanse of lawn some half acre or so (big by English standards) that fell away, after the pool, fairly sharply into the field. We had plans and dreams for that field – a waterfall, a tree-lined avenue, a thousand million wild flowers, a sweeping drive with big solid gates down in the valley … but of course it all came to nothing. We kept it simple. We had neither the time, the energy, or even the will to do anything other than lawn. The stoep was also on that side, facing directly south over the orchard. Euan laid the "cobbles" himself, faked ingeniously out of concrete, and we all put our footprints in the wet grey surface, here and there, his first, size twelve, then me, then Debbie, then Max who was about ten, and then little Bernie , three years old. I suppose those footprints are still there, being walked over by other feet. Perhaps somebody – another mother – looks down at them and wonders whose children they were and where they are now. Do other mothers wonder about other people's children?

We had our barbeques – or "bri" we called them, after my South African childhood word *bra'vlees* literally "burnt meat" – out there on those cobbles, wind and mosquitoes permitting. We built the barbeque out of huge sandy-coloured stones found there on the property, and we set other stones like "seats" around one side of it. It looked like a miniature Stone Henge.

We never picked the fruit from the orchard. Alain and Sylvaine were horrified. I never picked the fruit at Les Cypres either, except from the cherry tree that first brilliant summer when the tree was laden with fruit, before the big storm that brought it down.

"Whyever not?" Sylvaine exclaimed. "Good, fresh, un-polluted fruit from your own land!"

"Humph!"

"Full of vitamins. Full of goodness!"

I buy my fruit in jars and packets, I told her, tongue-in-cheek. I've done all that, I said, the picking fruit bit, the making jam and chutneys (she didn't understand about chutneys). I did that in our last house but three. I'm not doing it any more. I've even made apple wine, I told her. She didn't understand apple wine either – do you mean cider? she asked.

All the heart had gone out of things at that time. Picking fruit was something I couldn't be bothered with.

"You don't have time," my mother told me, emphasizing the word "time". You always have time for the things you want to do, I sighed. I just don't want to. I've done all that. It's all lost, gone, finished.

To the east of Tulips lay the farm rented by the Michaux family. Jean-Pierre Michaux, and his father before him, (and doubtless – he thought - his sons to come) rented the flat grey-brown farmhouse on the eastern slope and farmed the hectare upon hectare of land all around. Mostly maize. He bred geese for *foie gras* and you could often, even at that distance, hear them sqwalking and screeching under the corrugated roofs of the barns and sheds. The poor creatures are force-fed with fat-enducing food literally shoved in to their throats with (in this case) a stick. I have never eaten *foie gras* again.

Many of the barns and sheds were tagged on to the house itself, so that at a distance you couldn't tell which was which. There were hundreds of metres of crumbling wall where hollyhocks grew wild in with the brambles and in the yard a couple of ducks wandered about pecking at the earth.
Indoors the house had not altered since their wedding twenty-five years earlier and sported the same plastic tablecloth where you could see bright patterns had once been, and the same 1960s furniture and the same green wellies by the door.
Jean-Pierre loved the land and loved everything that surrounded him. Severine, for a while a play-mate of Debbie's, became a bank clerk. One of the sons joined the army and the other became a waiter. He stopped off to say hello at Les Cypres one day, years later, and he had gone bald and the Michaux farm was the last place he wanted to be.

A Call From France

It's all a long time ago now. Tulips has been bought and sold twice since, I understand, and the palm tree Euan planted for my fortieth birthday in the courtyard is now taller than the wall, and the hefty front gates he built were torn away the year of the big storm, and the shutters have been re-painted blue.

Oddly enough the day we viewed Tulips there was a thick and spongey white layer of snow. It was the first snow in the Charente Maritime for eighteen years and the local people stared at it in amazement. Many had never seen snow except in pictures.

"Of course you're used to this in Angleterre, aren't you?" said the post man.

"No, not really …" I corrected him, "we don't get a lot of snow."

The silent and stiff black branches bowed low under the weight and the house looked like a scene from a fairy-tale, crisp and ethereal in the motionless day. The eastern turret was shrouded in darkness, the oak trees forming a snow-layered blanket of shadow and, to the west, the grey-bright light of the clouded sun broke weakly through the January sky. Even the birds had died. The stillness was total. We stood, feeling the heat of the car engine behind us, shocked and quietened in our hearts, and we looked up at the lonely hugeness of the abandoned building and felt the finality of death and the excitement of birth.

"What d'you think?" my words made puffy white clouds in the air in front of me.

"Well," Euan almost whispered, " I'll have to take a closer look".

We had collected the key from Michaux "next door". He had half-heartedly offered to accompany us.

"*Non, non,*" we told him, smiling, waving, "*c'est bon, nous irons seuls merci* ..." instinctively knowing we should be alone for this.

The keys opened first of all the big iron front gates into the walled courtyard where we were to later – two years later –plant my palm tree. The courtyard was square and about 80 square metres in size, two sides flanked by stone out-buildings, the third with the front façade of the house and the southern wall, where the entrance was, with a high parapet and a couple of stone lions. Double shutters opened to a glazed front door and thence into a narrow passageway, tiled in beautiful Art Nouveau fleur-de-lys. A glance at the wallpaper told me that it had last been re-decorated in the 1930s. To the right a long narrow living room, thick with cobwebs and mouse droppings, led through to a small library. A few books still sat dustily on the shelves and a broken ladder, like a testament to the last reader, was propped against the wall. Here the loo from a room above had fallen through the rotted floorboards and lay, smashed into three neat pieces, on the library floor.

"Well," Euan laughed, "we're lucky there's a loo at all!"

We had seen many houses where there were no sanitary arrangements. Odd, that. France was very late in sorting out it's loos. Yet, once sorted out, I mean having twigged that a loo is a good idea, France and the French seemed to recover and swung into action – and suddenly sanitation was up to standard, water was drinkable, computers arrived, streets got cleaned up and the country entered the twentieth – not to mention the twenty-first – century. It overtook England in no time. Not even two years earlier, when we had arrived in France, supermarkets stocked no cereals at all, and the most mediocre selection of anything else. That all changed mercifully rapidly.

Beyond the library another door led in to a huge bedroom, with further Art Nouveau tiles on the floor We were to later to knock through the end wall into the bread oven, till then accessed from the courtyard, to create a kitchenette and bathroom. You'd be surprised how big a bread oven is. This became our guest suite. Double doors led out into the eastern side of the garden where the oak trees were. The flies were continual.. They never ever went away. But we were not to know that then.

On the other side of the narrow hall way there was the kitchen, little more than an old enamel sink and some grease-encrusted curtains over windows that looked out onto the courtyard. Beyond that was a small dining room. The barn on the other side of that part of the house soon became the kitchen extension and the office, utility room and another WC.

I have a wonderful photo of Debbie on her birthday, standing in the rubble in that part of the house, grinning into the camera, paper hat on her head. She leans forwards, hands on knees, alert and enthused. I can still hear her laughter. They always had a party, the babes, no matter where we were or how simple it was. I've been trying to work it out. She'd have been ... twelve, I think.

The staircase was small and narrow considering the size of the house. Seven bedrooms in varying states of abandon, and one derelict bathroom, led off two landings, one above the other. That roof never stopped leaking. It never ever got properly repaired despite vast efforts. Euan said it was because there were just so many pitches at so many different angles that unless we stripped the roof totally and started again, we would never get it watertight. We had no money, so there was no question of it. In the winter that place leaked like a sieve.

A Call From France

Diary entry. Bernie woke me early, clambered with frozen feet into bed with us. Little darling. Snuggled up and zozzed for an hour or so. I hated rushing him to get him ready for Maternelle. Visited a house.. The vendor – he used to be a tennis champion, apparently – a Mr Challumeau – you wouldn't think it to see him now – wants too much. I told him 280 000f was the most he could ask. Afternoon faxing and photocopying, always so much to deal with. The boys seemed so happy to see me after school, & Debbie happy to hop off the school bus. How lucky that it stops right outside the house! Euan has got the contract to do up the Wagstaff property. Spent last evening repairing clothes and altering things, some typing, lots of faxing. I try to fax after ten when its cheaper. Spoke to mummy and daddy on the phone. Seem well. Pleased with the way the house is shaping up and looking forward to showing it off.

***

We moved to France in 1989 at the time of the first big financial slump. It was a traumatic time. I didn't want to leave my lovely house in Sussex or wrench the babes out of school. But we had little choice. The recession had hit us in the back of the knees and we were all but crawling. Had we stuck it out would things have been different? Would Debbie have been all right ? Had we stayed in the middle-class comfort of a Sussex town, would she have met different people or had different values or made different friends?

Like so many of the people we were to later sell property to, we chose a house that was far too big for us and far too expensive. It just seemed such a brilliant deal at that time. It was called the Chateau Marcons, near Bourges in the centre of France. We stayed there barely ten months, realizing too late that we had made a dreadful mistake. What a desolate place! It seemed to us we had hit the Dark Ages. There was nothing, there was nobody, the shops were poorly stocked, the banks and chemists hopelessly out-of-date, the pavements broken, the school children still wrote on slates. Seriously, the school children wrote on slates. I tried to join in and attended a keep fit class with a couple of other mothers, but I truly cannot say that they tried to make me welcome. There was nothing. The pretty countryside soon turned in to a wet blotter of mud. With a miserable sensation of failure and

A Call From France

foolhardiness we admitted it was the back of
beyond of where we needed to be. It was only
because we had an unusual and frenetic energy that
we were able to sell on and move to the Charente
Maritime.

Was that where the rot set in? Max told me years
later that he used to lie in his bed at Marcons facing
what he hoped was England and long and long to go
home. Both he and Debbie started bed-wetting,
Max would walk and talk in his sleep. They were
unhappy and lost. We read them stories and let
them sleep in with us. Debbie was nine, Max
seven. Bernie was just a baby.

A teacher by trade I had naively thought that I
would simply get a teaching position, never
imagining the acres of bureaucracy you must go
through first. It seemed that what qualified me to
teach in the UK was not valid in France.

"*Ce n'est pas conforme*" I was told.

Setting up my little estate agency happened really
by accident. I kind of fell in to it. I was
immediately stunningly successful. I don't know

why. I had an enthusiasm born of ignorance, I was (though I didn't realize it then) beautiful, people liked me, and through sheer brash determination I convinced vendors I could sell their houses and I sold them to the British. I worked hard, really hard.

From there we moved – I've heard people say that moving house is one of the biggest worries you ever go through but to me it is old hat – to a seventeenth century house in a village called Breuil-Magne. Now why did we choose that place ? I have never been so cold in my life. That was the winter of the snow, when we viewed Tulips. There was no heating in Breuil-Magne and we had so little money that Euan sawed up bits of the innards of the barn for firewood. We stayed there eight months. Once again our inordinate energy enabled us to sell up and move on.

It was not easy to sell a house in France. Well, in the pits of that recession it wasn't easy to sell a house in England either. Property didn't have the same status symbol for the Frenchman as it had for his British counterpart. The French were quite happy to rent – that has changed over recent years.

41

It was quite common for a French house to remain on the market for several years. That was why they were so cheap, of course. The properties out in the countryside, where the French didn't want to live (that has also changed in recent years) could be stunningly cheap in those days. I once sold a little run-down farmhouse with a couple of barns and a couple of acres for just under £7,000 – that was in about 1990.

We spotted that hole in the market and filled it.

"Is there any reason I shouldn't be an estate agent?" I asked a friend who was a *notaire*.

"No, no reason at all," he replied.

Euan in turn set up a small building firm. I sold the houses: he got the renovation work.

Debbie was quick to learn French. Girls are quicker, I think. She was a friendly, chatty child, happy to join in all activities. She always had lots of friends. Max took nearly a year to become fluent. My motherly concern centered on him for he seemed so unhappy. He became violent and aggressive and, all of seven years old, would rip up his toys and throw them out of the window. We waited. We cuddled him a lot.

"Would you like to do karate?" we asked him, "there's karate down at the *Salle des Fetes*. How about that?"

"No, no I don't like karate."

"Goodness sweetheart – you've never done it! How can you say you don't like it? Why don't you try it? It'll be fun. You get a special outfit."

Reluctantly he went along with Debbie who also did ballet. Tall and skinny she had the grace of a giraffe! She wore a pink shiney leotard, white tights, pink shoes. She was totally beautiful. Her long curly hair cascaded down her back
and she had an adorable little expression of concentration as she danced. She was never any good at it, but all little girls need to do ballet.

Diary entry. Last night I dreamt about Hill Cottage. I dreamt we were all home again. I dreamt about the garden and the babes' bedrooms,

43

that Bernie was asleep in his cot and there were those yellow chickies on the wallpaper. In my dream some of the things had changed – the furniture was different and the arrangement of the rooms, but it was still Home and we were happy to be there.

When I'm trying to go to sleep at night I sort-of rock myself in my thoughts: I pretend I'm on the stoep at Hill Cottage, lying on a sun-lounger, wrapped in a blanket, and the apple and plum trees are there, and the rock garden I worked on, and the sound of English birds.

The school nearest to Tulips was two or three miles away in a place called Moragne.

The school consisted of three one-storey buildings, one of which was a pre-fab, set squarely around a tarmac playground. At one end were a few smelly hole-in-the-ground loos. There were perhaps 200 children at the most, ranging from the three year-olds in the *Maternelle*, to eleven year olds. Learning by rote was the thing, though Max never learnt anything at all, set drawings where you followed squares and coloured the colours indicated, no assembly or singing or music of any

44

kind and certainly nothing so avant-garde as drama or dance. In the school's defence I have to add that Max totally REFUSED to learn anything. Over a year went by before I realized that he was kept in detention every break time because he hadn't done any work. A whole year of detentions! Apparently he sat silently and sullenly at his desk, stalwartly refusing to write anything down at all.

"I thought it was a good idea," he told me years later, "I thought it was getting me out of work."

In the foreground of the playground was a sandpit where the little ones played at break time and whenever I drove past I would slow down in case I could see Bernie . Sometimes he would see me and we would wave to each other.

I was always there to meet my boys at the end of school. They were always so thrilled to see me. No matter who the client was or how exhausted I was I always met them from school and hugged them tight with a horrible awareness of how time flies, never to be had again.

That was one of the loneliest patches of my time in France, standing there outside the school waiting for the bell to go and no longer bothering to try to make conversation with the other mothers. They had no conversation for an English woman, least of all one who had bought and restored the famous old *manoir* at Touvent. Not that they were unkind – they weren't – they just had no need to make any kind of contact with me, were probably in awe of me, had known each other all their lives and my English input in to their village was completely irrelevant.

One morning I spotted a mother who I happened to know was a nurse at Rochefort hospital.

"*Bonjour!*" I called cheerfully, and shook her hand as one does.

Unlike most local women who, winter or shine, were invariably in carpet slippers and had nylon overalls over copious bellies, this woman was fairly well dressed and wore a short skirt showing shapely legs, fashionable shoes, a colourful T-shirt with "do you wanna dance?" written over it.

"*Bonjour Madame,*" she replied.

"Do you remember me?" I asked her, "we met at the hospital when my daughter was poorly?"

"Oh yes, I remember you, Madame," she replied formally. Then:

"Is your daughter better?"

"Oh – yes, thanks."

There was a moment of silence as she seemed to be about to speak to somebody else.

"My name is Catherine," I ventured, "and you?"

"I am Madame Dumas," she said.

Undaunted I smiled encouragingly and tried to chat about the children and the school. She had a boy the same age as Max. She worked three days a week.
She was not working that day but was going to the big market in Rochefort.

"Ah!" I exclaimed, "well, listen. I'm off to the market too. Why don't we go along together?"

"What for?" she asked, genuinely surprised.

"Well ... we could have a coffee ..."

"Coffee ...? Oh no, I've had my coffee."

I tried again.

"I always think it's more fun ..." but gave up.

I knew enough about the local people that she almost certainly meant no harm. I tried just once more.

"You see, I don't know anybody ..."

But now she did turn away to somebody else, greeting her by her Christian name and exchanging a flurry of little kisses. I realized she had had no intention of being rude, and I smiled broadly at the third party and said *bonjour* politely, but
I never spoke to the nurse again. Like a child who has been refused a toy I turned suddenly away from

her, fighting to hold back the tears. She must have wondered what she had said wrong, if she wondered anything at all. But I always ignored her after that.

I cried when I got home.

"What's up, mummy?" Debbie encircled me with her skinny little arms.

Over the years I have learnt that French women do not seem to have the same "chumminess" or the same "sisterhood" one finds among British women and, although I have a great many French friends, my close friends are, without exception, foreigners like me. Not necessarily British foreigners, but any girlfriend I might phone to accompany me to, say, the cinema or a shopping spree will invariably non-French, even if we nonetheless speak to each other only in French.

Debbie went to school in Tonnay Boutonne. This was an altogether bigger school, the equivalent of what we at that time called a comprehensive at that time. At first the school bus picked her up in the mornings and deposited her at about six in the evenings, having gone all round the dozens of little hamlets in the area. She was shattered when she got in, so after that first term I took to picking her up from school myself along with a child called Marie whose mother dropped both girls off in the morning. Debbie had lots of friends and, although she certainly didn't shine at school, she did all right. I attended parents' evening only once.

"Deborah's marks for this term are as follows," the bespectacled teacher read from the sheet in front of him, "Maths: 6 out of 10, 7 out of 10, 3 out of 10, 8 out of 10, 7 out of 10. For Geography: 6 out of 10, 4 out of 10, 8 out of 10 …"

"*Monsieur*," I interrupted, "thank you very much indeed, but I can read these marks for myself. I wanted to discuss Deborah's progress"

"*Mais oui!*" he exclaimed, surprised, "that is what this is! Her progress! History: 6 out of 10, 5 out of 10, 9 out of 10 …"

I stared at him in disbelief.

"Is he making fun of me?" I asked in English of Debbie who was leaning against my chair at my side.

"No ... of course not!" she replied.

I looked at the man closely, thinking perhaps I was missing an important point. He stared intently at the page in front of him, running his fingers down the columns to one side. Occasionally he pushed his spectacles further up the bridge of his nose. He wore dark red trousers and an open-necked shirt of a similar colour.

"Art, 7 out of ten, 8 out of ten, 6 out of ten, 7 out of ten. Biology: 2 out of ten, 6 out of ten ..."

"*Monsieur, excusez-moi,*" I tried again, "I was hoping to have a discussion with you ....?"

"*Mais oui!*" he exclaimed again, smiling broadly, "religious studies 4 out of 10, 8 out of 10, 6 out of 10 …………..

"*Monsieur,*" I insisted, hand flutteringly over my upper chest, "could we have a talk ? I want to talk about my daughter ...."

He looked seriously confused. He stared at me for a few moments, his finger still pointing to the spot he had reached on the marking forms, then looked down and continued ...... *Orthographe* 8 out of 10, 10 out of 10, 9 out of 10 ....

"Come on Debs, " I stood up and took my child's hand, "we're out of here."

"But mummy, wait! He's still talking to you!"

"No, he's not, he's reciting your marks."

"*Madame* ..." the teacher began surprised out of his recital by the sound of my chair scraping the floor.

"*Au revoir monsieur*," I said, hoping that the stinging tone of voice would put my message across. Debbie grabbed my hand.

"My other teachers want to see you ..."

"Well, they won't."

Debbie tripped along beside me, trotting to keep up as I strode out to the car. She tugged at my hand.

"I think you should stay," she insisted, "it's not finished."

"It is finished for us," I told her firmly. I turned and looked at her. "You won't get in to trouble if that's what is worrying you."

"No … it just seems rude …"

"Well, I suppose I am being rude," I said to her. A little strand of hair had escaped from her pony tail and I tucked this back behind her ear. She had naturally curly hair, very pretty. "We'll go to the supermarket instead."

<u>*Diary, ten years later.*</u>
Last night I dreamt about Debbie. I dreamt she was ill. Her legs were blue with bad circulation and she was thin and bruised. She didn't look like Debbie, totally different in fact, but I knew it was her. In the

dream somebody said to me "she is very ill" and I wanted to help her but she was rude and defiant. I said "you need me to help you" and then she let me. Then the dream ended. When I woke it was still dark and I got out of bed and stood for a long time by the window and watched the trees and the sky and the huge night all around me.

The supermarket was nearly half an hour's drive away, in Tonnay Charente, (town on the Charente – d'you see?) and it stayed open till fairly late; it was cheap and it was the nearest to us. I used it frequently in those early Tulips days. Every time I went I swore I would never go there again – and I have vowed this in many supermarkets in France – because the French, then as now, know nothing about customer service, and the till girl will to this day quite cheerfully stare at the ceiling rather than help with anything. If you ask for assistance from somebody stacking the shelves, they will perfectly happily flick their fingers in the general direction of the item you want, and will even turn their back on you as they do so. But in those days it was convenient and it sold – as supermarkets do – almost anything from food to envelopes to brooms and duvets.

Tonnay Charente has only one claim to fame and that is the impressive bridge over the river Charente, built in the 1700s. The river is wide and tidal for a long way, and ships in the old days would moor at Tonnay Charente and load there the barrels of cognac brought down river from Cognac, fifty miles away. The cognac trade carried on in this way for hundreds of years till after the Second World War. We went to visit Cognac, of course, and found the old chateau of Francois 1ier fascinating, but the rest of it is fascinating only is you're fascinated by cognac – which we're not. It was a fading town, however – that word described it well – it was fading. It has doubtless picked up since, as all of France has. Then, the cognac distilleries dominated everything and the grand houses had been split up in to offices and the rich had moved to Paris or Bordeaux. I remember the town centre only because of a man stark naked that evening, wandering with drunken hilarity round the *rue pietonne*, singing a song and half-heartedly keeping one hand over an extremely small and ineffective-looking penis.

Tonnay Charente straddles the river and is proud of its heritage as one of the main mooring places of the Charente. Every year the local people organize a great feast of sea food, a huge street party with fireworks and stalls which throng all along the embankment and between the shops. We went there from time to time ... I bought a couple of excellent side tables there, shaped to be elephants, for sale in a bric-a-brac stall in a market and worth I'm certain fifty times more than I paid for them. The nearest lab was there too for our analyses – the French love to have their urine analysed regularly and, under a French GP, we did not escape this treat.

Debbie was a brilliant help at the supermarket. From a very early age she would take one trolley and I another and we would set off at two different ends of the supermarket, grabbing the relevant produce off the shelves as quickly as we could before meeting again at the till. We never took more than fifteen minutes for a weekly shop and we virtually never got it wrong. She had a brilliant memory and plenty of sense, and I could leave her, even when she was only nine or ten, to fill her trolley with exactly the right things. Sometimes I would give her a list, sometimes I'd remind her of what to get.

"Tea bags – essential – milk – essential – red wine, Bordeaux, approx.25 francs – essential – apart from that it really doesn't matter."

And it didn't: I was not fussy. I didn't mind at all whether we ate pork or chicken for supper, whether the casserole had beans or carrots, which cereals, which shampoo. That was in the days before cook-in sauces had reached France, so preparing a meal for the five of us took a little more time than I wanted, but I nevertheless never fussed about the ingredients and if I couldn't prepare one meal I'd prepare another. Whatever. It was unimportant. We ate well, however, always with meat and always plenty of it. Euan ate huge quantities. Throughout our years in France he retained his preference for good old English bangers and mash, shepherd's pie, beef with Yorkshire pud – that sort of thing. I've often seen women in the supermarket carefully stacking their purchases in carrier bags, being certain to not put the washing powder next to the butter, but I was never like that and Debbie and I would hurl our items willy-nilly into bags, pay, and head for the car. At that time you put 10 francs into a slot to get the trolley, and this was Debbie's job except when Bernie was with us for all little children love to put coins in slots.

We were not rich, but we were not poor. I never carefully counted out what I was or was not spending, and all three children could always pick out biscuits or sweets or other goodies they wanted.

I read an article about spoilt children once. It said that if your child has whatever he or she wants but has nevertheless been able to retain the sense of fairness; if he or she can still think of others, be aware of cooperating and share his or her things in a cheerful and giving fashion, then he or she is not spoilt, no matter how much you give them. The word spoilt is mis-used. Spoilt means SPOILED like milk that has gone off. My children had not, I'm certain of it, "gone off" in any way, though they did have almost anything they wanted.

Poem written by Debbie, aged nine:
A chant that I am longer than the sea and bigger than the earth.

A Call From France

Je suis plus grande que la terre,
Et je suis plus longue que la mer.
C'est moi, Deborah,
Qui est la plus grande et la plus longue que la mer
et la terre.
Je suis plus grande que les arbres et les branches,
Haut, tres haut!
Et maintenant voici la fin de ma chanson.
En Anglais ... .
I am bigger than the sea
And longer than the earth.
It is me, Debbie, Debbie,
Who is the most longest and the biggest of the sea
and the earth.
Oh oh oh oh yes yes yes, it is me the most biggest on
the earth,
I am taller than the trees and the branches, high
high!

My working day varied enormously. Only people who run their own businesses really know what work is. If you are employed by somebody else, you go in to work, do whatever it is you have to do, then go home again. You get paid for it. It may be easy stuff or difficult stuff, but essentially you get paid for a specific job and it is up to you to do it properly.

People who run their own businesses have to create a situation, in our case out of thin air, out of which they can earn some money. Nobody said to us "do this and I will pay you for it". We had to cause ourselves to be paid. I, in the first instance, had to persuade my client (having got the client at all) to buy a house in France. Not just any house in France, but a house on my books. In order to get to this situation I first had to place advertisements in magazines and newspapers in the UK. This was long before the internet. I then had to answer the phone, the fax and the post several hundred times, enclosing details of five or six properties each time, in order to get one solitary client into my car. I worked out that for every 200 sets of details I posted, I got one client. Out of the clients who got as far as looking at properties with me, about one in every seven would buy.

Having got the client to agree to buy something – invariably an old *fermette* in need of repairs – I then had to get them to sign papers called a *Compromis de Vente*, which is a kind of promise to buy. At that stage I also had to persuade them to part with a cheque for 10% of the value of the property. This was sometimes done in the office of a *notaire*, but was also regularly done in my own little office at Tulips with the washing machine chugging away in the background , the smell of burnt toast and the sound of children playing. The cheque was always made out to the *notaire*. From that moment responsibility should have fallen off my shoulders and onto his, though it never really did, and it was his job to do a search while I kept the clients informed.

Of course, the clients always referred back to me, from sensible questions like the perimeter fences to silly questions about the height of the skirting boards. If something went wrong it was always my fault – even the weather seemed to be my domain – and people never wanted to pay for anything.

It was, however, a neat little business. My clients looked to me for sorting out utilities and insurances for their properties, and I was able to make a small charge which helped to swell my commission a little and – Lord knows – we needed every penny.

And before all this, of course, I had to find the property for sale, negotiate a sensible price with the vendor whereby he would get what he wanted and I would pick up a commission, take photos, type up details, photocopy them. The properties were all over the place, as much as an hour's drive away. As time wore on I learnt to not go further than half an hour in any one direction which gave me a good enough catchment area. Sometimes I would go to great lengths – taking Bernie to the child minder and making a detour into Tonnay Boutonne for another film for the camera, then drive off using up my precious petrol, only to find that the property was totally unsuitable for sale to the British. I rapidly learnt that the vendor's description over the phone was utterly meaningless.

My favourite *notaire*, Maitre Sarge, often kept me informed as to what was for sale. He was an invaluable help to me. He was a kind of dark brown person. Not the colour of his skin, but his personality ... unsmiling, deadly serious, infinitely careful, studious, sallow skin ... yet a consistent and unwavering ally for me who, over the years, saw me through several fraught events. Although he never spoke to me in English I gather he could speak it quite well. He certainly understood it well.

I very rarely advertised for properties for sale for the jungle drums worked a treat and word rapidly went round that I was the English agent who would work wonders and get the best price – as indeed I did.

It was a sharp, curt, cut-throat business. Not least of the stress was the bureaucracy for it seemed that whatever I was doing was *interdit* unless I had some piece of paper from some authority somewhere: yet nobody (the *notaire*, the accountant, the town hall) ever seemed to know which bit of paper, or where or how. We had to be very quick-off-the mark for competition from French estate agents was vicious, and so was the attitude of French building firms. We were intensely disliked by the local French and, although some British families made a happy move to France, the majority regretted their purchase within a year or two, blamed us, and disliked us too. It was a lonely job that I did alone. I grit my teeth, hardened my jaw-line, bit the bullet, just got on with it.

A Call From France

letter from Aggie:-
Catherine, la belle Catherine!
*That's French – you didn't know I could speak it
did you?   My dear, on a serious note, you sounded
frightfully depressed-o on the phone.   Don't be.
But they do say the French are not very friendly,
I've often heard it. The world is your oyster.   It is
certainly my oyster dear, so I'm sure it's yours too.
I miss you too.   Poor old ducky.   I think you are
stunningly STUNINGLY brave to do what you are
doing – most women wouldn't dare even try.   Jolly
good well done, it takes lots of initiative and
courage to run your own business.   Think about it!
In a FURRIN LANGUAGE apart from anything
else.   Be proud of yourself.   Don't let the bastards
who let you down get you down.*

*That is your advice from me, so you know it's jolly
good advice.   Grin into the mirror.   It's good for
you.   Toodle-oo.*
Yours friend,

Aggie   xxxxxxxxxxxxxxx   BUCKETS of kisses

I often took one of the children with me when I went out to view a property. I tried to take only the one child because it gave me a bit of one-to-one time with them. In the early years Bernie spent many an hour strapped in to his car seat next to clients; he had his nappies changed in barns and fields and sat on my hip around dozens of houses. He was my good luck mascot. As he reached school age I was able to see to clients without him, but tried to include Debbie and Max where I could. Many a lop-sided photo, taken by one of them, has been sent out to many a confused client. Perhaps that was where the success was. People nowadays don't realize how very much the internet has changed the life of people like the one I was then - digital cameras and sending things by e-mail has made life so much easier and cheaper. At that time photocopying and posting alone ate maddeningly in to my meagre budget, not to mention films for the camera, wasted photos posted to non-serious client.....

"This house is a traditional Charentais farmhouse," I told Debbie. "If you look at the roof you can see the red tiles – see? Well, apparently they are shaped on the thigh of a maiden."

"What's a maiden?"

"You're a maiden. A young girl. You're a lovely young maiden, like a precious jewel. See this front door? Well, traditionally the front door opened straight into the living room, but as local families started to learn about other families in other parts of France, they realized that smarter houses have an entrance hall. That is why there are these two doors. There isn't enough space to make a whole entrance hall, so the owners have put this tiny lobby ... with two doors ... see ? It makes like a weeny hallway. It made them feel more important."

"Humph!"

The owner showed us around, apologizing when he stepped ahead of us ...

"Excusez-moi, Madame, je passe devant vous ... "

Generally speaking the standard of accommodation was pretty low. A lot of the houses reminded me of childhood when Formica had just been discovered, and gloss paint and plastic tablecloths and gushy net curtains. Because most of the properties I sold were very cheap – the British loved a bargain – by necessity the standard of sanitation was regularly abysmal. If there was a WC at all it was invariably outside in a barn or a garage, and was frequently the hole-in-the ground type with a bucket to hand to that you could throw water in when you had finished. Almost everything was out-of-date, from the kitchen sink to the bright lozenges on the wall paper. *Toile tondue* was a cloth that was spread out of the walls in lieu of wallpaper, but not glued on to the walls as we did with our hessian wall coverings in the 1970s, but pinned on to batons that were themselves pinned to the wall, rather like batons ready for plasterboard. This was particularly common in the centre of France, but was still seen regularly in the Charentes. Another favourite was *lambris* which was a kind of tongue-and-groove wood panelling, positioned vertically on the lower half of the wall to hide (one assumed) a multitude of sins and, if the owner was especially in love with the system, the *lambris* would be not only over all the walls from ceiling to floor but over the ceiling too. Wallpaper likewise, often over the doors to boot.

Aspects of these properties were utterly charming, however, with huge copper pots hanging from beams, big circular earthenware bowls holding dried twigs and leaves of *tilleul*, huge old stone fireplaces and entire trees across the ceilings.

The more up-to-date properties of course varied, and the local people loved to boast a *cuisine Américaine* (a fitted kitchen) and fully tiled bathrooms and an indoor loo. The older properties could be quite magnificent with wonderful warm sandy-coloured cut stone and a left-over feeling of times of yore when life was good and some could prosper. There were no chateaux in the Loire Valley sense – or virtually none – but the Big House of the village was often called the chateau, as indeed was our own.

The countryside was generally flat, dotted with run-down little hamlets which contained huge dilapidated barns and small one-storey cottages by which sat old folk dressed in bright blue overalls and carpet slippers. Dogs barked furiously, making cycling on a Sunday – something we tried for a few months – a nightmare of avoiding irate animals, bicycle pedals and bitten ankles. Most of the dogs

68

were tied up and we never ascertained what they were kept for, though a fair few were for hunting.

Most of the local people had lived in the area all their lives and a terrifying percentage of them had lived in the same village since birth and regarded a trip in to the nearby town of Rochefort a rare treat. They had married local people and been married in the local church and would in due course be buried in the local cemetery. Even the professional people were mostly "Charentais", having never moved – or even studied – very far from home. As great travellers ourselves – Euan had spent three years in Australia and had travelled around a fair bit in the near east, and I had spent most of my childhood in Africa and the South Pacific, not to mention post-grad days in Spain and Morocco, we found this very local feel to everybody and everything really quite astonishing. One of the funnier aspects of it was that the more affluent people, who were able to afford a holiday house, would have their holiday house only a few miles away.

"I'll be away this week-end " Marc, an estate agent, told me, "we're going to my holiday house."

"Oooh, lovely!" I exclaimed, "where?" Pictures of Paris, Amsterdam, Madrid or even just Bordeaux flit through my mind.

"In Fouras," he told me, his expression completely bland.

This clearly was not right - I had misunderstood. Fouras was only a few miles away.

"Really? No, seriously, where are you going?"

In a moment of madness I allowed Tahiti to slip through the window of my mind, Prague, perhaps? California?

"Fouras," he repeated.

And it was. His holiday house – and we were to soon find that this is very common, is only a few miles from his normal house.

The Charentais people were friendly enough, though we never broke through the thick outer layer … and after a while didn't even try to. Why should we? The British in France have an astonishing vanity – I saw it over and again with the people I sold property to – in that they think that the locals are somehow honoured by their friendship ... which they may or may not be ... but they certainly don't need or seek that friendship in any way.

Typing-up details of the properties was a never-ending task. It was difficult to think of something different to say about each one, but it was essential to say as much as possible. The French have a dearth of information on their property details and everything seems to be based on the habitable surface area. Quick at writing, imaginative and literate, I dashed out details by the score, giving as much information as possible without being tedious and being as entertaining as possible without being silly.

La Charrue   265,000ff   (approx £28,000)
This charming old property, circa 1840, is situated at the edge of the village of Archingeay where there is .... not a lot. The inevitable Mairie is there, bien sur, and I'm told that if you peer hard through the dusky window of the place opposite the church, that is a bread shop, but there really is nothing else. The major town of Rochefort is barely twenty

71

minutes' drive, however, and of course there are all essential shops in Lussant, where you can buy most things providing you catch the shops while open ... which is not very often.

- *three big bedrooms, one with a fine marble fireplace, tall windows overlooking fields, floor boards in need of repairs in one room but the others seem OK-ish*

- *- another room which would be ideal as a bathroom, though it is under the eaves*

- *- wonderful living room with big traditional stone fireplace. Slightly over-enthusiastic wallpaper recently done in order to "modernize" and even more enthusiastic linoleum underfoot covering a very fine stone floor*

- *- utterly dreadful kitchen consisting of a stone sink (keep it as a curio) and masses of smelly drains; a big room however, just waiting for Somebody Clever*

- *a variety of barns in varying states of repair or disrepair*

- *- just over an acre of land, nice views, lots of stinging nettles*

Utterly shattered one evening, I asked Debbie to help me with the typing up of descriptions. She had been with me to view a house after school.

"Can you manage that?" I asked her.

"Oh yes, no problem," she said as she seated herself in front of the word processor.

I gave her one of my descriptions and my hastily-scribbled notes about the house we had seen.

"Just type the same as this," I told her, "but change things where you need to – for example, there was no fireplace in the kitchen, and there were two bedrooms, not three."

"All right, mummy," she said.

I watched for a moment as her slender little fingers flew rapidly over the keys. She was what the Scottish I believe call "canny"; all of eleven years old, she was full of confidence and in some ways was older than her years, the way the eldest child often is. I went into the kitchen and started preparing supper. Bernie sat at the table with his paints and had got paint all over his face, and I could hear Max going "broom-boooom-BROOOOOOOOM!" in the next room. For a while everything Max did was accompanied by the sound of a rocket taking off, but that day it was cars.

"I've finished!" called Debbie after a while.

I went in to look.

"Brilliant," I told her, "that's just the job. Except that you haven't said anything about the garden."

"There wasn't a garden," she frowned at me.

This was true, there was just a small courtyard.

"Well," I told her, "just write something about the small courtyard."

"CK" she said, and her little fingers flew over the keys once more.

I went back in to the kitchen and wiped the paint off Bernie 's face and stopped the potatoes from boiling over.

"I've finished!" called Debbie again.

I went in to look.

"There is a small and very pretty courtyard," she had written, "with some flowers and an old well, also a little girl aged about seven called Lucille and a little boy who is her brother called Ludovic who is about five, and they've got a kitten called Feline."

***

Kissing was a problem. We couldn't make out how often we should kiss people on each cheek, nor which people we should kiss. We studied others with interest, for the kissing – peck-peck-smack-peck – was clearly an important part of French culture. People, particularly women between the ages of one day and a hundred years, seemed to spend as much time kissing each other when they met as speaking to each other. If there were several of them they seemed to form a little circle, or perhaps a little line, and various members of the group, presumably at some secret given signal, would start – peck-peck-smack-peck – making small jerky bobbing movements of head and shoulders, depending on the height of the person they were kissing.

The quantity of kisses meted out seemed to follow no set rules, anything from one solitary peck on the proffered cheek to as many as two on each cheek, even two on one cheek and three on the other. We counted carefully and wondered if we should set up a chart of some kind so that we could note whether the kisses depended on colour of hair or beauty of beholder.

Truth of the matter was that we didn't really WANT to kiss anybody at all, except within the family, least of all the variety of snotty school pals that lined up in front of us by the school gates most days. All females and all children seemed to expect to be kissed once introduced, and the majority of men, and teenagers of both sexes too. I went through a patch of announcing that I was English and that in England we don't kiss each other, but soon discovered that it was quicker and easier to get on with the kissing and be done with it.

A problem we encountered with this was that, because of the constant proximity of the kissing fraternity, we seemed to pick up colds at the drop of a hat and – worse – nits. Debbie and I had nits, I assume because we both had long hair, off and on the entire time we were in France; we had never had them before and I have not had them since. I bought Debbie hair bands and "hair furniture" (as she called it) in general that had been pre-treated with anti-nit product. These are quite commonly available in chemists in France, which seems to me to prove my point, for they are virtually unheard-of in the UK. These hair bands helped keep the problem at bay to a degree but it didn't smell very nice.

It was easier to avoid the colds. We discovered that if we studied nose, eyes and mouth of the approaching kisser we could usually ascertain within reason if that kisser had a cold to impart to the kissee. If it seemed to be the case the trick was to take a gulp of clean air before approached too closely, hold the breath, let it out by, near or on the face of the kisser and then take another breath – in fact start breathing normally again, only once a suitable distance between kisser and kissee had been established. This was relatively easy to do for the kissing, although it could consist of several loud and enthusiastic smackeroonies, was generally aimed past the ear of the kissee and as long as the heads more-or-less touched (and nits more-or-less transferred) it seemed to be all right.

The only problem arose if required to speak. It is remarkably difficult to speak when holding one's breath, and many of our greetings to French friends and acquaintances came out as a gruff sort of *"Rumph!"*

Debbie was invited to act as "nanny" for one of my sisters and her two children one summer. They rented a house in Italy. Debbie loved her two little cousins and took on this nanny role three summers in a row. Although Debbie was never a rude and belligerent as the teenage years drew nigh, not in any noteworthy way, our personalities had started to sometimes grate, just slightly. She was too old to be babied and too young for us to really relate to each other as we did in later years. It gave me one less child to worry about – with all three babes I have experienced the Out-Of-Sight-Out-Of-Mind syndrome – and one less to deal with in every way. It was also very good for her for not only was it an experience in itself, she loved it, and it made her mix with a better (there is only one way to say this) class of person. We were miserably aware that we were surrounded by peasants – of course, peasants are all very excellent, but we wanted more for our children.

Debbie was volatile. I could see that look in her eyes that I remembered quite clearly from my own girlhood. She was easily influenced, by both good and bad. I could see her wings, almost tangible, growing and getting ready to spread.

"She is just a child," I said to Euan, "just a little girl."

"Why, of course!" he exclaimed.

There was something about her, even in those early years when she was twelve or thirteen or so, that was difficult to control – and even more difficult to fathom. The little girl clashed violently with the teenage girl; and the young woman in her who was longing – aching! - to break through, was totally quashed by the complete innocence and wide-eyed wonder of the child within. Her stay with my sister gave her something else to do and to think about. I could see the beginnings of ... I couldn't put my finger on it, but was glad she went off for the summer. When the autumn term started again I was thrilled to see her. She had had her hair coloured, she was more mature.

Article written for women's magazine
Those terrible teens.

The best way to deal with teenagers is to get rid of them.

Years ago, when my now-taller-than-I-am babes were just little, a girl-friend sent her thirteen year-old daughter to boarding school. They just didn't get on, she explained, and it was the best solution.

I was horrified. How dare this mother shirk her responsibilities and palm her child off elsewhere because she couldn't cope?!

A Call From France

As my little ones grew older, however, and the first signs of "lip" started to appear I declared unwaveringly that, if we could possibly afford it, ours would be packed off to boarding school at the first signs of nasty behaviour. As it happened by the time Debbie and Max reached teenagehood (Bernie is six years younger) we were living in France where boarding school is a fraction of the price.

Parents suffer, I have come to realize, from a kind of inverted vanity whereby they think – for no logical reason – that they are the best people to deal with their children and their children's behavioural difficulties. Parents go through a kind of self-inflicted martyrdom that really is quite unnecessary. The Masai tribes of East Africa, where I spent several childhood years, to this day pack their adolescent boys off in to the bush and don't allow them to return to the family circle till they are old enough to be married. This eliminates all the fighting and the fractious elements introduced to the family by a teenage boy whose sex hormones are invariably chugging around at a pace his brains can't keep up with.

81

A Call From France

Debbie started boarding school at her own request when she was thirteen. She loved it and remained a boarder till she left school at seventeen. Daughters are in some ways more difficult than sons and it is without shame that I admit to experiencing a sensation of considerable relief when I dropped Debbie off every Monday morning. Adversely, however, I was always thrilled to see her on a Friday evening. Max became a boarder at the same time, not because he was giving us any "lip" – quite the opposite – but as an experiment because Debz was already there. He hated boarding and regularly phoned me:

"Mummy! Come and get me! Come and get me!"

He tried it for just one term and, both his nerves and mine frayed beyond endurance, he came home as a day boy again.

Our children can sometimes be utterly dreadful. It is astonishing to see one's precious off-spring turn in a split second from an amiable budding adult to a red-faced and steaming pile of indignation. Back goes the chair – SCRAPE! Up goes the voice – SQUEAK! Tears spring to the eyes – GLOB! – and the scene is invariably accompanied by cries of "it's not fair!" or perhaps "why always me?!"

All three of our children seem to be consumed by rules of fairness and unfairness, and despite vast quantities, both physical and emotional, of Everything a Kid Could Wish For, are frequently telling us that one of us has been unfair over one thing or another. Money is the main issue, of course, and edible goodies another. At the other end of the spectrum loading and unloading the dishwasher (almost the only chore they ever do) is invariably "unfair", and for some totally inexplicable reason putting away their bikes, tidying up their video games and putting play things away all fall in to the "unfair" category. Most unfair of all, it seems, is walking the dog.

As we watch our teenagers grow tall and croaky, develop breasts and pubic hairs – and acne – there are vast quantities of acne in our household, it is difficult to remember what torture it was for us not so long ago. One thing I have learnt as a parent is NEVER criticise your own parents till your children are old enough to criticise you!!

A Call From France

Having said that, our children are essentially polite and pleasant. From the outset we put up with no rudeness whatsoever when they were little, so teenage rudeness has been considerably modified. The total ill-manneredness of some teenagers is extraordinary – some don't even realize they are being rude, supposedly because their parents don't know they are being rude ... or perhaps they go through a kind of madness like a menopause the wrong way round ...It is a source of great wonder that the world survives it. Debbie has been in and out of several Horrible Patches. Max is always sweet with me but can whip up a foaming anger with his dad at the drop of a hat. Bernie assures me he is going to be The Perfect Teenager.

Max has a friend, Jeremy, who stays with us off and on all the time. Until recently I thought it was because his father had died and his mother was depressed but no, I have come to realize that I am Jeremy's mother's buffer. Jeremy is always adorable with me but Max reports terrible screaming matches between Jeremy and his mother. She's not shirking her motherly duties – she is being sensible. Get rid of him.

A Call From France

A few months ago some clients gave me an important bit of advice. They said "try to think only about yourself".

These clients had had four children of their own and now boasted thirteen grandchildren. They nodded understandingly as I described the previous night's antics as we tried to convince Max that having lights on his bike when cycling at night was A Good Idea. The ensuing row as Max tried to persuade us that we had no idea what we were talking about left us both exhausted and me close to tears. My clients told me to remember that it is always us, the parents, who have to soldier through the various teenage crises and that as parents we should try to home-in on ourselves and not let our off-spring ruin what would otherwise be a nice time.

"You'll be with your husband in ten, twenty, thirty years' time," they said, "and your children will have grown up and left you. Sometimes they will come to visit you. They will expect you to pay for things for them, even when they are quite grown-up. It is essential that you, the parents, try to think of YOURSELVES and never let your children's

tantrums or demands interfere with you as a couple."

Lord only knows there is no recipe. If only there were! I have come to the conclusion that it doesn't matter what you or do not do, there are high chances of your children being utterly ghastly at one stage or another of their teen years, no matter how well you have brought them up. All we, as parents, can try to do is educate them about good old-fashioned Right and Wrong and then hope that they carry that message through to adulthood.

<u>Diary entry (five years later)</u> Today I came across that article I wrote for Woman (or whatever it was called). Goodness – it sounds right enough when you read it ! But Lord knows I wouldn't write it now. I don't have an opinion now. My opinions have all gone ....

We employed several people. I use the word loosely. Several people worked for us. If you actually employ somebody, ie have them on a payroll, you are absolutely punished for it. It costs a fortune, and the employee's "rights" go on and on forever. In the UK we had learnt the hard way that it was best for us if people were self-employed and France was no different.

However there were many obstacles to this. Because of the inordinate charges made on self-employed people, their estimates for any work were extortionate. A jobbing builder to help out here and there didn't exist. Well, he did exist, but only on the black. I was even advised by somebody at the Employment Office to take people on only on the black otherwise, I was told, *"c'est trop compliqué"* !!! We discovered that a massive percentage of workers in France, including government workers, work on the black. Their own system makes them do so.

This worried us hugely because we didn't want to find ourselves in trouble with the law. As it was there were so many rules and regulations (being an estate agent without the appropriate qualifications, licence and paperwork, carried a prison sentence – yes, a prison sentence!) I waged a constant and extremely fraught battle trying to keep work coming in on the one hand and stay on the right side of the law on the other hand; stupidly, it was very difficult to do both.

The British don't realize how lucky they are: if you, for example, decide tomorrow morning that you want to be a hairdresser – hey presto, you can be a hairdresser. There is no such luxury in France: you have to be *immatriculé* (we came across this word frequently), you have to have done *un stage* (another frequent word) lasting anything up to two years. You have to have a little badge to say you are a hairdresser. If you don't you are in big trouble. Big legal trouble. Yet despite this care of their citizens (which, one assumes, is how the government looked at it) there was far more unemployment in France that in the UK, for the same population. Far more bankruptcies, far more repossessions, far more debts, far more fraud, far more court cases.

Our most loyal workers in those early years were Michel and his son Bruno. By side-stepping the system and declaring both Michel and Bruno as employed by a UK firm, we were able to pay them cash and also keep them legal. That, of course, is what most of the French do – they simply side-step the system. They worked for us for twenty years. Bruno died of AIDS.

An English couple named Eric and Jean worked for us for several years; they were both hopeless cases who made good thanks to an extraordinary mixture of ignorance and determination. Eric and Jean had their own trendy language, despite both being in their forties:

"Hey, Eric! Check this out! "

"Wow, yes, cool, really wicked!"

"Wicked!"

"Wicked!"

My father, on one of his regular visits, found this hilarious and referred to Eric as Wicked thence forth.

"How is Wicked?" he would ask over the phone.

"Oh, he's fine, so is Mrs Wicked."

I nevertheless valued Jean's friendship and soon came to rely on it. She was the one I wailed down the phone to when things had gone wrong – and they often did – and because she worked for me she understood absolutely the ups and downs of the trade, the fighting and negotiating for a sale, the hopes rising as the all-important commission appears temptingly on the horizon, and then the depths of disappointment and anger when it all falls through. A commission invariably entailed hour upon hour of unseen work, miles of driving, hours of measuring and photographing, typing and photocopying, posting and negotiating. It represented all the people who phoned us at some ungodly hour in the evening, all the time-wasters, all the frustrations of dealing with somebody by fax or by phone or by post or even in the flesh … just to find out that they weren't serious buyers at all … they were just having a little look … and were blissfully oblivious to the effort and energy put in by the likes of me and Jean, not to mention the use of my meagre funds and the even more precious use of my rapidly wearying energy.

We confided everything to each other, whether business or personal, and Jean was a source of strength for me at a time in my life when I was fundamentally exhausted both mentally and physically.

Jean wore G-strings years before they became popular. Sex and sexual matters were a subject of great importance to Eric and both he and Jean were astonishingly frank about it.

"Well, I must go," she said on the phone to me one day after a long discussion about a contract she was getting a client to sign, "I must cut my pubes. Eric doesn't like it if they get too long."

Like me she usually wore denims for work but one day she appeared wearing a very full dress, nipped-in around the waist, the skirt section being almost a full circle.

"I love your dress," I told her.

It was early summer and I accompanied her with a client to see a house out in the countryside not far from St Porchaire. A warm wind blew. The house, unlike most houses in the area, was detached, situated in a small hamlet. It was potentially lovely, with nice country views and big spacious rooms still boasting ancient fireplaces and heavy beams. Jean and I had decided to try to do things together. This was for several reasons, the obvious one being for security to ourselves. Also, being two of us, the client somehow drained me less for I allowed Jean to do much of the talking and she took on to her shoulders the tense waiting for a difficult question or the thrilling sensation of knowing you've made a sale.

Standing outside by the car, and remembering what I had taught her, she said:

"And look at this lovely tree. It is called a *tilleul* ..."

At that moment, and without warning, her dress blew up. It woooshed right up over her face, making her lose her footing and revealing long slender legs and what at first glance seemed to be a bare bottom and pubic hair. She stumbled, trying to brush the dress down again, while our clients stood in open-mouthed stupefied silence, the man's astonishment changing unwittingly to a broad grin. Seconds passed while Jean flailed around with her skirts and I tried to rush forwards to help her.

"Oh!"

Finally the dress was back in place. Mortified, Jean took a step back and, like something out of a bad comedy, caught her foot and fell backwards, the dress going up again and the legs scissoring furiously. It was then clear that she was wearing a black lacey G-string. I stared in horrified amazement while she picked herself up again.

"And the price," she said with the greatest composure, brushing the skirt back in to place a second time, "is 400,000 French francs."

My business grew and with it Euan's business grew.

Jean also accompanied me on most of my visits to properties; this was very time-consuming and, although at first it was fascinating looking around other people's houses, it rapidly became stunningly

93

boring, particularly as most vendors wanted too much money and thought that the life history of their family would somehow enhance the value of the property. Very few vendors in that part of France, twenty years behind the rest of France (which was anyway in those days twenty years behind Britain to begin with) had any taste; bathroom tiles with imitation splashes on them were *de rigeur* in the few houses that had a bathroom at all, raised baths with imitation sheepskin bathmats, brown kitchen tiles left over from 1970 Britain with pictures of onions and coffee pots, and plenty of gloss paint.

Bearing poor Suzy Lamplugh in mind, I always made a note in my diary as to where I was going and who I was meeting. There were, in those eight or so years of my little estate agency, only two incidents worth noting where I did feel in danger. The first was simply an empty house in St Savinien … no danger at all, really, except that there seemed to be a "presence" there – I was far too practical to call it a ghost – and there was a strong smell of blood. You read about hair standing on the back of your neck – well, mine stood on the back of my neck, and I was filled with such a sensation of horror that I fled within a few minutes of starting to look around. The vendor hadn't accompanied me, and I understood why, and Jean wasn't with me that day either. Never one to waste the smallest iota of my time or energy I nevertheless typed up a description, calling the house The Haunted House and knowing I would never sell it. But just the description in my books was good … people liked it, and my aim was to sell something, anything, even if they were in fact attracted out by a house they knew they wouldn't buy.

The second incident was one spring day a year or so later. Again, Jean was not with me. It was one of those days were you feel a spring in your step, just because the sun is out, and I picked up my two clients at the designated place – probably outside the town hall – and took them to view an isolated farmhouse a few miles away. They were two men, both French, in their forties. This in itself was unusual because the French had no need to contact me – there were plenty of French agents.

The property was called Les Fellouins which, as far as I know, doesn't mean anything, and was in a near-idyllic setting between the villages of Lussant and Tonnay Boutonne, surrounded by fields and the few gentle hills available. It was in need of repairs, but had plenty of space and a good-sized plot of land. Altogether a very sought-after kind of thing. I showed the men around, through the empty rooms and round the plot of land, then opened the barn door and climbed the ladder into the loft. Lofts in this kind of property are often huge wasted space and can cover the entire surface area of the house and the barns. The barns are usually attached to the house. Treading gingerly over the ancient floorboards I made my way to a window and, after a bit of fumbling in the dark, threw the shutters open. The place was full of huge black cobwebs.

The two men stood to one side, surveying the dark space, and brushing dust and cobwebs from their trousers. Based on absolutely nothing at all suddenly an alarm bell started to ring loudly and insistently at the back of my mind.

"I'll go and fetch my torch from the car," I told them.

"Oh, don't worry about that," one replied, "we can see."

"No, no I insist! I'll only be a second!"

My mouth dry and my legs numb with fear I scrambled down the ladder and rushed to my car. I have never driven away so fast, instinctively locking the doors as I got in and sending mud spluttering up behind me. I don't know what happened to the men. They must have hitched home. But I know that if they had been up-front they'd have phoned – "hey, what the hell was up with you?!" – but they didn't phone, and I know I had a lucky escape.

Diary. Ten years later. Today we went boating in Port des Barques. It was sooooo hot! We had lunch at the top of the town and walked past Jean's estate agency. I wonder if she gets any trade there ? I can't imagine so. It had the Jean touch – everything very neat and professional. I remember the day we sacked her and Eric – goodness, that's years ago now! How she screeched at me and tried to defend Eric.......

A Call From France

Jean gave me a skirt to give to Debbie.

"It was mine," she explained, "I used to have such a wild time in that skirt! I'll never be slim enough for it again, so Debbie might as well have it."

It was a denim mini-skirt with lace pockets. I didn't like it at all. It looked tarty and was anyway too big for Debbie. I threw it out.

When Debbie was little I had made lots of clothes for her, mostly pretty dresses, but also coats and jackets and Andy Pandy suits. I used to run them up in an hour or two and I took a lot of pride in them. I made several things for Max too when he was a baby. Clothes that were shop bought, in English days, came from a shop in Forest Row called The Dandelion Clock. It was later burgled and had to close, but at the time it was a haven of goodies, usually terribly expensive, in which to dress my babes. From a very young age Max was quite particular about what he wore; he was the first in the designer cult that hit our youth a few years later. Max was only a tot when he used to insist on designer clothes, and that was long before the child market had been cornered.

In France it was a different matter. I had no energy, or even enthusiasm, for sewing. I made the odd pair of curtains here and there, but totally lost interest and my sewing machine, given to me by my mother on my twenty-first birthday and whose familiar electric buzz was once a regular sound, remained silent and idle, and even started to rust, before I used it again. Children's clothes – and adult clothes for that matter – seemed to fall in to two clear categories: there was very expensive designer stuff that I was no longer able to afford, or horrible cheap shoddy rubbish from shops like Prisunic or – worse – La Halle aux Vetements.

Debbie was getting tall. Euan is slightly under 6'5", so it was natural that his children should grow tall. She stopped growing when she was a little less than 6'. She always held herself well, though, shoulders back, head up. I think having such a tall father helped. She didn't feel big and gawky. She was considerably taller than any of her friends, however. Like me before her, she suffered badly with acne. Blackheads and pustules were an on-going battle in our household. The beginnings of a smashing figure were showing by the time she was thirteen, and one of her great assets was her hair – long and wavy and a wonderful auburn-brown in colour.

We had her teeth seen to. They had started protruding in a way that could not be ignored. The system was very good for, although it cost something in the region of £3000 altogether to have Deb's teeth braced and straightened (and this was back in the 1990s), almost all of it was paid back to us out of the system. Appointments were in Rochefort, about half an hour in each direction for me, but were generally punctual and stress-free. Each appointment cost about 500f - £50 – which I had to pay. I was then given a *Fiche de Soins*, a bit like a receipt, which I then had to post to my *Caisse*, duly completed along with special number, name and address, date of birth of Debbie and half a dozen other things, and within a couple of days most of the money was paid back into my bank account.

At first the filling-in of these forms drove me mad but, like so many things, it is only a question of getting used to it. It does make you think twice about going to the doctor, however, for the same system applies to all medical attention, including hospital but with the exception of accidents and emergencies. The French medical system was efficient and smart, precise, clean, friendly, prompt. But they pay for it.

We moved all three children to a privately-run school in Clion, a small market town nearly an hour's drive away. The village school was teaching nothing of any sort to either of the boys and, although Debs seemed happy at Tonnay Boutonne, we had our doubts about her education. We hoped that the new school, with a slightly more up-beat clientele, so to speak, might open the children's horizons rather more, especially – and most importantly – as there were a couple of other foreign children there.

While we were most concerned about the boys' academic education, we were rather more concerned about Debbie's social education. She made a point of only mixing with – and again I use the word very loosely and I certainly do not intend offence – her inferiors. She played with girls at least a year younger and, rather than chum-up with the few daughters of the few members of the

101

educated classes in the area, she seemed hell bent on finding her friends among the children of the pig swillers, the local drunk and the desperados.

It was at about this time that we met Mat. Dear darling Mat! I missed him terribly after he had gone. He brought an element of sincerity and calm into our household and although he was only twenty three, he was a good conversationalist and he filled a gaping void in my days.

Mat was a kind of "assistant" teacher at the school in Clion. The son of an Anglican priest in Yorkshire, he had taken this teaching post to learn French even though his degree was in Theology. He was paid a pittance and was lodged in a horrid room at the end of a corridor in the convent. Debbie phoned me one day.

"Mummy! There's an English guy at school!"

"Really? Who – how?"

"He's called Mat!! He's a kind of teacher."

"Aren't you supposed to be in lessons? Who is this Mat?"

"He's really cool, mummy. I've invited him back for the week-end! Yes, yes, I have to go, I'm supposed to be in Histoire right now. Bye!!"

That was my introduction to a young man who filled our lives for a year or so, bringing with him a kind of ... comfort. I think that perhaps as he was the son of a priest he had learnt, albeit unintentionally, a manner, a way of talking, an attitude that inspired confidence and opened conversation. He was tall and thin and covered in freckles. He had an allergy to dust particles and was constantly snuffling and croaking. I eventually paid for him to go to a doctor. He had no money, nothing, and was far from home wondering what idiot idea had made him come to France.

"Of all the places in the world," he said, " of all the amazing things I could have done ... not only do I land myself in France, but I land myself in Clion! "

He had a way of saying Clion– the way one might say "leprosy".

"I could have gone to Hawaii," he continued, "I could have gone to Jamaica! Even Paris would have been all right. But no, I come to Clion, blcomin' sodding Cliiii-onnn!!"

We gave him work so that he could earn pocket money, we housed and fed him every week-end, and in return he gave us – well, me – the pleasure of his company in a world where I felt everybody was out to "get" me if they could.

This sensation of being hunted got worse as time went on. I seemed to be on the receiving-end of so much aggro. I had had no business experience before and was unable to deal with aggressive situations.

"It's just part of it," Euan said, "it's just part of the job."

"They're virtually blaming me for the rain!" I wailed.

"That's not important. Let them blame whoever they want. It doesn't matter."

Worse, the local authority seemed to be constantly sending us aggressive letters about one thing or another. Because Euan did not speak French, and because he had developed a fairly mild (but nonetheless most unpleasant) form of Meniere's Syndrome which seemed to be triggered by stress, I dealt with these things myself. The tone of the letters always confused and upset me:

"Madame, because you have not filled in form number 123abc you will be guillotined at dawn ..."

We bought a second-hand caravan for holidays and all year round I kept spare clothes, non-perishable food and passports in there in case we needed to make a quick getaway.

"Getaway from what?" Euan asked.

"The Gestapo," I replied.

***

105

We took the babes to Paris. We stayed in a wonderful hotel called, oddly, Hotel du Bois d'Amour – hotel of the woods of love, such an odd name. It stuck in Debbie's mind. I had no idea how that hotel would play a role in our lives ten years later. We did the rounds including Versailles, and collapsed back in to our rooms at the hotel pleased and exhausted each evening. I think we were gone four days. The hotel had a pool so Euan kept the boys there one afternoon for me so that I could look around the Louvre with Debbie. You can't see the Louvre in one afternoon, and you can't see it at all when there are such crowds. Debbie was not interested really and was pleased at the end of the day to return to the Bois d'Amour.

She was ....almost fourteen, I think.

***

We converted the guest suite in to a little gite. It was the obvious thing to do. We didn't go out of our way to advertise but we had a steady collection of holiday-makers staying there during the summer, and this brought in a bit of much-needed cash. Really, the place wasn't suitable for it faced east so that it got only the early morning sun, and even then the sun was filtered through the trees, tall skinny oaks, clustered in a group of fifty or so over the land that bordered the Michaux farm. They were a feature, for there are few big trees in that part of France. The landscape is generally flat with small trees dotted here and there. When we sold Tulips those oak trees were listed as a point of interest on the agent's details. Many of them came crashing down the year of the big storm, years later, at the end of the millennium.

There was something about the shade of those oaks and the rotting vegetation there that attracted flies. Somebody told me that bay bushes attracted flies and we hacked away at the several that were there and burnt them. The whole area was riddled with flies and at about three every afternoon, even in the winter, flies would cluster all over the window panes of the southern side of the house. During the summer months these clusters were all but intolerable and – like so many things – you'd have to see it to believe it, for the panes of glass would be alive with a buzzing black mass.

The problem was so bad that I used some of our meagre funds to get in a pest control firm. They sprayed everything and, although the flies came every day, at least they died quickly and I went round with a dustpan and brush sweeping them up. The dust pan filled up so quickly with dead flies that I would have to empty it several times as I made my way round the house, going from window to window. I used to take a macabre delight in hoovering up live flies with the hoover attachments. The problem was half-solved for about a year, but then they came back almost as bad as before.

I sat down on the living room floor and dug out the encyclopaedias. I had no idea there were so many types of fly. I waded through the lists – black fly and buffalo fly, crane fly, dragonfly, firefly, sand fly and so on. The item said flies were worldwide and found in most habitats. Including my house. The smallest was 2mm and the largest 50mm – two inches! I must be glad of small mercies, I told myself.

Of all insects flies are almost the only one with just one pair of wings I read.

The eyes of the small-headed fly can almost entirely cover its head, said the next bit.

Flies lay eggs between five and twenty-five times a year. The eggs metamorphose from embryo to larva, pupa, and adults forms. The metamorphosis takes about two weeks. The average life span of the fly is around two months. The female common house fly will lay 600-1000 eggs in her lifetime. ... . Fly larva consume dead organic matter.

"What are you doing?" asked Debbie when she came in to the room.

"I'm looking up about flies, seeing if there isn't something I can do to get rid of them, or at least to stop them coming."

On the gite side of the house, perhaps because it was relatively undisturbed, the flies remained bad throughout the year. Windows had to be kept closed. We were not dishonest – we always had this idea that it would be all right on the night, so to speak.

Only couples stayed there for it was not suitable for children. I went in to clean up after one lot before the next lot arrived – there was a nasty smell of cigarettes and fried food, so I opened the windows and French doors wide to air the place and returned to my office. When the guests arrived I escorted them round to their side of the house.

"Did you have a good journey?" I chatted amiably as we walked.

"Oh, fine, fine, thanks."

"So, here we are, this is your …."

The place was thick with flies. They buzzed round and round the room in an incessant lunatic dance, hundreds of them.

"Oh!" the wife put her hand to her mouth in utter horror.

"Whatever is it?!" asked the man.

"I ... I don't know ... something must have attracted them in ... I'm so sorry, I'll get some spray."

Looking round at the woodland the couple, unbelievably, sat down by the barbeque and waited till I returned with the spray. I also brought a couple of cans of cold beer, which I think tipped the scales. I sprayed the room vigorously and the flies buzzed louder and fell to the ground where they finished their erratic dance in spinning death throes on the tiled floor. At last I swept them all up.

"I'm terribly sorry," I said repeated.

I never opened the windows again, but never got rid of the flies either. It was insect-riddled, mostly with the flies and also with beetles called *punaises*, which also means "drawing pin" for they look slightly like drawing pins – or perhaps drawing pins look slightly like the beetles – the children called them "stink bombs" because they let off an indescribably disgusting and lingering pong when

111

threatened. Actually, one of the biggest spiders I have ever seen in my life was in that room.

The gite consisted of one huge room with a wonderful 1920s tiled floor. There were French windows on either side, the guests' pair opening into the woodland and the other pair, firmly locked, opening on to our courtyard. A third door, also firmly locked, led in to the library. When friends and family came to stay they had access to the rest of the house via the library, of course, but paying guests got in to their gite only via the woodland, though they could drive their car and park right up virtually next to their door. Where a bread oven had once been at the far end we had knocked a doorway through and that space, combined with a stone shed also at that end, made a kitchen and bathroom. The kitchen featured the ancient bread oven door. Gran was always brilliant at finding cast-off curtains and similar odds and ends, invariably dug out of a box, all carefully wrapped in tissue paper, in her attic. I decorated the place with these, laboriously lugged over by her every time she came and including floor mats and mirrors and ornaments and pictures of various shapes and sizes. I hung net curtains in thick gushy quantities over the windows and this

hid the old paintwork or the cracked parts of the
wood. A few choice bits of furniture, bright
ornaments and accessories, and the gite - despite
the flies - was very pretty.

The *banque alimentaire* took place every autumn.
All school children all over the Charente Maritime
were issued with a carrier-bag which they brought
home and which the parents were expected to fill
with non-perishable food goods. These were then
taken back to school and collected by the local
charitable organizations such as the *Secours
Catholique* or the *Croix Rouge*.

I liked the system for it gave us an opportunity to
give to the poor in a land where there didn't seem to
be much in the way of charitable functions. In fact
France has an excellent support system for the
needy, and for charities, but you do not see street
collections or charity shops the way you do in
England, which means that you are generally less
aware of anything charitable going on. At home in
England I had been involved with several charities,
the way middle-class English women tend to be,
and I was part of a group raising funds for Cancer
Research, Prisoners Abroad and a couple of others.

These unofficial fund-raising groups provide not only substantial cash funds but a social life too, and I had had a wide circle of friends whose company I had enjoyed and who I now very much missed.

In France, of course, you have to be *immatraticulated* for fund-raising as you do for anything else. It took me a long time to understand this and when we first moved to Tulips I went down to the village *Mairie* and told them that I would be interested in joining a local fund-raising group.

"Comment, Madame?"

I didn't know how to say fund-raising. The word *les fonds* does indeed mean funds, but you can't apply the word "raising" in this context. You can raise a child from the bed or raise a carpet off the floor, or raise merry hell if you want, but you can't raise funds. The word "charity" didn't seem to fit either. If anything one could say *faire du bénevole*, but that somehow didn't seem to fit either. The fact of the matter is that they just don't do it. Fund-raising is very organized, seen to by specific groups of people.

After a bit of discussion the woman at the town hall suggested I join the village committee and said she would give my phone number to the appropriate person. I tried to ask her a bit about the village committee but she replied with a logic that could only be admired that I would do best to go along and see for myself. A couple of days later the phone rang.

"Bonjour, Madame, je suis Madame Clemenceau."

Oh good, I thought. I wonder who she is ? So long as she's called Madame Clemenceau all will be well, I'm convinced.

"Bonjour Madame," I replied formally.

"How can I help you?" she asked.

I wasn't aware that I needed help. My mind raced around at a million miles an hour while I went mentally through all the things I needed help with – the cooking and ironing, difficult clients, taking photos of houses, massaging Euan's back, washing the car, translating a contract ... After a few confused moments I worked out who she was. I do

115

apologize, *Madame*, I explained, but so many people phone me … I didn't know.

I was duly invited to a meeting in the church hall and I went along on the appropriate day. It was terribly hot but I nonetheless rejected my habitual shorts and vest T-shirt for a dress, a floral little number that I thought made me look serious. Several wooden school-type benches were arranged in the room, lined up as though in a church. On these sat a variety of local people, mainly in their fifties and sixties. My heart sank. There was no friendly chatty group of women of my age with children like mine. On a kind of small stage arrangement was a long wooden table, probably nicked out of a scene from Jane Eyre, (or *Le Grand Meaulnes* at any rate) and at this table sat a couple of men and a heavily be-spectacled woman. Everybody seemed to be smoking. I sat down on a bench in the middle of the room, close to some women, one of whom nodded *bonjour* at me.

.

After a while I realized that one of the men was talking. It was difficult to work out whether he was talking to us or to himself. Upon further investigation I spotted a blackboard in one corner

116

and somebody got up from the front row and wrote down four names including my own. So! They realize I am here! I thought.

I gathered that the subject for discussion was to be whether or not the village could afford to have the town hall shutters re-painted. This was not at all the kind of fund-raising thing I had had in mind but ... one has to start somewhere, I told myself, and I daresay even the shutters of the *Mairie* are a good cause.

A Vote By Slow Motion then began. I hadn't gathered who or what we were voting for – I mean was it to raise the money for the shutters, for the paint, or was it to just decide whether we were going to give it a go – or what? but voted for myself as I was clearly the best candidate there, whatever it was. This took about two hours - two hours ! I flapped a magazine in front of my face to keep both flies and cigarette smoke away and battled against simply getting up and walking out. The faces of my old friends in England loomed before me ... I felt the treacherous tears pricking. Happy coffee mornings in Aggie's house flit through my mind, some six or seven of us all chatting about our husbands and donations from local shops and middle-class English things ... like a nice pub, or an antiques store, or the milkman. Suddenly I could picture my old garden and my parent's house .... I am far too busy for all this anyway, I thought. What am I doing here ? I waited till the end, then, as one or two people seemed to be moving around, I got up and left, nodding a farewell in the general direction of the table as I went.

Madame Clemenceau phoned me that evening.

"*Bonsoir Madame,*" she said.

"*Bonsoir Madame*," I replied.

"*Je suis Madame Clemenceau,*" she said.

I refrained from saying "*et je suis Madame Broughton*". Why did you leave, she asked. I didn't know you knew I was there, I replied.

"*Mais oui! Bien sur, Madame!*"

I told her I was terribly sorry to have wasted her time but that the village committee was just not what I was looking for. She was flabbergasted. I explained that I was looking for a group of people like myself, something to take part in … and I was again aware of that vague feeling that I ought to be feeling bad about it, but that I didn't.

So the *Banque Alimentaire*, although it did not provide me with any kind of social life, was welcomed by me every year as my one chance to do something for somebody else, and I filled my babes carrier bags up to bursting point without fail.

A year or two later an English woman moved with her seven children to the village. I have never seen anybody quite so hard-up, nor quite so brave. Her name was Monica. I struck-up a friendship with her, for she was my age, and I tried to be a good friend for she was clearly a person in need. One day she told me that she got most of the food for her seven children from the *Secours Catholique* who in turn got it from the *Banque Alimentaire*.

"It's always beans and pasta, pasta and beans," she said. "I'm grateful, whatever it is, but it would be

119

lovely to have something other than pasta and beans."

From then on I made a point of filling the carrier bags with chocolate biscuits and tins of salmon, cereals, dried or tinned fruit, sweets, coffee, juice, always hoping that some of it would one day reach one of the Monicas of this world.

Poor Monica. She was one of the world's losers. Her husband was French and, she explained to me, her mother had taken out a mortgage on her house in England in order for Monica and family to move to France. I sold them a big draughty barracks of a house at the edge of the village. It was potentially lovely, but had no sanitation of any sort – not even outdoors. There were several acres of land and lovely views out over the fields. They had a female Labrador, appropriately named Bisto for she was dark brown.

"Bisto is going to love all this space!" Monica exclaimed.

It seemed to me that Bisto wasn't even moderately interested in all that space, for she lay almost completely motionless on a rug in the back of the van.

"Perhaps something smaller with at least a loo
.........?" I ventured.

But no. She wanted that house, and despite her poor choice Monica was quite clever. She spoke good French and had clearly been educated. Looking at her, thin and bedraggled, I wondered what had gone wrong.

"Cyril will join us in a few weeks' time," Monica explained to me as her seven children milled around her ankles. "He is selling our house and business and then he will bring the furniture out."

"It seems odd to me," I told Euan later that day, "that this Cyril person should allow his wife and SEVEN children to come out without him. She clearly hasn't got a penny. That van of theirs is on its last legs. The children are filthy."

There was something about Monica that spelt trouble. Some people are like that. They are born under the wrong star, perhaps. She seemed to be

121

always involved in one problem or another. All seven children attended the village school – in fact saved it from closing for numbers were down to such an extent that the seven extra made all the difference. It closed a year later, after they'd all gone.

Cyril didn't turn up. The weeks tripped by and winter came round. Monica and her children hadn't even got a WC. She dug a pit in the garden and they all used a potty and tipped the contents in to the pit several times a day. She instructed the children to do as much of their doings while at school – not that the school loo was much better than a pit – and to eat as much as they could of the school lunches. Monica came round to me for a bath two or three times a week, bringing with her her youngest who I nicknamed Buttons, aged about two. Buttons sat on the bathroom floor – or perhaps she was in the bath too. In the meantime, Monica's washing chugged around in my washing machine. By the time she had finished her bath and had a cup of tea with me, the washing was finished and it was then transferred to my tumble drier. All the laundry was a grey-beige colour for it all got thrown in together and was invariably far too much

122

for the tub. Often it came out looking – and certainly smelling – as bad as when it had gone in.

"The children all wet the beds," Monica said, " and when they've wet the bed they come and get in to bed with me and then they wet that too …"

She had very little bed linen though the village had given her quite a lot of warm clothes for the children, if not for her. I dug out a couple of old cotton sheets I never used. Monica was clearly constantly struggling to survive not just financial demands but demands on her nerves and energy too. It was clear that her husband was not going to join her, for no man who loved his children, even if he didn't love his wife, would allow them to live in this state.

"Where is your husband?" I asked her bluntly one day, "where is Cyril?"

"Oh, he's coming, he's just very busy."

"Monica, has he left you?"

"No! No! He hasn't left me …"

Suddenly she dropped her face in to her hands and loud anguished sobs racked her poor dishevelled body. Her hair was still wet from her bath and it fell in long dark strands over her shoulders. I went to her side and put my arm over her shoulders.

"He's in prison, isn't he?" I asked.

She nodded yes. The sobbing abated a little.

"Tell me about it," I said gently, "how long as he got?"

"Seven years," she whispered hoarsely. I waited while she calmed herself.

"Seven years," she repeated. "He's a printer. He forged money. He was brilliant at it."

We both sat silently for a moment.

"I wouldn't mind quite so much," she smiled wryly, " if I had had use of the money. But we never used it. He did it with my uncle. It was my uncle shopped him to the police."

124

"Goodness …"

"If we'd had a few good holidays and been able to buy a house and a car – in some ways I'd say it was worth going to prison over. But I never even saw the money, let alone spent any!"

"Oh, Monica …"

"I know he shouldn't have done it," she said, "but at the time it didn't seem wrong – I dunno – but they're punishing me more than punishing him. That's what is so cruel."

I didn't know what to say. Her eyes had swollen from crying and Button had fallen asleep on her lap, grubby thumb in her mouth.

"I know it can't be nice in prison – of course I know that – but we … we haven't even got a loo! We've got nothing. The children don't understand what has happened. I thought it would be better in France. With seven children I can get lots of child allowance – about double what I'd get in England. Cyril is French. But I haven't had anything, not a centime. Mum bought the house – Christ, she took a mortgage out on her own house! – just so we could buy this place. I was to get rent allowance, you see, and that was to pay mum back with ... but you can't get rent allowance if it's your own family that owns the house ... I didn't know."

The sobbing started again. She was at the end of her tether.

"Well," I said, "you can count on me for support where I can ... obviously. Tell me what would be helpful, tell me what you need the most."

"Hot water, a loo and firewood," she replied without hesitation.

She wiped her nose loudly on the back of her sleeve and tried to smile. I passed her a roll of kitchen paper.

"I try to be normal in front of the children ..."

"Of course...."

The electrics in her house were ancient and it wasn't possible to rig up a hot water tank, but we did have, tucked away in the attic an old water heater that would give just enough to fill a basin if nothing else. It ran off gas so we had to buy a bottle of gas for there were no gas mains in the area. We took the portaloo out of the caravan and gave it to her. Six months or so later, when mains drainage had been installed in the village, Euan put in a proper loo for her. Monica helped herself to firewood from our extensive piles of logs. She had nothing – just a few sticks of furniture, mattresses on the floor, some pots and pans. Her house was cold and dirty. Worse, it stank, truly stank.

Bisto was mated with a local Labrador and produced four puppies. Debbie loved them and begged me to buy all of them. One by one the puppies were sold, as planned. It brought much needed money into Monica's dark, frozen household. The house stank even more.

It made me very aware of how lucky I was with my wonderful husband and my three gorgeous children. Whenever I came home after going to Monica's – which I avoided like the plague – the

127

pretty and cheerful orderliness of my own home particularly struck me and made me appreciate all my lovely things. A little bell at the back of my mind told me I ought to help Monica clean up in her house, and I did try a few times ....

During the winter months when there was usually nobody staying in the gite Monica used that washing machine and tumble drier, also that bathroom, rather than mine in the main part of the house.

"So you have a bit of privacy," I told her.

The truth of the matter was that the smell of her washing, especially when it was in the tumble drier, was nauseating. It truly made me gag. The children complained loudly.

"Ugh! That Monica-person has been here doing her washing!"

Poor Monica! Rumour about her was rife. The entire village seemed to despise her long before they knew her husband was in prison – word got out doubtless via one of her older children. Their dislike of her seemed to stem from a curiosity that could not be satisfied. People like to have an explanation for things.

"What is she doing here with all those children?"

or

"Does she work? Is she going to work?"

Mostly, she was just so dirty. Her poor skinny body, invariably dressed in a dreadful old pair of black baggy trousers and a black top of some description, was often bent with back pain and her hair, which had clearly once been beautiful, fell in thin broken strands over boney shoulders. In her face there was pain and suffering and worry. Her eyes darted maddeningly as she spoke. She had nothing, absolutely nothing, and what little she had was old and dirty and broken.

"You realize she's a prostitute?" the postman confided to me one day.

"Of course she's not!" I exclaimed.

"Believe you me, Madame, I know," he replied, "and there's only one way I can know, now isn't there?"

I told him to go away. I wanted to tell him to never come back. After that he just threw our post in the general direction of the letterbox. I frequently picked it up wet.

I don't know what happened to Monica. After fourteen months or so she asked me to sell the house, which I did mercifully quickly. Selling a house in rural France can take months, even years. She piled her children in to her van and, waving bye-bye to me, she set off for the south of France. It has to be said, she had plenty of courage. Some weeks later the police phoned me from a place near Toulouse.

"What information can you give me about this family?" asked the *gendarme*.

"Why, none at all, " I replied, "is she in trouble? Can I help?"

"She has seven children," came the reply.

"Yes, I know. Are they all right?"

"That is why we wish to speak with you, Madame. The child called Sophie tells me you are a friend of her *maman.*"

Sophie and Button were the only two girls out of the seven children; she was about eight. I had given her a couple of Debbie's dolls and she had decapitated them; it had horrified me.

I wished the *gendarme* would get to the point.

"Do you have any reason to think these children are abused?" he asked at last.

"By their mother? Good Heavens, no! She is a devoted and caring mother in every way."

"The children are under-fed, barely clothed and very dirty," came the reply.

"That is because she is poor," I said, "not because she is bad."

"I know that," replied the man tetchily, "but we wish to know what she is doing here in our village."

"She should be encouraged to return to her own country," I said, ignoring him, "surely there is a social worker there who deals with this sort of thing? This is absolutely not my concern but, as you ask me for information, I'm telling you that she would be better in her own home with her family nearby."

It was left at that, though a social worker did phone a few days later. The child called Sophie, the social worker said, needed psychiatric attention. This was doubtless true for she was a peculiar child with a slightly frightening violent streak in her. A few months later I got a letter from Monica from England.

Dear Catherine,
Here we are back in merry old England. Guess what – it is raining! I'm glad to be back, though. Mum found us a big house not far from her. It's a kind of council house. France wasn't for us. I had thought that as Cyril is French it would work, but the system there is so slow we'd all have died of

starvation before they were going to shell out any dosh. We had to leave Bisto behind – we sold her. The kids were devastated but they'll get over it. I visit Cyril every Friday and I know he likes me to go to see him. He wants to see the kids too so I suppose I'll take the older ones along. He is going to appeal next month. The solicitor says he's got a good chance, what with 7 kids and all that. I hope I can forgive him for doing this to us. But he didn't mean to do it – not really. It'll all be all right.

Tommy is doing really well at school. They'll all be good at French, of course. If Cyril gets out of prison soon he'll be able to get a job and then hopefully we can all have a holiday. France is fine for a holiday. We'll come to see you . I hope things work out well for you, you're very lucky, you've got everything.

Love

Monica.

I sent her a post-card in reply – just a few quickly scribbled lines to thank her for her letter and to wish her well. I didn't want to say or do anything to encourage her to come and see me with her seven children. I'd have liked to have seen her, but not with seven children on tow! About a year later, after we'd moved, she sent me a fax to say that Cyril was out and that it was wonderful to have a normal family life once more. I didn't reply. I never heard from her again.

***

We moved house. The isolation of Tulips took its toll on all of us and the babes in particular needed to be able to see friends more regularly. With the help of our workers we packed everything up - office, workshop, garage and 7 bed roomed house, loaded it all on to the trailer and drove back and forth till it was done. It took a couple of weeks and we moved in to Les Cypres just a few days before Christmas.

We also acquired a dog. Big Harry. I don't know why we got a dog because we are not pet-people, but we got Big Harry. He was a Great Dane, black, three months old when we bought him and nearly twelve years old when he died. Great Danes usually only live seven or eight years, so old Big Harry did

well. There is some corner of a foreign field ….
Big Harry accompanied us to Istanbul (well, you
do, don't you? Take your Great Dane to Istanbul
with you?) and he died while we were there.
Forever England. Or forever France, as the case
may be.

Big Harry was a totally excellent dog - if one has to
have a dog. Very intelligent, very obedient, totally
devoted.

Debbie got knocked down by a ram.

We were wandering around Les Cypres, just a few
weeks before Completion, and the babes had been
in the field where there were some sheep and a
ram. The vendors kept them there to keep the worst
of the grass down. I'd never had animals around
me and felt a bit dubious about the sheep and the
ram, but also felt it was good for the babes. They
seemed peaceful enough, wandering about the
cropped grass, heads down. A slight farm-like
smell accompanied them; it was not unpleasant.

"How do you say *un bouc* in English?" asked Debbie.

"A ram," I replied.

"And the *moutons* ?" chimed in Bernie

"Sheeps," Max told him.

"Sheep," I corrected him, "it is sheep, whether one or several of them."

We looked over the *domaine* several times, wandering through the huge, dark, empty rooms and round the dilapidated gardens. An ancient stone wall, some two metres in height, surrounded the entire plot of land – three or four acres – crumbling away in places. Ivy grew in dark green leafy strands through the broken stones and in parts the stinging nettles and brambles were so high you couldn't see the wall at all.

"The garden was once lovely," Euan commented.

He indicated an old stone bench hidden by overgrown shrubbery.

"Somebody once loved this place," he said.

Here and there were the wild remains of trimmed and shaped hedges, roses, flower beds, stone urns, decorative trees and shrubs of all sorts. Lilac and forsythia spread haphazardly across what used to be lawn, and there were huge clusters of irises and even some agapanthus – which I hadn't seen growing wild since South Africa - and all the while the sheep wandered lazily around, chumping at the grass. Most of the shutters had fallen off, or were hanging dubiously. The sturdy iron gates had rusted. The entire place was heaped with fascinating ancient features, from the wells and iron hand-pumps in the grounds, to the weedy remains of a vineyard. There were a couple of massive ancient stone sinks, dating back to the 1600s, lying in the bushes, clearly flung out during a "modernization" period before World War Two. The entire place was hugely romantic and we liked the idea of being near the sea – barely three miles away – and nearer Royan and Oleron, places that were lively if only in the summer. We both longed and longed for company and action of some kind.

A Call From France

"You really want to go back home," Euan said, putting an arm over my shoulders.

"Yes, I do. I want to go home. But I don't mind giving it one last shot. We've been here ..." I counted, " six years. I'd rather just pack up and go home, but if we can't afford a house in England, this will do."

"You could put up with a chateau in France, could you?" he asked, grinning.

I looked up at the crumbling building. The Chateau des Cypres. There was something about it that attracted us both. Only people like us could possibly take it on. There were several big old stone barns in varying forms of dereliction. Euan could turn his hand to any kind of DIY, anything at all.

Funnily enough I read an article at the hairdresser's this morning about a house that had been renovated in Yorkshire and the writer (a woman) said "our friends thought we were mad to take it on". Yet, by our standards, that house in Yorkshire was in perfect order.

138

The babes seemed happy with the move and it would also mean that they wouldn't have to board at school because we were relatively close to Clion. We tried hard to not talk about "going home" in front of the babes, fearing it might upset them at some level. All three were so French in many ways.

"Come on, then!" Euan called out to the children, "time to go!"

"Ice-kweeem!" volunteered Bernie ..

"I expect so," said Euan and helped him to strap himself in to the car. Debbie and Max turned away from the ram and sauntered towards us. I heard afterwards that you must never turn your back on a ram or a billy goat. He just calmly walked up behind Debbie and butted her in the back. With a cry of astonishment and alarm she fell forwards onto both knees, straight on to the stone path. I rushed forward.

"C'mon! Quick!" I grabbed her under the arms, frightened the ram was going to somehow attack. But he sauntered off back to the sheep almost as

139

though he had his nose in the air. Debbie wailed and wailed.

"Max! Get in to the car!" I yelled, still frightened.

"It's all right, it's all right," Euan, ever calm, came over and helped Debbie onto her feet.

"Are you hurt?" I asked.

She wailed and wailed.

"Debbie!" I said more sternly, "we need to know if you are hurt."

"My back! My knees!"

I turned to Euan.

"She went down with quite a whack," I said.

Debbie hobbled between us to the car where she eased herself in to her seat, still crying loudly. We looked at her knees. She had been able to get up and move with no problem so we judged there was nothing broken. The knees weren't even scratched.

"She's shocked," I said.

"C'mon Baby," Euan cajoled her, "it's not as bad as all that. I expect that was a nasty fright, but you're not hurt."

The wailing continued.

"Cry quietly," I said to her in desperation.

Gradually the tears subsided. Bernie stared at her with his mouth open. Max enquired where we would stop for ice-cream and the incident was put to the back of our minds.
The following day I looked at Debbie's knees: they were neither swollen nor bruised and nor was her back. She said her knees hurt and that she couldn't possibly go to school.

"Up you get," I told her, "into the car by eight."

"Mummy!" she said crossly.

To help her feel a bit better about the incident I gave her some deep heat to rub in to her knees which she did. She smelt – and hobbled – like a little old lady. Having finished with my client in good time at the end of that day, I got to school earlier than usual. I watched my babes come running out of their classrooms, Debbie included, towards the car.

"Your knees better?" I asked.

"I've been in pain all day," she said, looking at me accusingly.

"Oh dear," I patted her thin little thigh, "never mind. If you don't feel better this evening you can have half a paracetomol when you go to bed."

But a few days later Debbie was still insisting that her knees hurt her. She seemed able to move freely, and frequently quite clearly forgot all about her knees. Her appetite was normal, still no bruising appeared, and she slept as soundly as ever. I put it down to Deb's usual behaviour and ignored it. The following week, however, she said to me:

"I can't believe you're not taking me to the doctor!"

"But, Debs, I think there's nothing wrong …"

"The pain comes and goes," she insisted.

So I reluctantly took her to our GP. You rarely have to wait long in France. We knew him quite well, a young man with fair hair and a deep tan, named Jean Demenders. He examined Debbie's knees and asked her several questions.

"I think she should see a specialist," he said at length.

A look of "I told you so" crossed Debbie's face as she glanced over at me. I was horrified.

"What do you think might be wrong?" I asked.

"I don't think there is anything in fact, but it's not <u>impossible</u> there is a fracture," he said, " and she might have a nerve caught. Knees are funny things. I'll get you an appointment at Rochefort hospital. In the meantime she should keep her weight off her legs, just to be on the safe side."

"Oh dear," I said to Debbie as I strapped Bernie in to the car, "looks as though you were right."

"I need some *bequilles,*" she told me.

"What are *bequilles*?" I asked.

"I don't know how you say it in English ," she said and, as soon as we got home she went running indoors shouting, "Max! How d'you say *bequilles* in English?"

Max didn't know the word in either language, but Debbie described to me what she meant.

"CRUTCHES?" I asked, aghast, "you don't need crutches, do you?!"

Just then Jean phoned to say he'd got an appointment for us at Rochefort Hospital in three days' time. I told him Debbie wanted crutches and he said I could go back to the surgery and pick up a prescription for some. Poor little Bernie couldn't believe he had to be strapped in to the car again. I picked up the appropriate prescription and took it to

144

the chemist. Bernie was heavy to carry but he was too tired to walk.

I handed the crutches over to her. She couldn't keep the pleasure from her face. Euan and I grinned at each other. That's our girl! we thought.

I had no choice but to cancel my client on the day of the appointment and to arrange for the child minder to pick Bernie and Max up from school. I felt really bad that I hadn't taken more notice of her when she fell, but she was such a terror for making a big fuss about nothing ... I was determined to look after her properly today and not rush her because of clients and her brothers. He knees were X-rayed and examined. Eventually the doctor put down his notebook and leant back in his chair. He looked at me.

"There is nothing wrong with her knees" he said bluntly.

"Oh good!" I was greatly relieved, even though I could see Debbie was disappointed, "it's just a bit bruised, is it?"

"No," he replied, "there is no sign of any bruising, or of any trapped nerve, or of anything of any sort that might cause pain."

There was a moment of silence.

"Debs," I said , "go and wait outside a minute, please."

Limping determinedly she grabbed her crutches and stood up.

"Leave the crutches!" the doctor barked at her, "if you use those you really will have bad knees!"

I took the crutches from her and she hobbled, close to tears, from the room. I spoke with the doctor for some time. She was not really quite faking it, he told me, but close to it. I could hardly believe she would be so naughty. Why? I asked him. Why in the world would she fake it? Even unintentionally ?

"Ah, Madame! That I cannot tell you! All I can tell you is that there is absolutely nothing of any sort whatsoever wrong with her knees. They are not bruised, they are not fractured, they are not dislocated – nothing. There is no pain. Teenage girls are funny things (where had I heard this before?) and it is possible she has been able to convince herself she has pain, perhaps even bad pain. The brain works in ways we do not fully understand yet."

"In which case ....?"

"I am not a psychiatrist, Madame, I do not know the answer you need. All I can tell you is that there is nothing wrong and that there is no pain."

I took Debbie home. She was pale and close to tears. I didn't say anything but tried hard not to show that I too was close to tears. I asked her if she was thirsty or hungry for the traffic was building up around the eastern side of Rochefort and Tonnay Charente and another forty minutes would elapse before we got home. Yes, she said, she was thirsty and so we stopped at a supermarket near the bridge and bought a small carton of juice and a Mars bar. She pierced the carton with the straw and sucked noisily.

"I'll have to dig out some money to pay Celine for looking after the boys," I said conversationally, "see how much is in the purse, would you?"

She counted the money out cheerfully enough. That's one thing that could always be said for her – she was a cheerful child. She had missed the point, however, and clearly felt no sense of responsibility for having caused me the expense.

"Pity I missed my client today," I tried again, "they sounded really keen. Would have been a good commission."

But again it fell on deaf ears. I battled against getting cross, and the familiar thickness over my temples started and I knew that a bad headache was on its way.

"Why?!" exclaimed Euan when I told him about it later that evening, "what could be her motive?!"

"Actually," I said, "the doctor thought that in a weird sort of way she really thinks she has got painful knees. She has sort-of persuaded herself that they hurt."

148

"But what for?"

"It's as though she wants extra attention – from anybody!"

"Even from herself. Perhaps especially from herself."

Should we have punished her? Hugged her more ? Should we have talked to her? How can parents ever know if they're doing the right thing? The following day Debbie was as bouncey and cheerful as ever. The incident, with us firm in the belief that things would right themselves, was essentially never mentioned again.

Diary entry.
Sometimes I worry about Debbie. On the one hand she is so bright and confident, but on the other hand there is a kind of pragmatic insolence to her. It's just the teenage years, I suppose, but it is a bit hurtful. I try really hard to be chummy with her so that she knows that whatever happens, I am her

149

*friend. Oh! Why am I going on about it?! She's
fine, absolutely fine. I think it's just the sex
hormones that seem to be oozing out of her every
pore that makes it all a bit shocking. I daresay I
was the same.*

*I bought a length of gingham yesterday and helped
Debbie cut it out. I showed her how to make a
skirt. She seemed to enjoy it, though the hem is so
bad I'll have to give it to Josie to alter. I did a lot
of it myself, especially the zip. But the aim was not
to make a skirt, it was to spend a bit of time doing
something with her. Sometimes I feel she is slipping
away, falling off my lap, so to speak. Well, they do
spread their wings, don't they? What can I expect?
She's a really nice kid on the whole and she knows
right from wrong.*

Buying Les Cypres created quite stir in the area for
the old house had been empty, looming like a
ghostly grey hulk at the edge of the village, for
almost twenty years.

Not only was it suddenly sold, it was suddenly sold
to an English family who, in the space of ten
months or less, largely renovated it. While moving
our stuff in to Les Cypres we were burgled, and this

also created a stir for the culprits were rapidly found and turned out to be a crowd of village boys. They appeared in juvenile court a year later and the judge condemned them all to come round and apologize to us and each pay us 330f. I'm not certain where the judge got that figure from, but it totalled something in the region of 2,000f (about £200) which didn't even begin to cover what had been stolen. Not that we intended to make a fuss about that, for the whole thing, bearing in mind this was a small community, was best forgotten as quickly as possible.

Most of the parents of the boys who had burgled us were mortified, but there were some who were bitterly resentful, as though it was somehow our fault. We made a statement in the local paper when the reporter came round, as was inevitable, saying that we understood that young people do silly things and that it didn't matter. Nonetheless local opinion of us was intrinsically coloured – whether lighter or darker – for good.

"Whatever you do," I told the babes, "remember that we are in a different kind of situation to most people. We live in the chateau AND we are not French. If any one of us does something – anything

151

– it will be gossiped about far more than if you were local children living in a village house. Try to bear that in mind."

(Did I imagine they listened ? Did I think these reasonable words sunk in ?)

From the top balcony at Les Cypres you could see for miles, almost as far as the sea. I enjoyed quiet moments up there, watching the traffic go by. Occasionally I could see somebody in a car, far below, point up towards me, obviously saying to the driver "there's somebody up there", or perhaps "that must be that English woman".
I often took a tray of tea with me up. South-facing it was far too hot to sit there during the summer months, but during the spring and autumn months it was a pleasant little haven of escape for me, just sitting and watching. On the opposite side of the road was a small farm, really not much more than a smallholding I suppose. The barn was derelict and what little there was left of it came down during the Big Storm a few years later, killing the two dogs that were almost permanently tied up in there. You couldn't see the village from the front, and I liked that, but over the marshes were the rusty-coloured

roof tops of other villages and hamlets ... les Touches, Luzac, Nieulle ... and beyond the river Seudre lay La Tremblade. You could see the lights all along the river for miles and miles at night time, like Christmas decorations strung out along the horizon. Off to the right lay Arabor, its impressive and lop-sided church steeple looming up in to the brilliant sky, a beacon of yore for the pilgrims heading south. The landscape is very flat and dotted with just a few small trees. In those days being at the edge of the marshes meant that it was impossible to sit outside for long in the summer evenings for the mosquitoes moved in as soon as the heat faded. We learnt to keep an array of anti-mozzi barbeque candles and flame torches. Nowadays the marshes are treated, the local authorities having recognized the value of tourists and the fact that tourists don't like mosquitoes. The sun set was perhaps the most spectacular thing, a huge scarlet and gleaming ball of fire, descending over Arabor, filling the sky all around with a myriad shades of red and orange and orange-red, and evening birds flitting by, black silhouettes against the scarlet.

A Call From France

In the summer I kept trailing geraniums on both balconies, though I seemed to be the only person who ever thought to water them. Facing the blast of the southern sun, they never really grew particularly well. I haven't got green fingers. I tried putting winter plants on the balconies too – small pine-like shrubs and little trees – but the Atlantic winter winds soon obliterated them.

The house was very beautiful and both Euan and I were extremely proud of what we achieved there. Constantly on a shoe-string budget, I decorated the place with art-nouveau type drapery and pictures done by my father or myself. The babes rooms were the last to be decorated, over a year later, though we did slosh cream-coloured wash over the walls in Debbie's rooms to make it less spidery for her. One of the first things we did, because the house was so huge, was to install a bell system so that I could ring for the children's attention when needed, for supper or to do their homework and so on. We named it the Calling Bell.

Being in the line of work we were in we frequently came across furniture, sometimes left abandoned in the house in question and sometimes going very cheaply. At that time the local French hadn't twigged that old French furniture was of any value and the things that I paid £30 for then now sell for £1000 and more. This meant that our huge house was soon full of furniture, ranging from dilapidated farmhouse stuff that I either re-painted, stressed or stripped, to quite nice quality antiques dug out of somebody's attic or bought for a song at the market.

I painted an old linen chest for Debbie and decorated it with little flowers and her initials.

"This is where you can keep all your treasures," I said to her. "All the things that are best, you can put them in here. And when you are grown-up and have a house of your own, this chest will be yours. It's not valuable, but it's a collectable."

Inside she arranged a little pair of wooden chairs Euan had made for her dolls when she was only two or three years old, an Indian frame Gran had given her, a leather camel from Egypt, a shell-encrusted box from Spain. Also her dolls – an Indian doll, a porcelaine doll, a doll that had been mine.

Diary, two years later
Today I looked in Debbie's chest. Her treasures.
Her dolls. They stare out in glassy silence .
"Where is Debbie?" they ask.

I was happier at Les Cypres.

I was physically, if not mentally, considerably less isolated. It was only once we'd moved in that I realized just how much the distance between Tulips and everything else had added to my work load, just in sheer driving time. I hadn't even been able to post a letter or buy a stick of bread without getting out the car and, worse, any form of entertainment or relaxation – beaches, restaurants, cinemas – were all miles away.

Les Cypres offered us more and at closer proximity. As the months flit by we tried a variety of things from jazz sessions to yoga, from archery to Amnesty International. It may be that we asked too much of life, but we were never able to become immersed in any way and remained permanently sitting at the edge. One of the things we got involved in was the village committee for saving the *patrimoine* – the local heritage – and we attended

156

several village meetings where the restoration of an ancient bread oven was discussed. I suppose the problem was that it was not our country, not our village – hey, not even our language! – and we found it difficult to take any realistic interest in renovating a bread oven, not least because we had an ancient bread oven of our own.

I can't say I actively enjoyed the proximity of the village shops or the supermarket in Arabor, but I was aware it was an advantage. St Sylvain , the village, offered the basic essentials, despite being closed half the time, and Arabor was at least a town with real live people around, if not very many. It's funny how you just don't see French people in the streets in a French town, the way you do in England.

On a Sunday morning, particularly in winter, Euan and I went to the supermarket in Bourcefranc, some five minutes in the car. Afterwards we walked on the beach. I loved looking out over the sea to the island of Oleron opposite, seeing the boats bobbing about in the estuary and the cars passing by over the bridge.

157

There is something undeniably exhilarating about walking along a beach, even in the winter when that wind whipped in off the Atlantic, searing like a knife through our cagoules and thrashing my hair into a tangled nest. We always parked at the eastern end of the beach, at that time little more than a dirt road and utterly stinking with seaweed and shell fish, and walked directly along the shore line as far as the little sailing club at the far end.

We walked briskly, breathing deeply, trying to counteract the stress and strains of the punitive week we had terminated. Big Harry always came too and would charge along that beach barking and leaping through the waves. We still walk on that beach, quite regularly. Sometimes we see Big Harry's shadow, his ghost, still leaping joyfully in the sand. Bernie joined the little sailing club in the summer and spent many a sunny day out in the estuary, sailing sometimes beyond the bridge and out in to the huge ocean.

Our move to Les Cypres coincided with my little estate agency fizzling out. That is the only way to describe it: it just fizzled out. That last summer at Tulips I had made many sales and had had clients almost every day; by the following spring it was over. At that time the expression "burn out" hadn't been coined but, looking back on it now, I realize I was all burnt out. Competition was greater, of course, for the proximity of civilization also meant not only proximity of other agents but sparsity of properties available: the abandoned little farmhouses simply didn't exist, people moved house less frequently, abandoned their houses never, and there was generally little of any interest on the market. My great strength as an agent had been that I was willing and able to drive around all the isolated little hamlets in the countryside, spotting the potential for British clients in the huge old beams and stone fireplaces, which at that time were the very things the French were abandoning. I had seen how to play the market. But it wasn't just that: somehow the energy and enthusiasm had gone. The need to earn money kept my agency limping along for a while, perhaps six months.

"I'm not doing this any more," I said aloud as I drove home one day, "I've finished."

And that was it: I finished.

A Call From France

Letter from Aggie, Lewes, Sussex.
Hello my dear old thing-o!   How's the sex life ?!
How's the French life ?!
Things tootling along as ever here.   Not enough
sex. Or too much. Depends.
Went to a lovely pub last night.   We'll treat you
when you come back. Proper ye olde English stuff,
none of your continental rubbish.   Big open fire.
Landlord as common as muck.   Bar girl with far
too much make-up.   Just the job.
Went to the market and ran in to Giles.   Deary me.
What can one say ?!
The girls are fine and ask after Debbie.   Pity you
left. Has Hill Cottage sold ?   Such a nice house.
Did the bank re-posess ?   Is that what you told me
?   How traumatic for you ducky!   But you will
recover, you know, you will.
Love forever xxxxxxxxxxx Aggie xxxxxxxxxxxxxxx

My nephew Richie came to stay with us that summer. He was seventeen. He was a gorgeous boy with his mother's good looks. Not very tall, but well-built. He had beautiful eyes and long lashes. He was quiet and shy. He seemed to be frequently deep in thought, mulling over some dream, his dark eyes on the horizon and a small

160

smile, almost as though his thoughts were bordering on a joke, playing about his mouth.   There was something Rupert Brooke-ish about his profile.

«Got a girlfriend ?» I asked.

«No!» he seemed embarrassed.

He was wonderful with the children, especially Bernie .   Together - Bernie was about five - they built a go-cart and hurtled down our field, narrowly missing the apple trees, and then clambering laboriously up again.   Over and over again in the summer heat under the shade of the trees, the lad and the child, legs scratched from the brambles, dusty, sweating and laughing. Kids.   I can picture it so clearly.   After a week or so Euan paid Richie some pocket money to help repair the perimeter wall.   There were almost 200 metres of it, old stone, and in need of constant repairs.   Debbie held the bucket of cement for Richie, and she chatted and chatted (Lord how she chatted!), half-heartedly picking at the ivy that Richie tried to persuade her to pull off, the cement slowly making its way over her chest and ruining her T-shirt. We all enjoyed Richie being there.

He stayed all summer - six weeks or so. It can be exhausting having somebody else in your house but Richie was no trouble at all and he slotted in as though he had always been there. I was so sad the day he left. Debbie and I drove him to the railway station in Rochefort. We hugged him. He seemed to cling on.

«You can stay, Richie» I said. «you can come back any time you like. Count this as your second home. That bedroom you slept in is called Richie's room.»

«Nah … mum is expecting me back, thanks.» He was close to his mother and had talked about her a bit, affectionate boyish stuff, half-embarrassed at himself.

I wanted to say «we love you» but didn't. I so wish I had. I will always wish I had.

He smiled that slightly awkward smile, those beautiful eyes dark with a mix of pleasure and emotion. He turned, waved, and went through to the platform.

A Call From France

We never saw him again.

The morning that Euan came up to our bedroom, a few weeks later, to tell me that had been my mother on the phone, and that Richie had met with an accident and had died, is etched on to my brain like a black-white scar, like a slow-motion film that has curled at the edges. Shock makes you behave in a way you don't imagine. I was angry. I lashed out at Euan and shouted «no! no!» as though it was somehow his fault. He gripped my wrists.

The loss of a child is the greatest grief. I couldn't even begin to imagine how my brother and sister-in-law would cope. There was something so horribly out-of-kilter with the world in those weeks as we tried to come to terms with it. Bernie didn't understand. Max was shaken, didn't really believe it. Debbie cried. She cried and cried almost all of that first day and off and on for weeks afterwards.

As the weeks drifted by normality returned for us. I removed the photo of Richie from our sideboard because it made me cry every time I saw it. My sister-in-law would have no such luxury. I know. I have known the loss of loved ones, but it is said that is not even on the Richter scale compared to the loss of a child.

***

Do you remember that Louise Woodward case ? The au-pair who was accused of murdering an American baby ? I always supported Louise Woodward, because bizarre things do happen. It is possible she whacked that baby so hard she accidentally killed him, we'll never know. If she did lose her temper and whack him that hard, who can blame her? We have all wanted to whack our babies, or certainly be shod of them for a while. I can't imagine what the parents thought they were doing, leaving a teenager in sole full-time charge of a baby and a toddler. No wonder she lost her rag. She maintained she didn't know what happened, and I feel that is equally possible. The argument was "how can she possibly pretend to not know that the baby had hurt himself so dreadfully?" How can such a horrific accident have happened without her knowing about it? Without the baby's parents knowing about it? But odd things do happen.

When Bernie was a baby he pulled the iron off the ironing board. It landed harmlessly on the floor beside him. I didn't see it happen, however. Heavens ... even all these years later I shudder when I think of it. When I was a baby my brother, eighteen months older, picked up a hammer and my father was able to intercept him a split second before it came crashing down on my head.

Debbie disappeared.

We don't know what happened there either. Debbie had had an idyllic childhood. She had parents who adored her, she was great pals with both her brothers, she came from a big happy and caring family. She got cuddles and kisses, the odd spurt of parental temper, the odd sibling fight. She had horse riding, skiing, judo, piano, ballet, cycling, boating ... the lot. She not only had her own room but she had a living room too, with TV and video and stereo. Friends came to stay, she went to stay with friends. She joined-in happily all family activities from baking a cake to playing silly games. Life, although very hectic and certainly action-packed, was comfortable and easy-going.

We were affectionate, undemanding but firm. She was a happy child. Some metaphoric iron fell on her head when I wasn't looking.

That summer term she had to do work experience for four weeks. I found her a place in a nearby five-star campsite, belonging to a couple I knew vaguely, Saskia and Sergio. It was ideal for it was barely two miles away and she could cycle there. Saskia and Sergio had bought –as so many foreigners to France do, ourselves included – an old chateau, unused for many years. It was twice the size of our chateau. Unfortunately somebody had ransacked it and there was not one iota of interest left in it: each and every chandelier, every fireplace, every stone parapet had gone. All the original doors, all the interior panelling, the lot had been removed by some bright spark after a profit. It was nonetheless an attractive building surrounded by fifteen hectares of woodland and farmland and, just two miles from the beach, an idyllic spot for a campsite.

Sergio and Saskia aimed at the top and in under a year had transformed the place in to a five-star site with two swimming pools, shops, tennis, bar and restaurant. They restored a small section of the main house for themselves and left the bulk of the old chateau empty, to be used one day – far away perhaps – for conferences and similar venues.

The local Rotary club held their annual *ecclade* there, which was how we met Sergio and Saskia. The campsite was still very much in its nursery stages, but it was nonetheless a good choice of venue for all the local people were interested – including us – in finding out what was happening and, in turn, it created publicity for the campsite, not to mention general bonhomie for the village.

An *ecclade* is a traditional cooking of muscles in the Charente Maritime. The entire coastline is renowned for its seafood – as indeed is any coastline, I guess – muscles and oysters being the staple diet of the local people. An entire culture has evolved around muscles and oysters, accompanied by a whole world of "knowledge" about the type of oyster or muscle, and an entire vocabulary to go with it. For this particular speciality, the muscles are arranged, tier by tier, in a circle on a fireproof – usually a large cast iron platter - dish or even just on the sand. They are carefully balanced, facing

167

inwards (this is important) so that they eventually make a kind of rounded pyramid. All guests must stand in a circle and admire. Pine needles are then placed over them, about two inches thick, and everybody must again admire. Words like "*ooh la-la*" are uttered. At a given signal (a mystery to this day) the pine needles are set alight. They are allowed to burn (along with further *ooh la-la*) for about three minutes and then are brushed away, hopefully onto sand or similar where they will die out. All guests then help themselves to the pine-scented cooked muscles.

This is altogether more complicated than it seems. The muscles are not only too hot to touch but also black with pine ashes, and the ones that were not facing inwards – or which fell to one side during the various *ooh la-la-ings* – are also filled with black pine ash. After we'd attended two or three of these functions we discovered that vast quantities of kitchen roll are essential for wiping blackened fingers, and vast quantities of chilled white wine for washing down the ash. Even so, we didn't bother with them again.

A Call From France

Debbie was given a little work experience job at reception and as she was bi-lingual this suited the owners quite well. Her duties also involved helping to make sign-boards and general light clearing. She could have use of the pool during her time off and was provided with a light lunch at the restaurant. The owners were people I respected. Sergio was an Italian who kept telling me we must go round for dinner sometime but who never actually got round to inviting us. Saskia was Dutch, tall and pretty and very clever. As fellow foreigners Euan and I hoped we might strike up a friendship.

I was very pleased with myself for finding Debbie's little job and it seemed to please her too. When the four weeks were up she returned to school with a glowing report and I managed, not without some difficulty, to secure her a summer job at the same campsite. Never push it. I've learnt that over the years. If the thing – whatever it is – doesn't seem to be moving, don't push it. The owners were very slow to respond to my enquiry after a summer job for Debbie and, despite having sung her praises when she was there for her work experience, seemed reluctant to take her on.

Debbie was not over-keen at working there either.

"But you loved it!" I exclaimed.

"I know. But I want to go to the beach with Ghislaine. I don't want to work."

"I daresay Ghislaine will be working too," I replied.

"No she won't. There are no jobs."

This was true. Unemployment was very high in that area, made worse by poverty for the few jobs available were frequently on the oyster farms where people without cars had little hope of going, or else they were in some other village or small town and as there is no bus service to speak of access to work was a problem that exacerbated an existing scourge.

"Well, you're very lucky to have got a job. You wouldn't if you weren't bi-lingual."

"So! I'm being penalized because I'm bi-lingual!"

"Debbie! You really are so naughty! Why can't you be glad you've got an opportunity to earn some money? Most young people would be glad!"

"Well, I'm not glad. Max isn't working."

"Max is too young to work. You have to be sixteen as you well know. Anyway, he'll be helping daddy." (By the time he was twenty, Max was one of the best DIY people in Christendom.)

Debbie turned sixteen in early June, a couple of days after starting work. We had celebrated her birthday on the beach with a crowd of friends. As always she had played in the muddy sand flats with younger children, caking herself in the grey-brown mud and collecting small shells and building little dams. I took a photo of her. It showed her standing with bucket and spade, clad in a tiny blue bikini she had chosen as one of her presents, covered in mud. She was blissfully unaware of her stunning figure and I affectionately labelled the photo: *Debbie, aged sixteen, going on twelve.*

For her main present that year we gave her the *Conduite Accompagnée*, which was what she

171

wanted. This was an excellent, and optional, system for learning to drive and so far as I know was in those days unique to the French. Youngsters start when they are only sixteen with a proper driving school. They have to do a multiple-choice test and attend so many hours of classroom lessons. They then, if they pass the multiple choice test and fulfil the required amount of classroom hours, have a set amount of driving hours with a qualified instructor. The entire thing takes them up to age seventeen, when they can then complete a further mileage of driving experience with any adult before taking their test. This means that when they hit the road at age seventeen they have a year of experience and qualified instruction behind them. The system is very expensive so only a few youngsters are able to participate – about 7000f then, £700-ish.

This year she also wanted a party. We turned over one of the barns to her and provided vast quantities of food and soft drink. Between them she and Max rigged up loudspeakers and lights. Several of her friends had to be fetched. This was typical of the local French, I had long since discovered, for other mothers just didn't seem to do the fetching and carrying of children that I did. I was very frequently the only mother to fetch and take any of the youngsters, not to mention feed them and put them up for the night and then take them home again. I didn't mind at all, however, for I had always enjoyed teenagers and, although it was often very difficult fitting it all in it gave me great pleasure seeing them having such fun. And they had a lot of fun! That barn became known as The Party Barn and for years many a wild party happened within the confines of its now completely unshockable walls.

We went to eat at the campsite restaurant a couple of times and Debbie served us, politely taking the order and quietly muttering things under her breath:

"That woman over there can't decide whether she wants fish or fish!"

or

"I'm expecting a good tip from that German lot ..."

We were glad to see she had started enjoying it. She was very adaptable, extremely quick-witted so that she was never phased by a guest asking something difficult; she always had her answer ready or, if she had no answer, had the ability to turn the situation around. She had seen me handle clients many a time of course and, as Gran pointed out, she had also seen me speak to employees. She was confident and versatile and so lovely. We were terribly proud of her.

Sergio came over and slapped Euan on the shoulder in a hail-fellow-well-met gesture that was characteristic of him.

"U-annn, my friend! We must go out for deeeena togezzer! I will phone you!"

(Odd, the way some people will do this kind of thing, knowing full well it is vacuous.)

"I can stay tonight at the camp," Debbie told me one morning as she set off.

"Oh? Where?"

"There's a place. Several of us can sleep there."

"But what? I need to know where you are …"

"Oh, don't worry about it mummy!"

"Does Saskia know about it? Does she know you're staying?"

"Of course! It's her that suggested it!"

"I see. That's all right then."

That was fine. I was glad Debbie was at last mixing with her own age-group. Her tan had deepened and her hair had taken on the golden glow of hours spent under the sun. It suited her. We went to the campsite for a drink; there was a nice little bar at the restaurant. Debbie introduced us to the barman:

"This is Manolo," she said. We shook hands. Another man came out of a back room. "This is Louis, the chef" she said, and we shook hand s again. Louis disappeared into the back of a van.

Manolo served us a gin and tonic each. He had stunning eyes, a bright, bright blue. He was very good-looking in a rakish sort of way, aged in his

175

mid-thirties. We chatted lightly. We told him we felt there was really nowhere to go in the area and that we hoped the campsite, for just that reason, would be a great success. He came from Marseille, of Italian extract. Euan and I carried our drinks out on to the patio and enjoyed the evening sun. There were hundreds of campers around, mostly Dutch.

Euan's brother, John, came to stay for a few days, accompanied by his two children, Jez and Colin. Jez was two years younger than Max, so aged thirteen then. On Debbie's day off the two girls set off in to Arabor on bicycles. It was about three miles, not .far. Although mobile phones had been in reasonably regular use in the UK for a couple of years, they had only just hit France. We nonetheless frequently loaned Debbie our mobile phone so that she could phone us should the need arise.

"You never know," I said to her. "If ever you find yourself in an awkward situation just say you're going to the loo and quickly phone me. I'll come and fetch you."

"What sort of situation?!" she scoffed.

"Oh Debbie ... I don't know. I realize you think I am silly. It's just so that you can call for help if you need it. Hopefully you will never need it." I hesitated and, just out of curiosity really, I asked her:

"Actually, what would you do if you found yourself in a dangerous situation and you couldn't get to a phone?"

She shrugged.

"Scream ?" she suggested. Then, cocking her head to one side: " – why ? What would you do, mummy?"

"Depends ......" I stroked her little brown nose teasingly, "I'd check myself in to an expensive hotel and then phone daddy!"

After the two girls had been gone several hours, the phone rang.

"Mummy! It's me!" Debbie had an adorable way of putting excitement into her voice, as though everything was good news.

"Where are you?"

"In Arabor. Can you come and fetch us in about an hour?"

"What about your bikes?"

"We'll put them in the car."

"Yes, I realize, but I thought you were going to cycle back?"

"It's too hot. We're tired. We can't."

"I see. OK then. I'll meet you outside the post office, okay?"

She said that was okay and rang off. I called John-o.

"The girls want to be picked up in an hour's time, "
I said, " but we might as well go in to Arabor now
because I need a few things. You coming?"

I parked outside the post office and was about to
turn towards the supermarket when John-o spotted
Jez and Debbie sitting outside a café with Manolo.
We stood silently for a while and watched them.
Jez looked moderately bored but Debbie was
crossing an uncrossing her legs, giggling and
smiling and tossing her hair. A shudder went
through me.

"Girls are such silly things," I said to John-o.

Jez spotted us at that moment and leapt up, waving.
She grabbed her bike and wheeled it over, her face
flushed in the sun, and she helped her dad load the
bike in to the car.

"Debbie says she'll be over in a minute," she
announced.

I nipped in to the shop and purchased the items I
needed. When I came out Debbie was still with

Manolo. They were talking animatedly. They leant towards each other over the table.

"Go and tell Debbie we're ready to go," I said to Jez.

Jez went trotting over to the café.

"What d'you think?" I asked John-o.

"Hmmm… looks a bit seedy …" he replied.

"Shall I say something?"

He hesitated.

"Yes," he said at length, "I would."

I smiled cheerfully at Debbie as she came over with her bike. As she loaded it in to the car I crossed the street and went over to Manolo. He stood as I approached, his hand outstretched and those stunning eyes smiling at me.

"Bonjour!" he exclaimed.

A Call From France

He shook my hand vigorously, clasping it in both his, as though he were genuinely pleased to see me. I realized I was doubtless making a fuss about nothing.

"I don't want Deborah sitting in cafes with older men," I said bluntly, "I know you mean no harm, but girls are funny things ..."

"Ah, Madame! I understand absolutely! I do apologize! I have a daughter of my own – I can see what you mean – don't worry, it won't happen again."

Well, there was not a reason in the world for me to think it would happen again. Or was I just so naïve ....?

We went cycling on the island of Oleron and found a pretty little port called La Cotiniere where I did a water-colour sketch of Bernie sitting under a fishing boat. I mentally ear-marked the port as a good place for me and my father to go and paint in a few weeks' time.

A Call From France

"I'd have loved to go to art school," I said to Euan, "I'd love to be able to do it properly.

Letter from Aggie, Lewes, Sussex.
Do be patient with Debbie. She's only young. My girls are also difficult sometimes and my dear – I have two of them! Odd, though – isn't it? Your Debbie has 100% parent-daughter attention. I'm afraid I think she's like you deary, truly I do. The good side of this is that she will turn out to be as excellent as you are and the (temporary) down side is that .... hmmm, can't think of anything.
On a serious note, I really believe that one should never ever shout at children or really punish them. They're only kids, after all. Just be patient. Like me. I am The Perfect Mother. Didn't you know? I wonder if I'll be made to eat my words....?
Your wise friend, Aggie   xxxxxxxxxxxxxx

A tattoo.   In my dictionary it said:

A Call From France

Tattoo. Mark (skin) with permanent pattern or design by puncturing it or inserting pigment; make (design) thus. Tattooing. Tahitian tatua.

Well, I thought, I knew that. Of course I knew it, I just wanted to look it up in case … in case of what ? Somehow looking it up made it real. This was not the next episode of a story. In my medical dictionary I read:

Tattooing: a method of obtaining a permanent mark or design on the skin by puncturing and the introduction of colour. It is of very ancient origin and is found worldwide, except in the darkest-skinned communities and in China. Various methods are used to produce tattooing, the most common being with needles and pigment, though small cuts with special knives are also used. During the past twenty years tattooing has become increasingly popular among young people in the Western world. In unskilled hands, however, it can be dangerous and had been implicated as a possible cause of some forms of skin cancer. In 1961 the New York City administration severely restricted the practice because of the spread of hepatitis caused by contaminated instruments. Tattooing can be erased only by the removal of the tattooed skin and the grafting on of new skin.

Tattoos hit France a few years after they hit England. I wasn't really aware of them. From time to time one saw somebody with a tattoo on the beach, sometimes a discreet little butterfly on a shoulder, or a tiny flower on an upper arm. The huge and ghastly snakes and "I love Michelle", associated with workmen, seemed to be less common on men's chests – or at any rate we didn't see many of them.

"Do you like tattoos?" Debbie asked me one day.

"Depends on what it is, where it is, and who it is," I replied.

"Mmmm …"

"Why d'you ask?"

"I was just thinking I might get a tattoo done."

"I'd rather you didn't. For goodness' sake check it out with me before, at any rate!"

184

"Mmmm ..."

"Debs, are you listening to me?"

"Oh ... yeh ... sure ... it was only an idea ..."

So why was I so surprised and shocked when she got the tattoo done? Funny, the way mothers think they know their children. I had so often made the mistake of crediting her with more sense that she really had. She was sixteen, the age of consent, old enough to know her own mind, yet I had thought my light words of warning had sunk in. She pulled back the V-neck of her T-shirt and showed me the tattoo. Her eyes were full of defiance.

The other day a friend asked me how I defined the word "ugly". I couldn't answer in a simple sentence. Ugly: repulsive, vile. Initiates a sensation of recoil. The tattoo was ugly. It was vile. It was offensive in every sense and worse – had it not been on the breast of my young daughter – would have been terribly funny.

On her left breast, stretching from the edge of the nipple right up to beyond where her bra covered, was the head of a donkey.

My mouth dropped open in astonishment.

"It's a horse," Debbie told me.

It was a child's drawing of a donkey's head. She – my little girl, my child who I thought was so bright and so beautiful, had had this monster tattooed on to her pink young flesh. It was hideous.

I turned suddenly and left the room, afraid of shouting and struggling not to wail. Debbie remained on the sofa, silent. There is some way round this, I thought. This is a joke, not real. I pottered noisily about the kitchen, trying to be calm. It wasn't as though I could command her "take it off immediately!" I unloaded the dishwasher with a great deal of vigour, cracking a tea cup in the process. I wished I smoked. It was too early for a drink. After a while Debbie came in. I looked at her.

"I did ask you to consult me first," I said hoarsely.

186

"Please don't tell daddy," she replied, ignoring me.

"He'll see it, won't he?" I found I had to whisper as though it might somehow help it to not exist.

Suddenly I realized she was on the verge of tears.

"Who did the drawing?" I asked.

"Pamela."

"Pamela! For goodness' sake! Pamela is a CHILD!"

"No, she's not, she's fifteen."

"Debbie! Fifteen is a CHILD!"

Debbie looked down at her feet. I struggled for calm. I wanted to slap her, I wanted to hit her really really hard, I wanted to hug her, I wanted to cry.

"Where did you get the tattoo done?" I put my arm around her and tried to reassure her. She was white and had started to shake slightly, "did it hurt?"

187

"I hate it!" she burst out.

(Yes, my little girl, I expect you do hate it. Soon you will hate yourself for it. I don't know how to help you with this one.)

"Where did you get it done?" I repeated.

"A friend," she said bluntly.

"But who? Where?"

"In Manolo's flat," she said, her voice hardening in a nasty way that was soon to become familiar to me. "That's all I can tell you. I promised I wouldn't say."

"Manolo's flat ?!! You must NOT go in to a man's flat ! But anyway - why the secrecy?!"

She didn't answer.

"Well, it is good to keep your word," I said, "but if you know anything about me at all, my girl, you

188

know that I will find out. So you might as well tell me. I take it it wasn't Manolo?"

"No!"

"How much did you pay?"

"Five hundred francs."

"And where did you get five hundred francs?"

She didn't answer but made a small shrugging movement ......
 With a sinking sensation I saw a stranger forming in front of me as the child that I had raised started to disappear.

"I want it removed!" she blurted out suddenly.

"I expect you do," I said, "but I fear it won't be that easy."

"There's always a way," she said, quoting something I said frequently, "it is just a question of finding the way."

189

"I hope so," I said giving her another little hug. She didn't respond to me and I felt she hated me while asking for my help. I didn't understand why she should hate me and I flailed around in my mother's heart to find a way of reaching out to her and letting her know I was her friend.

The French medical system being what it is – and it is excellent - I got straight on to the phone and made a series of appointments, one after the other, with dermatologists and plastic surgeons over the next few days. Most were pretty booked-up but I got appointments as promptly as I could within the next couple of days, fearful that the tattoo had some kind of "setting" quality that would make it harder to remove the longer it was left. There were a couple of dermatologists in Rochefort, one Euan had seen several times about his scalp, as well as a plastic surgeon, and another two of each in Royan and several in La Rochelle.

"I'm pretty certain a tattoo can't come out," I warned her.

"It's got to come out!"

"We can only do our best, Debbie. I'm doing my best."

"I don't want it! I want to see somebody TODAY!"

"I've already got too much to do," I said, my anger and hurt steadily brewing up towards the surface, "without carting you around doctors all day tomorrow! I can't do it today – there is nobody available."

"Why not?!" she all but stamped her foot.

"Because unlike you, young lady," I said between grit teeth, "other people have other things to do. Especially doctors. Other people are not your mother, ie willing to drop everything for your sake."

I crashed angrily around the kitchen, preparing the evening meal. Part of my fury was directed straight at Debbie for being such a fool but another part was about her rather than at her, for although she kept sobbing she was not sorry. Certainly, she wished she hadn't had it done and could see how utterly ghastly it was, but she wasn't even remotely

191

contrite and appeared to have no sense of responsibility vis-à-vis me, her mother, or any of my needs or emotions. Her entire upset was for herself, but not in a How-could-I-have-been-such-a-fool way – more as though it was somehow somebody else's fault.

Worse, I was concerned about how Euan was going to react to this. Had it been a discreet little flower on her bottom or shoulder, or something similar, I could have persuaded him it was pretty – as indeed it might have been. But Debbie was the apple of his eye and a great donkey head on her young breast was … sick. I hoped against hope that there was some way we could have it removed without him seeing it, but knew it was useless.

"Well," I said, barely keeping the sting out of my voice, "you've always enjoyed plenty of medical attention – you're certainly going to be getting it now!"

She didn't answer, but fingered the wound under her T-shirt, gently probing it with her finger tips.

"Don't do that!" I snapped, "it'll get infected on top of everything else!"

I sat down suddenly, struggling not to cry, but slowly letting my anger dissolve into tears. I looked at the faded blue tea-towel in my lap and turned it round and round my hands.

"I remember buying this tea-towel," I said, "we were in the supermarket in Buzancais, you and me and Bernie in the buggy."

"Where was Max?" she asked as though it was of great importance.

"I can't remember – with daddy I expect."

Silently we both looked at the floor.

"Debs," I said at length, "I will do everything I can to help you with this. In return I want you to promise me something."

"What?"

"Promise me faithfully that whenever you are thinking of doing something ... a bit ... radical ... when ever you have got an idea about something that is not just ordinary every day stuff ... promise me you will always consult me first."

"Oh mummy! That's hardly likely!"

"Well," I managed to keep my voice steady, "at least promise me you will talk it over with a mature and sensible person – not Pamela!"

"Pamela IS mature and sensible, mummy! You hardly even know her!"

"Debbie!" I roared, my temper snapping totally, "Pamela is a CHILD! I don't need to know her. Now listen, and listen carefully. You have done something extremely stupid, something we may well not be able to undo. Daddy will be devastated. I could – and believe me, my girl, I am tempted – tell you to simply stuff it! I could say – tough, your problem, live with it. But I won't. If you want me to I will give up my time in order to drive you around all those doctors tomorrow and the day after. Do you or do you not want me to help you with that?"

"Yes," she said quietly.

"Right. I will help you. I will do whatever I can. But in return I want you to promise you will NEVER do anything – ANYTHING! – even remotely different from the norm without first consulting a mature and SENSIBLE PERSON!!"

It wasn't possible to hide it from Euan though Debbie begged me to. At least she feels ashamed in front of him, I thought. As predicted, Euan was shattered. He looked at her lovely young breast and wept. He sat down on the edge of the chair and his face fell forwards in to his hands and he wept.

"You stupid girl," he said, "you stupid **stupid** girl."

Debbie and I spent most of that week going round doctors in the local towns. Most didn't hold out much hope. One wanted to do a skin graft.

"I can remove the skin," he explained, "and then take some off her bottom and graft it on top."

"But that will then leave a huge scar on her bottom?"

"Yes, of course."

"And the skin graft – it will show, won't it? Surely it'll look ugly?"

"Not as ugly as a donkey's head!" he smiled.

"I want him to do it," Debbie said to me, "mummy – this week – straight away."

"She is right," said the doctor, "it is the only solution."

I'll bet it is, I thought, along with a nice fee for you.

Debbie was furious with me for not agreeing to the operation.

Neither Euan nor I were prone to getting cross with the children; we barely ever smacked them – in fact, I don't think we did ever smack them at all. We never became angry over a broken cup or spilt milk and never made an issue over things that really didn't need an issue making over them. But we made an issue now. We were both extremely angry. Debbie remained defiant, almost cold.

Back at Les Cypres I phoned Hugh who had done a patch of plastic surgery at medical school.

"Technology is advancing all the time," he advised me, "so don't do anything for now. There's nothing that can be done, but in ten years' time there might be. The only possibility is a laser. I don't know much about it."

My other brother, Rupert, also a doctor, said more-or-less the same thing. They turned out to be absolutely right.

"It's only a tattoo," Rupert said, "kids can do a lot worse."

That helped me keep it in proportion and although I was still furious with my daft child, I calmed down considerably and managed to adopt an oh-dear-lets-

A Call From France

see-what-we-can-do attitude which Debbie appreciated.

A doctor in La Rochelle recommended laser treatment. He explained there was only one place in France do get it done and that was in a plastic surgery hospital in Tours – about four hours' drive away. I made the appropriate phone calls. Over the next year we went to Tours six times. Each session cost about £100. The tattoo was faded slightly and small sections of it disappeared, but essentially the donkey remained. There was nothing to be done.

We did lodge a complaint against the man who did the tattoo. As the police pointed out, Debbie was over sixteen and therefore past the age of consent. But, as I pointed out, you have to be licensed to do this sort of thing, and this man – clearly a total amateur – not only obviously had no qualifications whatsoever but had also charged Debbie 500 francs for it. Debbie was unwilling to give the name of the person in question.

"Do you want him to do this to another girl?" Euan asked her. "Do you think he did a good job and earned his 500 francs? "

"No, I don't …"

She didn't know his address of his surname, or even have his phone number, only that he was called Pierre and lived in Royan.

"He's a friend of Manolo's," she said.

We talked it through and it was agreed that she would phone Manolo (I noticed she knew his number off by heart) and try to get the number or address off him.

"Hi!" she sounded totally cheerful, leaning down in to the receiver as she spoke. "I want to phone Pierre to let him know how my tattoo is healing." She lied with such ease.

"There!" she slammed the bit of paper with the appropriate number on it down on the table in front of us.

199

"Now phone him for his address," said Euan.

She picked the receiver up again and dialled the number.

"I'm coming to Royan this afternoon," she told him, "I've got a present for you. I'll pop by ... what's your address ...?"

"She lied with such complete ease," Euan said to me after we'd returned from the police station, "she didn't bat an eye lid."

"I lie with ease too," I told Aggie later on the phone, "I suppose she gets it from me ..."

"Not lying, my dear – acting! It's not the same thing!"

It was at about this time that Debbie suddenly declared she had been gang raped. I stared at her (........ *Debbie, what are you talking about you daft kid.. .? Don't give me this rubbish ... ...)*

"When ?!!"

A Call From France

"About a month ago," she said.

She explained that she has blotted it out of her mind all this time. My reaction swung wildly from horror that this had happened, to fury that she would pretend, and back again …… It didn't seem possible that such a huge thing could happen to my daughter and not only she be able to blot it out, but me – her mother – not have the faintest inkling. I had not seen any sign of distress in her, no bruises, no abnormal behaviour in any way. I asked her a few questions about it and – even now I cannot bear to think about it, let alone write it – decided to go and see a solicitor. I didn't take Debbie with me; after all, she *seemed* to be fine and I was not convinced it was true.

"Teenage girls do sometimes cry rape," the solicitor told me, "I think because they want attention. They don't take on board how devastating the accusation can be for the man if he is innocent ……"

"**If** he is innocent!" I interrupted. "That is what I need to know."

"But in order to find out, *Madame*, you will subject your daughter to a very traumatic situation which may just make things worse. It will certainly make things worse for all concerned, including you and *Monsieur*, if it didn't really happen. By your own admission your daughter is a bit melodramatic. Imagine yourself being cross-examined by a barrister who is determined to defend these boys. Imagine Deborah being cross-examined. People do not realize how shattering a cross-examination of this nature can be. A good lawyer can make a witness look foolish very quickly! I am not sure I can take on this case; there is no evidence at any level. *Au contraire* there is evidence which, believe me, will be used to prove your daughter to be .... how can I put this ?   Let's say rather imaginative. It will be used against her by the defence and, make no mistake, they will rip her to pieces regardless of the truth, they will show no mercy."

I felt ashamed. Ashamed at myself, at the solicitor, at Debbie, even at those boys ..... how does a mother decide how to handle this kind of situation ? There is no book where you can look up "what to do if your daughter may have been raped". The main thing on my mind was Debbie's well-being, and she seemed to be fine ……

"Whatever you do," said my father, "it's going to be the wrong thing, I'm afraid."

So I did nothing.

That summer Les Cypres was let for the entire month of August to a certain Lady Winbolt and her family. June came and went and, part of the way in to July, Lady Winbolt phoned to ask if I knew of a local young girl who could help entertain her seven year-old son. Six days a week, she said, and she'd pay £10 a day. Debbie was happy at the campsite but there was something about it that tasted bad … I couldn't pinpoint it … I often felt she was hiding something from me, she seemed evasive, as though there was something about the campsite that was unhealthy ... yet I knew there couldn't be. I was glad to have her work for Lady Winbolt instead. It was agreed. To my surprise Debbie was very happy with the sudden job change. I arranged for her to stay with a friend, Claire, in the village and Euan and I set off on our own holiday along with Max,

Jeremy, Julien, Bernie and Big Harry. Both car
and caravan were all but bursting at the seams.

"Are those all your boys?" asked a woman on the
ferry.

"Near as damn it," I replied.

  We are unconventional people. Unconventional
people do unconventional things. Years later, when
Max set off to Explore The World, we sat in a pub –
a lovely English pub in the heart of Sussex - and he
said:

"I had an unconventional childhood – it was
fantastic – you were such unconventional parents –
that's what made us so different."

We left Euan's mobile with Debbie because,
although we knew she was safe in the hands of
Claire and Lady Winbolt, we wanted her to be able
to get hold of us at the drop of a hat should the need
arise. It wasn't long before almost everybody,
young or old, had mobiles of their own, but at that
time mobiles were fantastically expensive and not
common.

"If things go wrong – and I'm sure they won't – just phone us."

"All right," she said.

Lady Winbolt and her family were charming, though I didn't meet them myself. Euan told me he had never seen such a fat person – though that was before we went to Las Vegas. Debbie had to be in by ten every morning and stay with Robin, the little boy, till five. I sorted out Meccano and Monopoly, Scrabble and cards and vast quantities of paper and crayons.

"I expect he'll have some toys of his own," I told Debbie.

"There are Bernie's things," she said.

"No, that's not fair on Bernie. Those are his things. I don't want you to touch them."

"Okay."

A week tripped by under the hot Medoc sun and we started to unwind. We usually ate in a little restaurant on the campsite after spending most of the afternoon on the beach. A shower is utterly wonderful after an afternoon on the beach. The breakers had a cleansing effect on us. Euan would say:

"Let's go and wash it all away!" and we would jump in to the waves, sometimes being positively battered by them, and the cold salty water would wash away all our cares and we would emerge dripping and laughing and collapse onto our towels to dry off in the sun. There are a lot of naturist beaches in France, and about 4 miles of beach there is naturist. It shocked me at first but, like anything, you rapidly get used to it. There is something wholesome about naturist people – I suppose that, because they don't mind stripping down to the full monty, they have no inhibitions, no hang-ups. They are what the French call "*bien dans leur peau*" – comfortable in their own skins. It has nothing to do with looks – quite the opposite, for most people look far better with their clothes on – and it certainly has nothing to do with sex or pornography. It is just a comfortable way to swim, to dry off and to sun bathe.

Life at the camp tripped by at a slow and lazy pace. Normally active to the point of being hyper-active, we slept with the zonked-out sleep of the exhausted, till gone nine or ten. Euan and Bernie , after umpteen cups of tea, would then set off on their bikes, usually accompanied by Big Harry who was strong enough to tow Euan (albeit accidentally) for croissants while I made yet more tea. Under the hot August morning sun we ate our breakfast in slow motion and then sat and read. I at last took up sketching a bit more seriously again that summer and produced dozens of sketches of nudes, lightly washed with water colour, and several sketches of the pine forests and the mile upon mile of golden sand.

Walking on the beach in the morning is lovely. Dogs are permitted on the northern beach and the doggy fraternity met there, in varying states of nudity and, as the years went by we all got to know each other, sometimes with the same dogs year after year and sometimes with different ones as our canine friends left us. The morning air is fresh and warm, fanned by the Atlantic waves and warmed by the summer sun. The sand is raked over every night, clean scars of tracks underfoot, and little pink shells and a feeling of having got there somehow … wherever "there" might be …

Most evenings we drove Max, Jeremy and Julien in to Montalivet, or perhaps in to Soulac, which was slightly further but slightly bigger, so that they could "chill out". We had the constant problem of pocket-money for neither Jeremy nor Julien ever had a penny – or a centime, I should say –on them, yet we wanted Max to have a good time. He was very mature about it and understood we simply couldn't pay for all of them all of the time. They nonetheless seemed to enjoy themselves, and it was good for them. They looked like a trio of ruffians, with long hair and roll-up cigarettes and torn jeans. Jeremy in particular had a kind of cowboy-like amble, slightly aggressive to the uninitiated. It was perhaps because he was smaller than the other two, though he grew every bit as tall.

At sixteen, Debbie had the body of a grown woman and while in some ways she was bright and responsible, in other ways she was just a little girl.

A Call From France

We phoned her fairly regularly, concerned that she felt somehow left out of the holiday – which she didn't – and also concerned that … something was afoot. As with her job at Sergio's camp site, something tasted bad …………

"Hello, Claire" I said, "everything OK?"

"Mais oui," she said, "except that I wish Deborah had told me earlier that she had been asked to stay with the little English boy tonight. She didn't tell me till after I had prepared our supper. Not that it matters, really. I would like her to let me know in good time in future, though."

"I see," I replied, "of course. I'll tell her. So she's babysitting all night?"

"It's a nice little job she's got there. I hope they pay her extra for babysitting all night!"

I told Euan this. We judged it best to check this out with Debbie and she answered her mobile within seconds.

"Yes!" she exclaimed happily, "he's asleep, so I can watch telly."

"Where have the Winbolts gone?"

"In to La Rochelle or something. I'll see them in the morning – well, tomorrow sometime."

"Great. You're happy about everything? Not frightened alone in that big house?"

"Oh, MUMMY!"

We sat down to our own supper and afterwards strolled along the beach with Big Harry and Bernie . We had bought a kite which Euan and Bernie now tried to launch. It made Big Harry bark furiously. The tide was a long way out and it had left warm lagoons of seawater through which our dog, who loathed getting wet, waded. We scrunched the wet sand between our toes. The life guards had gone home and the red flag was out, telling us it was dangerous to swim. We waded in as far as our waists, gasping in the cold water, Big Harry barking at us from the shore. We stayed till it started turning dark and then found our bikes, and cycled back to the camp.

My mobile phone was ringing when we got back.

"*C'est moi*," came Claire's voice, "problems, I'm afraid."

"Oh dear, what's the matter?"

"Lady Winbolt has just been round. She wanted to speak to Debbie, to tell her she doesn't need to be in till lunch-time tomorrow. But, of course, Debbie is not here."

"I don't understand …"

"I fear Debbie has lost her job*, ma pauvre*, for when I told Lady Winbolt that Debbie was babysitting all night for her son – well, she was angry!"

"Where is Debbie, then, is she's not with you and she's not at the chateau?"

"*Ma chere amie*! Where do you think? She is with her boyfriend, of course!"

211

It took me a while to work this out. Boyfriend ? Which boyfriend ?

"Perhaps she feels you won't like the boyfriend?" suggested Claire.

I sighed. I felt I had tried really hard to show Debbie that I was her ally where I could be. I was wounded that she had lied. I had just spoken to her on her mobile – and she had lied through her teeth. It's true, I thought, I am constantly criticising the local people, and am not likely to particularly like a local boy, but even so it was unlikely that I'd put my foot down over any of them. I decided to phone Lady Winbolt, determined there was some kind of misunderstanding in all this.

"There's no misunderstanding," she replied gently. " I am so sorry but Debbie has lied constantly about dozens of things since we arrived, and I'm afraid I don't want her back."

My mouth went dry and a tight, strangled feeling started in my throat.

"Lied about what, for example?" I asked.

"Oh, one thing after another … usually to get her off work so that she can go and meet her boyfriend. She has done so little work with my son there's no point …"

"I thought she was there every day?!"

"No, I'm afraid not – she turns up all right but there is always some reason why she has to leave early or take a few hours off."

I was mortified.

"I had no idea … Lady Winbolt, I am so sorry … "

"So am I. I have an abhorrence of lies. And as for alcohol …"

"Alcohol …..?!!!"

"Did that French lady – Claire – not tell you? She thought Debbie was having a fit of some kind and called the doctor – but she was just drunk. Too drunk to stand up or speak."

213

"Good God …"

"I am sorry for you – I'm sure Debbie will grow out of it – I did silly things when I was her age. In the meantime, she'll have to find another holiday job."

I phoned Claire back.

"Do you know who the boyfriend is?" I asked.

"I hardly dare tell you …"

"Who …?"

"It's Manolo."

You know how an entire paragraph – Lord, an entire book! – can go through your mind in a split second ? My brain raced as I tried to take this in – clearly not the only Manolo I knew ....?

"Surely not … he must be knocking forty! I just don't believe it!"

"Well, it is. I have tried to talk to her, but she pretends to be listening carefully and then completely ignores me. Listen to me, *ma pauvre*, do not be too angry with her for you will simply drive her away. She thinks she is in love with this man."

"Good God ... it doesn't seem possible. What can she possibly see in him?! He's so much older ... he's broke ... a part-time barman .... I doubt he even owns a car ...!"

"Worse than that, he has been sacked from the campsite, so he has no work at all. He was sacked for stealing money. That is why he has latched on to Debbie: a pretty young demoiselle from the chateau. He reckons he's on to a good thing!"

"She must stop this folly immediately!" I was almost shouting down the phone. "How can she be so stupid ?!"

"Do not be too angry," cautioned Claire again. "Girls do foolish things."

Euan was furious. He ranted like a mad man.

"What's the matter with her? How can she be so revolting ?! Is she doing IT with this man?!"

"Don't ... darling ... don't ..."

Euan left early the next morning having decided that the best course of action was to fetch her. She could be with us for the fortnight left at the camp, she got on well with Max and his friends. Although so naughty – and the thought of her with Manolo was pretty disgusting – she was our daughter and we wanted her safely with us.

When Euan reached Claire's house, some two hours later, Debbie was back from her night out and had collapsed exhausted in to her bed. Euan unceremoniously woke her.

"Get up!" he shouted at her.

"Daddy ... what's gone wrong?"

"You know perfectly well, you bloody stupid girl! You're carrying on with that Manolo creature!

You've been sacked by Lady Winbolt! You have lied and lied and LIED!"

She started to cry.

"Apologize immediately to Claire!"

He made her apologize to Lady Winbolt too, then took the ferry, with her, back over the Seudre to the camp. She was crying when she got out of the car.

"Mummy! I'm sorry!" she said and flung herself in to my arms.

I patted her fair head and hugged her.

"Never mind, sweetheart, it was just a silly patch. Let's forget it."

And forget it she did. We helped her pitch a little tent and luckily I had enough extra bedding – anticipating more of Max's friends – and I helped her arrange her things. She had brought very little with her, having left it at Claire's, but there was enough to muddle through with. She perched on to the back of Max's bike and set off with the boys to

217

the beach and it was with considerable relief that we saw her mucking around with them on the sand and joining in the chatter with her usual animated loquaciousness at meal time. She's OK, I thought. It was just a silly patch.

After a few days Debbie had her period and we had to rush around getting what she needed and even buying an extra pair of shorts and some knickers for her. Unlike me at her age she never seemed to have tummy cramps. The boys wanted to know why she wouldn't go swimming and she told them to mind their own business.

The last two weeks of our holiday went by very quickly. Euan seemed relaxed and said his ears had almost totally stopped buzzing, though any high-pitched noise was likely to trigger off a Meniere's attack.
We spent the last three nights of our holiday at the campsite in Saintes, because Euan had got an important client to see and we couldn't go back to Les Cypres till Lady Winbolt had left.

As we were pitching camp that evening I fell on the caravan step and – I presume knocking my head

218

against something hard – I knocked myself unconscious. It was the silliest accident and an odd thing about it was that I fell no more than two feet at the most, though admittedly at top speed and at full weight, and in the short fall not only did I manage to knock myself out, but I injured my leg and sustained extensive bruising to one side of my bottom.

The pain ripped through my leg as I came in and out of consciousness and I felt very sick.

"Oh mummy!" the children, including Jeremy and Julien, gathered round me and Debbie rushed to my side.

"I'm OK," I said.

Debbie, remembering a first aid course she'd done at school, padded ice around my leg, wrapped in a towel. I could put my weight on it so I knew it was nothing much. However, I kept losing consciousness again, drifting in and out of a sick-y world of white and yellow flashing lights and could feel a dull thudding ache in the back of my head.

"I think mummy should go to hospital," she told Euan.

Saintes hospital was wonderful. Everything was clean and bright and cheerful, and I was kept under observation overnight. I felt bad about leaving poor Euan to cope with all those children, the dog and his client, but it couldn't be helped. I couldn't keep awake and slept almost the whole day the next day, and in to the night, but by the second day I was fine apart from a massive bruise on my bottom – really most impressive – and a bad leg. Euan had to carry me to the loo, otherwise I hobbled around. Evelyne, Ben's mother, came to fetch Jeremy and Julien. Both Euan and I looked forward to getting our house back. Our holiday was over. We timed our return so that the Winbolts would already have gone when we arrived, for I couldn't face them and doubted Debbie could either.

"I bet Claire has told everybody in the village!" said Debbie crossly.

"I doubt it," I replied.

"Ha! You don't know what people are like!"

"One thing is for certain and that is that people are never thinking things about you as much as you think they are. It has happened to me loads of times – I've done something embarrassing or stupid and felt mortified – only to find that nobody else even gave it a thought."

I was interested to realize that Debbie was sensitive enough to worry about what might be said about her, and although I was quite certain that the entire village was laughing and gossiping about that English family from the chateau, I didn't want Debbie to have to feel any worse that she already felt. Our imminent return to Les Cypres seemed to awaken her sense of shame and, the holiday forgotten, she became aware of the feeling of having to face the music.

There is a very good Italian restaurant in the centre of the old part of Saintes, not far from the cathedral, and we ate there that last night. It was a wonderful evening, all of us tanned and relaxed – against all odds – and the children chatted enthusiastically about what they had done and what they would do.

I was quite glad to have my little family back to myself at last, fond as I was of Max's friends. We had no privacy. There are things you can do and say in front of your own children but not in front of other people's children. By anybody's standards, three teenage boys, a child and a volatile teenage girl (not to mention the dog!) was quite enough.

"Still," I said half to myself, "they're young for such a short time."

Debbie was very clever at card tricks. I think she had learnt them in boarding school. She had a quick wit that meant energetic conversation and lots of laughter. Very few females can tell a joke but Debbie seemed able to do so and we tucked in to our pizzas and carbonaras, washed down with plenty of Chianti, and it was one of the best family evenings of my life. I shall never forget it. Euan caught my eye and winked at me. She's fine, our eyes said to each other.

She got on very well with Max and so the following evening when we finally got back in to our house, I took Max to one side.

"If you go out later try to keep your eye on Debs," I said, "I'm concerned that now she is back that Manolo creature will influence her. I don't want her to phone him. Try to keep her with you."

"OK," he said, "fine."

Max would have been ... I've been counting ... fifteen that year. He has always had a wise kind of maturity in with that boyish fun-loving front. I didn't want to make him feel a kind of guardian or spy in any way ... yet I needed him to keep me posted.

"Don't worry, *maman*" he said.

" Does she realize how daft she was?" I asked him.

"Oh *tout a fait, bien sur*! She just wants things to be normal again."

"Fine. They will be. Reassure her if you get the chance."

"Don't worry about it, *maman*," he repeated.

223

A Call From France

There was something terrible on the News. Dreadful that I don't even remember what it was. Somebody else's life somewhere else was snuffed out, perhaps hundreds of somebody elses – I can't recall – I have forgotten. Our own troubles took over our lives. We had no inkling then how long it would last. It doesn't matter how much you try to compare your troubles to those who are worse off, it never seems to help. Max and Debbie had gone out briefly but had been back within the hour. There's nowhere much to go in St Sylvain . Euan and I stared at the screen in horror as the news came in. I hobbled up to bed, leaning inexpertly on Max on one side and Bernie on the other, in good time, ready for a good long sleep. I kissed Debbie.

"Night-night," I said to her. Did I detect a slight frisson? Was that a kind of wooden kiss she gave back? What was that look in her eye …?

"Night, mummy," she replied. She continued to stare at the screen.

"Dreadful news," I said.

"Mmmm …"

Bernie washed and changed quickly and hopped in to Euan's side of the bed. He did that for years, and when Euan came to bed he would pick him up, all floppy and sleepy, and carry him up to his bedroom on the floor above. Bernie would sleep through the whole thing.

I shook myself as I got undressed. Despite our successful holiday and the lovely evening the previous night, I could see a dark void was opening, just a little, between me and my daughter. Quickly I banished the thought. It is so easy to be paranoid. The News had made me over-sensitive. On an impulse I phoned my father.

"You're still coming in a few days I hope?" I asked him.

"Why yes, of course. Rupert will bring me."

"Good."

"Night-night, my dear. God bless."

"Night-night, daddy. Be safe. See you then, then."

225

I lay on my back staring up at the dark ceiling and listening to the faint hum-drum of the TV in the living room below. Euan and the elder two were still watching the News. Next to me Bernie had already fallen asleep, one arm flung out towards me, long lashes on little pink cheeks. Gently I leant forwards and kissed him.

Our lives were about to change.

The following morning I was moderately irritated to find that Debbie was not up. Having taken something to help me sleep, even though my leg was not really hurting, I slept till nine and it was gone ten by the time I had had my tea and got dressed. Max was downstairs and had clearly been there for some time, judging by the quantities of things he had unloaded from the caravan and piled on to the kitchen table. The debris of breakfast also covered the table, with bits of sugar and cereal stuck on to sleeping bags and milk slopping over the picnic basket. Euan had long since gone over to his client's place.

Every mother knows what a lot of clearing up there is to do after a camping holiday. No teenager wants to help.

"Debbie not up yet?" asked Max

"No ..." I looked at my watch, "I'll give her a bit longer ..."

"I've been up for ages."

"Yes, so I see. You've unloaded a lot."

"I want to meet Matthieu later," he said.

I sat at the kitchen table with my foot up on the stool opposite, and I instructed Max and Bernie on how to put the dirty washing in to the machine, and which items to take to which rooms. Because of the recent rain a lot of things were damp and muddy, and because I hadn't been around to organize the packing, items were flung haphazardly on top of each other and things that should have stayed in the caravan had come in to the kitchen and vice-versa.
I felt terribly tired and my foot and ankle had

swollen to magnificent proportions. The boys were great.

"Can I watch telly now?" asked Bernie

"OK then. Half an hour of telly then come back here. Max , make me a cup of tea, would you ? And then go and wake Debs please. I need her to help."

Having been raised in France it was odd what a good cup of tea Max could make. He popped outside while it was brewing and returned with a little wild flower picked out of the grass and put it in an egg-cup on my tray. We chatted for a while and then he went up to wake Debbie.

"She's already up," he told me when he returned.

"Tell her to come down here to help me," I said, "at least with her own stuff."

"She's not up there. She must be outside."

"Oh – yes, silly me – I did say she was to clean out the caravan – could you go and fetch her, Max ? I'd rather she helped with the washing."

Max disappeared and I hobbled around the kitchen trying to clean up. Thank goodness I'm so fit, I thought. Bernie finished his TV programme and came back in, this time wanting ice-cream and unwilling to carry his stuff up to his room.

"Just do it, " I said wearily, "take it up. You can do it nicely, or you can do it crossly, but you will still do it."

"I'm going to do it crossly!" he declared.

Max came back He gulped down some water and fed Big Harry. The minutes ticked by.

"When is Debs coming?" I asked, "You did tell her?"

"Oh? Oh – no. I didn't. She's not there."

"Well, find her, would you?"

229

A Call From France

Les Cypres is a large property. Max went all over the house, calling as he went, and then round the grounds. The barns alone covered over a thousand square metres and he walked through each one, shouting:

"Debs! Debs!"

I could hear him calling. Boys and men can never find things – or people. Debbie had probably answered "yes?" several times. I listened. I could tell he was covering the grounds now. It wasn't possible she hadn't heard, I decided. Eventually Max came back in.

"Well, I dunno where she is, I can't find her. I don't think she's here at all."

"The NAUGHTY girl!" I exclaimed, "she's gone off without saying a word. Phone Pamela – she's bound to be there."

A slightly cold feeling started to creep about my throat.

Instinctively I knew that Debbie was not at Pamela's. She was not at Claire's. She was nowhere in the grounds nor in the house. The children never ever went out without telling me they were going and even then they told me where they were going and when they would be back. I tried paging her.

"Your message please," said the blank voice of the page.

"*Reviens immediatement. Maman.*" – return immediately, I said.

"I'll transmit your message, Madame," said the voice.

I had bought pagers for all three children a year or so earlier. They were very useful little gadgets, soon to be replaced by mobile phones. You had a to dial a number and give the number of the person you wanted to page, then give your message. Your message was then transmitted to the pager which in turn made a little buzzing noise to tell the child a message was coming in. These messages would vary from "supper is ready" (though always in

231

French of course) to "buy some milk on your way home" to "homework!" I used Max 's pager the most, partly because he tended to be out and about with his mates the most but also because he particularly needed that contact, especially when he was away at school.

"See you soon!" my message would read, or "miss you!"

I paged Debbie five or six times and got no response. I became increasingly irritated with her but the irritation became steadily more and more laced with fear. Although we had had our ups and downs, and although in recent months she had behaved exceptionally badly, she was nonetheless a thoughtful kid who wouldn't just wander off for the sake of it. It was very difficult getting anything done and my usual manic tidiness was utterly thwarted as I tried to get the boys helping me; everything took an eternity and constantly resting one leg was in itself exhausting. Soon the boys got annoyed.

A Call From France

"Why doesn't Debbie help you?" asked Bernie , "she's better at washing machines and stuff than I am."

"She'll be along soon," I reassured him, "then she'll take over."

Max finished emptying the caravan and sorted – in the way only a lad knows how – his own stuff out, plonking dirty washing in with the clean and leaving a trail of his belongings up the staircase. I could tell where he had been for oddments had dropped from the pile he was carrying, almost like a secret treasure hunt … a sock that used to be white, the sole stiff with sweat and dirt, a cassette case, a lighter (a lighter? where? Oh, that's not mine, mummy!), a small pile of sand fallen out of a shoe, a T-shirt with a deliberately cut-out hole in the front, a revolting postcard.

"Is Michel here?" I asked.

"Yes," Max replied, "daddy asked him to dig the trench out at the back."

"Ask him to come here, " I said.

233

I had got Bernie to bring me some deep heat and a tubigrip and I sat in the kitchen vigorously rubbing my ankle with it. It smelt delightful.

"*Salut, Michel, ca va?*" I said when Michel arrived, covered in sweat and determined to plant vigorous kisses on both sides of my face. Max fetched him a beer which he drank straight from the bottle, and he turned his head, trying to camouflage a loud belch when he had finished. I told him I couldn't find Debbie.

"Eh? Where is she, then?"

"Michel, I don't know. I want you to drive into the village, see if she's in the bar or in the park or something."

"*Tres bien*," he said and set off.

Word got round quite quickly, as I knew it would. By evening Claire had phoned to ask if we'd located Debbie, then Michel's wife phoned and two or three others. I wanted to locate her before Euan got back, whether she was sitting sulking

234

somewhere or partying with friends, I didn't want Euan to be put through any further stress because of her. The holiday had done him good, despite Debbie, and he seemed relaxed and happy for a change.

"It is odd," I said to Max , "I can't think she's sulking – she seemed fine last night."

I looked at him closely.

"Is there anything you want to tell me?" I asked him.

"Well," he hesitated slightly, "you told me to stay with her, but she did go off and make a phone call."

"Oh no! Just what I wanted to avoid!"

"I couldn't help it – it's easier said than done, keeping an eye on her you know! She told me she wanted cigarettes but she bought a phone card and before I knew it she was outside in the call box talking to somebody."

"Who?"

"Dunno."

"I can't think it was that horrid man – I just don't believe that HE would be so stupid, even if she would!"

"She told me she was never going to speak to him again," Max informed me.

"Where did she get the money?"

"Dunno."

He nipped upstairs for me and soon came back with Debbie's address book. When Euan got back I was still laboriously phoning all her friends. Nobody knew anything. Nobody had seen her.

I felt sick.

As predicted, Euan was shattered.

"She can't possibly have run off," he reasoned, "we were getting on so well!"

"We mustn't over-react," I said, "she hasn't run off – she is just sulking somewhere because she's home again and she doesn't want to be … or something…"

Debbie had behaved like such a spoilt brat the past few weeks.

"We're far too soft on her," said Euan, "we give in too quickly – she gets everything she wants and that's the trouble – she can't stand it when she doesn't have what she wants."

"Yes – no – perhaps … who knows …?"

Bernie sensed rather than heard that something was wrong and asked for Debbie several times. I tried to act casual.

"Where's Debbie gone?" he asked.

"Oh … just out for a while …"

We decided that a night out in the dark by herself would do her good, and we settled down to supper in front of the TV, fully expecting her to return at any moment. Our minds wandered from the item on the TV and back again. We ate our supper quietly, watching the screen and, despite ourselves, glancing towards the window. Every now and then I thought I heard a little noise and twice I sent poor Max up to her room to see if she had sneaked back in. Before going to bed Euan wandered around the grounds with a torch, shining it in to the darkness, trying to peer in to the obscure recesses by walls and the small dark mantles of bushes. I watched from the window for a while, and could see his lonely figure out there, occasionally calling "Debbie! Debbie!" in to the darkness. Big Harry went with him and even if I couldn't see Euan I could hear the faint tinkle sound of Big Harry's chain collar hitting his name tag. The sky had cleared and it was a bright starlit night. From our window I could see the lights shining on the opposite bank, all along the Seudre, from La Tremblade as far as Arvert and beyond, glinting in the darkness like little fires on the horizon. Euan continued his steady progress round the grounds, undoubtedly more carefully than Max had done earlier in the day. Sometimes I could see him in the obscurity, sometimes he was out of sight, working his way doggedly through every building and over each section of ground, calling, always calling, quietly in to the night "Debbie! Debbie!"

Eventually he came back in.

"I'm tired," he said.

"We'll leave the door unlocked so that she can creep back in when she's ready."

It was tempting to lock it so that she'd be forced to ring or sit outside all night. Euan sighed heavily.

"I thought we'd got over the worst of it," he said, "she seemed fine, cheerful, our old Debs again, the way she used to be."

I took a sleeping tablet, fearful that the event of the day would give me sleepless night. I dropped off immediately but was woken in the small wee hours by Euan shaking me.

"Wake up! Wake up!"

"God – what's happened …?"

"Nothing – but I know she's hurt – we just went to bed – Christ! How can we have been so stupid?! She's hurt! She needs us!"

Suddenly wide awake I sat up.

"What …?"

"Listen to me! She was fine – she was OK – we'd got over all that business with Manolo! She was sorry. Something has happened to her! It's obvious! She has fallen – or has been kidnapped!"

The night does terrible things to the brain. I tried hard to remain calm and logical, but Euan's fear was infectious.

"It's true we've been assuming that she's sulking somewhere … perhaps she is hurt after all – God, we'd better find her and fast!"

"But Euan ... you already looked, Max already looked ...."

"She might have fallen down the well!"

"Why ever would she fall down the well, Euan
.........?"

But nonetheless we both got dressed and Euan went
up to wake Max . Leaving Bernie sound asleep and
Big Harry on guard we set out with torches, me
starting by the abandoned pig huts and feeling a
fool hobbling around like an old woman, Euan at
the far end by the broken wall and Max at the back
where the path was. If she was hiding and was
feeling hungry and contrite, she was more likely to
talk to Max than to us, and the path was her most
likely hiding place on the property, the woodland
offering shelter and the area being familiar to her. I
was slightly frightened of the dark and seemed to
hear odd noises at every turn, and the black looming
brooding tress took on ghostly forms that waved
and teased in the night.

"Debbie!" I called not too loudly, almost as though
I was afraid of waking the birds, "Debbie!"

But nobody answered.

At six the following morning we phoned the police.
We also phoned Michel who, although it was a

A Call From France

Sunday, came round with the other men and we organized an inch-by-inch search of the grounds. Nothing.

"She has been kidnapped," Euan told the police.

"Whatever for?" I asked him in English, "why would anybody kidnap her?"

"To the local people we must seem like millionaires," he replied.

This was true.

"*Monsieur*," said the policeman, "do you have any particular reason to think she has been kidnapped – anything precise, apart from just a feeling? Do you think Manolo Costa has kidnapped her?"

"Yes! Yes, I do! I cannot – I CANNOT – believe she would just run off – she was happy with us! She had a happy holiday with us! We saw her dancing with friends, laughing, we went out to dinner, played card games …" His voice broke. The policeman reached out a hand to Euan's shoulder.

242

"We will find her, *monsieur*, don't worry."

Debbie was only sixteen and so a Missing Child programme was launched by the local police. It was terrifying because it seemed so ineffectual and it made me realize just how utterly ghastly it must be for the parents of a small child. Apart from informing other police stations and keeping a general eye out, the *gendarmes* could do little. They interviewed the local gipsies. Claire's husband, Joel, and their son, Matthieu, were very helpful, and went around the village talking to people who might know something.

"If it were a small kiddy missing they would do more," I said to Euan, "but Debbie is sixteen and they know she is almost certainly being terribly naughty. That's all."

Euan was half the time convinced she was dead, and the rest of the time convinced she was in grave danger. He was totally desperate to find her.

"My honey," I said, "we've got a lot to cope with here without you going over the top about it."

243

"Over the top?! Over the top?! My little girl is missing and you tell me I'm over the top?!"

We held each other close. That evening we put on an old "Love Songs" CD and we danced slowly, round and round in little circles in our big empty living room, clinging on to one another and listening to the gentle music. Max went out with his friends and Bernie watched the cartoon channel while we continued our hypnotic little dance, on and on, through several CDs till we were too tired to go on.

I realized one of our best chances of finding Debbie was via Max . He knew nothing, but was well positioned with the village people to find out something. We were careful to not allow him to feel like some kind of spy, yet we needed him to tell us anything he could find out.

"Nobody has seen her," he said when he got in, "but lots of people think they know a lot of things about her."

"Like what?"

"I've heard that she's a drunk, a drug addict, an escaped convict – the lot!" he said crossly.

It was to be expected. I didn't feel annoyed or hurt for what the local people did or did not think about us was of absolutely no interest to me at all. They could all go to hell as far as I was concerned, though I felt badly about it for Max 's sake. His lack of information from them did tell me one thing, however. It told me that whoever she was involved with or where ever she had disappeared to, it was not the immediate village. It was further afield than that. This pointed to Manolo, but despite everything I still could not believe that she had run off with him.

The police came back the following morning in case Debbie had turned up.

"No – nothing," we said.

The police woman who this time accompanied the **gendarme** seemed far too young to know what she was doing, and she looked more like a model than the long arm of the law.

245

"*Reflechissez,*" she said gently to us, - think, "try to think of something – anything – that she said or did. If she has been kidnapped we will find her, but whether she had been kidnapped or she has run away the clue to her whereabouts is almost certainly here in this house."

"I can't think of anything," I bit my lip, "everything was just ordinary. We had been through a difficult patch, but nothing disastrous, she came on holiday with us, she had agreed to go to college in Brighton – *en Angleterre* – to do A-levels. Just ordinary stuff. She wanted her hair coloured, she wanted some new shoes, she had gone off fish, she likes Brian Adams ... just ordinary stuff ..."

"Had she been in touch with Manolo Costa?"

"Our elder son tells us she made a phone call last night, and the fact that she did it from a call box and not from here shows she didn't want us to know ... but I do not believe it was to Costa ... she had told her brother that she wanted nothing more to do with him, she told me she was sorry and felt foolish and she was looking forward to leaving this area and going to England to make new friends."

"She has been kidnapped," Euan repeated, "or she is hurt, needs us, it's ghastly … we must find her quickly…"

"The most likely explanation is that she has run away," said the policeman. "You'd be surprised how common it is, even in the happiest families. Kidnapping is very rare, on the other hand. Also, she is a big girl. It would not be easy for somebody to bundle her up in to the back of a car. There is the possibility that she is hurt, but you have already searched the grounds. I will arrange some men to search the area. If she has run away with Costa that is not good either – he got out of prison only recently …….."

"What?!!!" Yet somehow this did not surprise me. It fitted. "What was he in for?"

"Assault. Assault and robbery. It was his second time in prison for a violent offence. I'm sorry."

247

I was lost for words. The enormity of the horrible possibilities hit us.

"She is so SELFISH!" shouted Max .

"What is your opinion?" I asked him. "Do you think she's with Manolo?"

"I've no idea – truly, *maman,* I've no idea at all. If she is with him she deserves all she gets. He'll beat her up."

"Oh Max …"

I tried hard to keep the two boys out of it, but they picked up the tension and Bernie cried for his sister several times. He wanted to move down from his bedroom in to our room, which we allowed, realizing that it was important he should feel secure and that his little world, despite his sister, was all right. He slept on a mattress by the side of my bed, on the floor, for several weeks, and then migrated in to our dressing room where we rigged up a camp bed for him. He was eight. Such was the tension and the fear in his little mind that he was to never return to his own bedroom. Although that top bedroom at Les Cypres is to this day called "Bernie's room", he never slept up there again and remained close to us at night till well in to his teens. I had problems forgiving Debbie for that.

Although I experienced moments of utter panic for her safety, and although at odd moments – usually in the middle of the night – I felt nauseous with fear as to what had happened to her, during those first few days I was not really particularly worried. I was quite certain that she was fine and was being not only very naughty but very stupid. I racked my brains for what I would do if I wanted to hide somewhere and give everybody a fright. The sensible and logical side of me was remarkably cool and I mentally waded through all the possibilities, making notes on scraps of paper … things she had done or said, friends she could be with.

On the fourth day I said to Euan:

"I have it! Of course! She's at Tulips!"

We knew that Primrose was empty and we knew that Debbie was aware of it. Having spent four of her precious childhood years there, she knew every nook and cranny, including how to get in via the boiler room. By car it was at least an hour's journey, but it was not inconceivable that she was there. I phoned Michel, who lived far closer than we did.

"Tres bien," he said, "I'll go up there and have a look."

Euan and I tried to get on.
"Go to work," I told him, "it'll be several hours before Michel gets back –he may not even be able to go straight away … I'll phone you."

Euan set off. The hours ticked by. I kept looking at the phone. Josie was doing extra hours for me, helping me to wade through the inordinate quantities of washing and ironing, much of it Debbie's. Poor Josie. She tried to chat lightly to me, tried to reassure me, tried to remember things that might be helpful.

Eventually Michel rang back.

"*Eh oui*," he said, "there's somebody there all right. I didn't go in but somebody has been burning a candle on the kitchen floor, I could see it, and there are empty pizza boxes and cans strewn about. Two of the windows at the back are open."

"Did you call out?" I asked.

"Ah no, I just left, *Madame*. Didn't call out, no."

"Did there seem to be only one person? Could you tell?"

"Ah no, I couldn't tell. Didn't look. Ah, it's in a bad state the old house. When I think of the work we did there and how pretty your garden used to be! All overgrown. Gone to weed. Snakes, I saw, several snakes. They like it in the courtyard, see. Warm for them. They bask in the sunshine, see. Shutters have come off at the back, you know –

round the back where the wind gets it, by Max's room."

"Thank you, Michel"

"The roof'll be bad," he continued regardless, "must be leaking everywhere by now. And that's no good. Timber will rot. Termites. Termites like damp timber, see. That grass will need a scythe to cut it. Shame. We had it looking nice, didn't we? The grass? We had it looking nice?"

"Yes, Michel, very nice. Can you tell me nothing else – not about the house – about who was there ? Were there clothes ? Clothes that might be Debbie's ?"

"Ah non, Madame ...."

As soon as Euan got it I told him. So tall and strong, his shoulders slumped, he looked older, grey, drawn.

"It'll be all right ...." I started, but fell silent.

He gulped down a cup of tea and had some toast then, dirty and weary after a day at work, he set off to Primrose. Had he had a whip he'd have taken it. Had he been able to hold his heart in his hand, he'd have done so. His suntan was fading already and all the good the holiday had done him had gone; the shadows around his eyes had darkened and deepened. His skin had a grey pallor.

I waited.

I fully expected him to frog-march Debbie in to the kitchen when he returned nearly three hours later. It had turned dark and a bit of a wind, the first sign of autumn, was coming in off the sea. The van's headlights shone bright yellow at the gate. Big Harry barked. I watched the van pull in to the drive and saw Euan's dark silhouette emerge alone.

"It wasn't her," he said dully, "there have been squatters there, but not her."

"Are you sure?" I asked stupidly, "did you look?!"

He sat down heavily, leaning forwards with his elbows on his knees.

"Oh I'm sure, love, I looked. She's not there."

My disappointment was total. A huge dark cloak settled over our shoulders. I opened a bottle of wine and poured a glass for each of us. Euan turned his around on the plastic table cloth, round and round in a tiny circle, silently watching the dark red liquid swill round the sides of the glass. He downed it in one gulp and poured another. I did likewise.

"I thought it would be her," I said quietly, "I thought you'd bring her home".

"I know my love," he didn't raise his head but recommenced the hypnotic turning of his glass, "I'm sorry."

I realized he was crying. I reached out to his face and wiped a tear from his cheek. Another fell, and another, soundless.

"It'll be all right," I told him again, "she is just being naughty. It'll work out well in the end. It's odd how things have a way of working out ...."

My voice trailed off. There was no conviction to my words. I adored this man, now slightly drunk, slumped at the table. The pain etched in to his big frame as he sat turning and turning that glass drove a knife in to my guts. I wanted to cry out to him. But I remained silent. There was no crying out to do as the fears and the doubts gnawed at us both.

My father arrived the following day, driven down by one of my brothers. We said nothing. The warm and comforting presence of my father meant a lot to me and I was so pleased to see him that for a moment or two I forgot about Debbie as I listened to his tale of the journey and poured us each a gin and tonic.

"Ah!" he exclaimed as we sat down with our drinks in the bright sunshine by the well in the courtyard. He looked around, as he always did, at the old pump and the fig tree and the expanse of dry lawn. He breathed deeply, smiling happily. "Ah, this is what it's all about!"

We raised our glasses to each other. He had deep dark brown eyes and a ready smile. Constant pottering in his garden in Kent had given him a tan, and his hands – beautiful hands – were gnarled from wielding a spade, even at his age, and he was all of eighty-two that year, yet somehow remained the soft and caring hands of the doctor. He always wore the most extraordinary clothes, ranging from an old suit he'd bought with tokens during the war, to brilliant South Pacific short-sleeved shirts. He kept everything forever, and the straw hat perched on his head, with a band of shells stitched into the brim, I could remember from girlhood in New Caledonia.

"Goodness, that hat!" I said. "I can remember that in Nouméa – it must be twenty-five years old!"
He removed the hat and turned it round in his hands a few times, adjusting the shells a little, and smiling to himself as memories of the south Pacific came back to him.

 Glancing over at his one grip bag I could see the inevitable books – mostly about Africa and African folklore – and just one change of clothes. Whenever he came to stay getting his clothes washed and ironed and back in his wardrobe before he needed them was a mad dash which became a joke between us and which I attended to with great pleasure.   Also sticking out of his bag were his paints.

"We'll go painting," he said, seeing me looking.

"That would be fun. Perhaps to the beach?"

Daddy's painting was not very successful – he was good at landscapes and skies, but his portrayal of me on the beach was poor. I kept it nonetheless. Fond memories. I did a biro and watercolour sketch of an elderly couple sitting in deck chairs. I framed it and hung it in one of our gites a couple of years later. It got stolen. I suppose I should be flattered.

We also drove up to La Cotiniere and did a few sketches there but both got too engrossed in *gauffres*,   covered in thick layers of jam and whipped cream, to take the painting seriously. We bought a scarf for my mother in the market there and then motored on up to the northern tip of the island where there is a lighthouse. Desperate for the tourist trade the island people had pulled out all stops in and around the lighthouse and had opened a funny little museum and several shops and cafes. We ate another *gauffre* and then, feeling fat and naughty, slowly drove back down through the centre of Oleron towards the bridge.

"Time for a gin and tonic," declared my father, spotting a bar at St Pierre.

"Only if you're going to drive," I said which, of course, he wouldn't.

Bernie was waiting for us crossly, annoyed with me that I had left him with Josie the whole day. Big Harry needed a walk. Josie had piled the ironing up in the utility room and I started to put this away, working my way through the clothes and trying to keep Debbie off my mind.

<u>*Diary entry.*</u>
The forest is lovely, dark and deep,
But I have promises to keep,
And a long way to go before I sleep,
A long way to go before I sleep.........

For some reason Euan suddenly decided that Debbie had gone off on a ship.

"Gone off on a ship?! Whatever for ?!" I exclaimed.

"I'm sure I'm right. I know I'm right. She was talking about going to Alaska ..... she was saying she wished she lived in Alaska!"

"Euan, she's only sixteen. I rather doubt she even knows where Alaska is. Anyway, she'd hate it." I added this last as though it somehow solved the issue.

Stress makes you behave in a way you don't normally behave. You do and say things you don't really believe, it is difficult to think straight, you flail about trying to find things to grab on to. The "fight or flight" response does not work for long enough .... There was no question of flight, yet the fight part seemed to have nowhere to go. We felt our world was out of control and although we were strong and experienced people, and my inherent feeling was always that it would work out okay, that modicum of confidence did not counter-balance the fear I felt, and in no way whatsoever alleviated the stress for Euan.

"Well," my father shook his head slowly, "boys much younger than sixteen used to run away to sea all the time ...."

I remembered then that at the camp Debbie had been reading a novel. I had thought it was set in Norway, not Alaska, but it didn't matter – all about some female who fell in love with some hero and was rescued by a dog ...... some rubbish story typical of that age group.

"Surely not?" I glanced from my father to Euan and back.

"I rather doubt it ...." My father didn't want to increase our fear but didn't want to prevent us from searching in the one area she may have gone.

I phoned the police station. We think she has run off with Costa, they said, we have seen this sort of thing many times; she will not have gone far; she will simply be hiding somewhere nearby.

"No," Euan was adamant. "She's very smart. She's clever. She would know how to go to the other end of the earth if she wanted to.

I thought about it, and the more I thought about it the more I realized it was a possibility. I was inclined to agree with the police on the whole, and felt it vastly more likely she wasn't far away, but it had to be said that Debbie had travelled a bit – way over the French average, and certainly way over the average of the average *Charentais* bobby.

So we set off for the port in La Rochelle. Why La Rochelle ? I don't know. There are other ports all up and down the area. But we started in La Rochelle. That first day, armed with one hundred black-and-white photo copies of her, we went systematically round each bar, each café, each office, pinning up the photos and asking questions.

The following day we split up and went to other ports. I was home again soon after lunch, preferring to be with my father and still feeling unsure about Euan's certainty. It was gone midnight when he got in. His head buzzed and ached, and the tell-tale Meniere's symptom of a greenish tinge around his temples was clear. He was exhausted. He kept drawing his hand down over his face as though he was trying to wipe away the nightmare.

My father .... we shared the same humour and the same eye for things, from art to landscapes. I had always been very fond of Byron as a poet and, although it was not to my father's taste, he nonetheless enjoyed poetry and between us we quoted vast reams, often testing each other .... "who wrote this ?"

He could turn his hand to anything. Whenever he stayed with us he would wade through a list of jobs ranging from helping Euan build a wall, to fixing locks on my cupboards. He was multi-talented. He could sing – old Frankie and Johnny-type songs, Way Down Upon the Swanny River .... that sort of thing. He made his own picture frames that year and brought me a knife holder made out of a bit of wood fallen off Brighton pier.

"Fallen off Brighton pier?!" I asked, incredulous, "how in the world did you come by that?!"

We had made good money letting the house to Lady Winbolt, and we decided we would do the same every summer.

"Not bad," I said, "we go off on holiday while somebody pays to stay in our house!"

The locks on the cupboards were for just that reason, so we could stash away our belongings while the house was let. At precisely six o'clock (which was frequently closer to half past five) my father and I would meet in the kitchen, grab the juice from the 'fridge and saunter, glass in hand, over to the drinks cabinet in the living room. Drinks poured, he's raise his glass to me and say

"This is what it's all about!"

By the end of supper both of us were invariably too tiddly to do anything, but my father had been writing his memoirs and we sat in the living room while he read them out to me in that deep velvet voice that I remembered from bedtime stories as a child. I loved him massively.

Women have often said to me that they wouldn't want to let their house because the thought of a stranger wandering through their rooms is off-putting.   But it was something that never bothered me. As a product of colonial Africa I had always had servants in the house as a child, had shared flats with other girls as a student and, once the broke years were over, had always had a nanny or help of some sort with the children and housework.

We tried to be cheerful and positive in front of Euan who was macabre in his determination that something dreadful had happened to Debbie.   He couldn't get it out of his mind.   Sixteen days limped by. I was wondering if we should try to start facing the fact that we may not see her for a very long time. She was an adult of sorts, after all, and presumably with somebody older. Every time the phone rang we leapt at it, but eventually we got used to even that.

At last one day it was her.

"Debbie!" my father and I rushed in to the hall when we heard Euan answer the phone. "Debbie! Thank God! Where are you?!"

I reached over and flicked the phone on to loud speaker.

"Listen to me," Debbie's voice was crisp. "I'm pregnant. We want a flat, money and a car. You will give us these things or you will never see me again."

"What in the world are you talking about?" Euan's voice was shaking. "We have been worried sick. Who are you with ? Where?"

"I'm with Manolo."

"Manolo?!!"

"And where we are is none of your business. I'm going to ring off now. Remember we want those things. I'll phone you again in a few days' time."

"Debbie! Wait!"

The line went dead. Euan looked a thousand years old.

"She's pregnant," he said dully.

I let this sink in. Slowly realization dawned on me.

"No, she's not!" My fury knew no bounds. "She had her period at the camp. She is not pregnant – or if she is, she doesn't know about it yet! She is pretending"

"But whatever for?!" exclaimed my father.

"Worse," I continued, "she is pretending to this man. Why, I don't know. She is sixteen, a minor. No wonder he whisked her off with him."

"I feel sick," said Euan.

The phone rang again, its screech shrill in the big hallway.

"And another thing," came Debbie's voice. "Manolo needs a job. You must give him a job. Bur first we want the money. Deliver it within twelve hours to the Café de Paris in Arabor."

Again the line went dead.

A Call From France

"So, she is in Arabor," said my father.

Is this our little girl ? The baby I gave birth to and breast fed? That little pink bottom, that first little pair of royal blue shoes, those white socks with the butterfly on the side …..? My Little Pony, Barbie dolls ? The small child with the fair curly hair ? The little girl who snuggled up in bed between us and who watched almost every TV programme available ? Was this her ?

In silence we all looked at each other. Debbie was being manipulated by Manolo, and his assumption that we would give him work and money was bordering on hilarious. My father poured us drinks. I could see in his dear old face that he was trying to think of the right thing to say. I looked at him expectantly, turning to my father for support at this time. His dark eyes looked back at me.

"Goodness," he said at length, "what a naughty girl …"

A Call From France

The following morning I phoned the police and told them what had happened. I found it ridiculous that nobody had the slightest idea where Manolo was.

"He's a criminal!" I spat at the police woman, "why don't you know where he is ?!"

"He is not a criminal, *Madame*," she corrected me gently, "he has served his time. He is out of prison and where he is now is not our concern."

This just didn't seem possible.

"You mean he has to murder my daughter before you will take any action?!"

"What action should we take, *Madame*? He has done nothing wrong. Your daughter is past the age of consent and she went with him willingly."

I could understand, of course.

"All you have to do is make a few basic enquiries ...." I tried.

"We are not detectives," came the reply.

Well, I thought, I shall be the detective. No way would I allow this man to lead off my child like this. No way would I sit back and wait.

"I'll find out where he is living," I said firmly.

"Be careful, Madame," warned the police woman, "he can be dangerous!"

"Precisely!" I replied.

Diagnoses:-
Claire: Debbie is so spoilt, so very spoilt, Catherine. She has everything. Whatever she wants, you just give it to her! She wants driving lessons – you give them. Une fortune, ma chere! Not only that but you drive her to the lessons, you fetch her, all of it! She wants a guitar, you buy it. She wants a new dress, you buy it. This is not how to raise a child. She knows no limits. That is the problem.

No, no, that's not true. That isn't the reason. Certainly Debbie is very spoilt in some ways and doubtless seems terribly spoilt to the people round here … but it is perfectly natural for her to have driving lessons – how else will she learn to drive, for goodness' sake?! As for the guitar, that's just a hobby, no more (in fact considerably less) expensive than horse-riding … or ice-skating or photography or whatever.

Gran: It's hormones. She's got hormone trouble. It's a kind of madness they go through sometimes. She'll come to her senses all in good time.

Madness? Yes, she must be temporarily mad. She'll grow out of it.

Aggie: perhaps she feels she can't keep up with you? Perhaps she feels the stakes are too high, the competition is too great? You are so clever, attractive, big flash car, chateau, tri-lingual, successful, witty. You are multi-talented, you handle contracts and Big Important Things … perhaps she feels it is all just too much to try to follow?

But why would she feel she has to try to follow? I never thought I should try to emulate my own mother. I have never suggested to her that she should be like me. I just get on with my own life and try to guide her as any mother would. What's more I would never describe myself – thanks, though – as multi-talented or particularly attractive ..

My father: perhaps she just wants something to love and to love her. All of a sudden she is too big to sit on her daddy's knee; she is too big to hop in to bed with you in the mornings. She badly needs to be hugged and cuddled and she feels, albeit wrongly, that she will get it from this Manolo rather than from you.

Yes, yes, that sounds right. Maybe that's it. She had lots and lots of cuddles as she grew up. She can still have them now. We've never done or said anything to make her feel cuddles were no longer available.

The psychiatrist: it is all of these things and none of these things. Teenage girls are fragile

271

creatures, very volatile, easily led, even two-faced. Debbie certainly has got hormone trouble, she certainly is spoilt, she certainly not only wants but NEEDS plenty of attention. Even more attention than she has already. Her mind and her body are trying to go in two different ways and she is searching, reaching out, trying to tell you something ... and unfortunately for everybody she had chosen this way to do it ...

I thought she knew better. We were so close. She must surely realize the anguish she is causing? I hope we are able to forgive her.

Fran: oh dear, poor thing! She is going to feel horribly embarrassed about all this one day!

Do you think so? I wonder.

The psychiatrist composed a letter for us to reply to Debbie. You must not give in to any of her demands, he told us, you must be brief and to the point. Your letter must show her that you love her and that she can come home at any moment, but that you will not give in to her demands or put up with any further nonsense.

272

Dearest Debbie,
We were happy to hear your voice on the phone.
Clearly, we will not give you and Manolo a flat,
or money, and nor can we give any work. You
know where your home is; we love you very
much and miss you a lot. But if you prefer to be
elsewhere, we understand. Live your life and be
happy. We're here if you need us.
lots of love from mummy and daddy.

My father and I drove in to Arabor and handed
the letter over to the barman as requested.

"It's the only thing to do," said my father seeing
my tight-lipped face, "I know you want to storm
around and demand to know where she is, but
it's best to remain calm. Almost as if the whole
thing is a bore."

He was right. He was always right. Debbie
wanted <u>A Happening</u>, she wanted <u>Action</u>. I
could remember being a bit like that myself.
Well, my girl, I thought, you're not getting any
action from me.

A Call From France

Most of my concern was for Euan who was coping very badly with the stress. His Meniere's problems had become almost intolerable and the nurse had to come round every morning to give him an injection to alleviate the dizziness and subsequent nausea. His ears buzzed constantly, the pitch in the buzzing rising and falling according to the level of stress. Worse, he suffered from blinding headaches that were sometimes so bad that all he could do was lie on the sofa, and even then he curled up, bringing his knees up towards his head, as if trying to ward off the pain. It's terrible to see a big man sob. I didn't know how to help him. I was so grateful my father was there, a warm and reassuring presence that kept me calm and focused. We tried hard not to talk about Debbie in front of Max and Bernie who were both suffering from the tension in the house, but what with the police popping in at regular intervals and the constant phone calls, it was nigh-on impossible to keep them unaffected by Debbie's behaviour.

We got no response to our letter and the days slipped by. Euan felt slightly better and we drove in to La Rochelle with daddy and Bernie for a meal and a stroll around the yachting marina. I always liked the atmosphere in La Rochelle during the summer when there were plenty of people around and shops teeming with goodies to look at or buy. All along the promenade artists of one form or another tried to earn a few pence, many of them English students. They ranged from fire-eaters to pavement artists, from guitarists to magicians. We always threw a few coins in to the proffered hats for they helped to create the atmosphere that was such fun, and we were happy to pay for it. I never give to the ones who just stand there with a hand out, wherever we are, but am always pleased to give to all those wonderful buskers - all over the world – who put a song in to the air and music onto the streets.

I don't know where Max was that evening ... chilling out with his mates, no doubt.

My father and I chatted constantly. His knowledge and understanding of a huge variety of subjects always astounded us, and he was interesting to listen to. As he grew older his speech slowed down, as did his movements, but that summer he was sprightly as a spring chicken and ready for a night out on the tiles. We both shared a weakness for red wine and would often end up quite silly, with Euan and Bernie patiently steering us back to the car and laughing with us at the world which – drunkenly – we found so funny.

It was difficult to relax that evening, however, and Euan was very heavy and solemn. His eyes kept glazing over and I knew he was thinking about his little girl and how nice it all used to be.

"You must try to keep it in proportion," I said to him, "it's not so bad. Her behaviour is heart-breaking, I know, but it's not as though she is dead or anything truly dreadful."

My words were strangely prophetic for driving home again the mobile phone rang.

"Hello?" I held the receiver close to my face, listening above the noise of the car.

"Mummy, it's me," came Debbie's voice.

"Hi sweetheart," I said casually and motioned to Euan to pull in somewhere because I was afraid of being cut off or going out of range. He pulled in next to Mac Donald's just outside La Rochelle.

"I'm phoning to say goodbye," said Debbie.

"Oh ? Where are you going?"

"Away. Forever. You will never see me again."

"Oh," I tried hard to sound casual, "I see."

"I want you to phone me back because I've got almost no talk-time left," she said.

I almost laughed. Kids! Rapidly I scribbled down the number, praying that she would answer it, which she did.

"So," I said conversationally, "how are you?"

"Not good, we've decided to end it all. Together."

"I see. Where are you?"

"In Paris."

"Ah – Paris! It's a lovely city, isn't it?"

"Did you hear what I said to you, mummy?"

"That you're in Paris – yes."

"No! Not that!"

"Well, I wouldn't do anything silly," I said carefully. "Ending it all, as you put it, wouldn't solve anything would it?"

"That's for us to decide."

"Let me have your address," I said, taking the bull by the horns. Euan was leaning over towards me, hoping to hear what she was saying. I could almost hear his poor heart thumping in his chest. The silence in the car was total as my father and Bernie also listened. I tried to remain calm and spoke coolly to her.

"I don't know the address," she faltered. I could hear her say something rapidly in French.

"Is that Manolo you're talking to?"

"No, it's his friend. Manolo has gone out to get some beer."

That was good news. It seemed unlikely that they were truly on the brink of a suicide pact if he had gone out to buy beer.

"Ask your friend for the address," I said, "then we can post you a bit of dosh to tide you over."

A bit more conferring in French and then she said:

"We're in the rue du 14 *juillet*, I don't know which number."

"There must be dozens of rue 14 *juillet* in Paris!" I exclaimed, "can't you do better than that?"

279

Euan leapt out of the car and rushed in to a call box. My father went after him.

"There's a café opposite, called Café de Paris," she volunteered.

"Oh, I see. Well, never mind." Almost every town in France has a Café de Paris.

"Don't send any money here," she said, "it won't reach us and anyway we'll soon be gone where you'll never see us ever again."

In view of Richie's recent death this was astoundingly cruel of her. I didn't believe her for a moment and wondered at her indefatigable lies. I didn't reply.

"I have to go now," she said suddenly and rang off.

Outside Euan was frantically dialling the police. Afterwards he told me how he nearly went mad because he was unable to tell the police the *arondissement* (area) of Paris the supposed suicide was to take place. I remembered then

280

that his own father had committed suicide and understood some of the panic he must have gone through. My father was trying to calm him.

"It's bluff," I told him, "don't worry about it. She wants to upset us."

He had gone completely white. Occasionally you hear of people going completely white but I had never witnessed it before – or since. The skin on his face appeared to have thickened, like dough, and a silvery layer of sweat had broken out over it. He walked woodenly to the side of the car and was sick in to the gutter.

I will forgive you, Debbie, I thought. Mothers do.

Why? Why does she want to upset us? Is it something I did? Something I didn't do? I suppose it might even be something I did during pregnancy? She was a forceps delivery after a long hard labour … is that where it all went wrong? When I held that dear baby, still woozy from the shot of pethidene, my heart burst with joy and love, and little did I realize what pain a child can bring.

The psychiatrist: no, I doubt you did anything "wrong", you know.   All parents make mistakes. All people make mistakes with all things – whether it is raising a child or driving a car. Unfortunately children don't come with an instruction manual.   All we can do is what seems to be the right thing.   It seems to me you raised her well.   She seems unbalanced right now, but many teenagers seem unbalanced.   That is normal.   She has a vicious streak in her ... or has had a vicious streak introduced.   How can we know?   She is punishing you because you are her mother and she has nobody else to punish.   She wants to hurt you because she doesn't feel quite right in her self.   The very core of her is in turmoil.   Most teenagers are like this.   Luckily for us all only a few teenagers behave so badly over it.   You must just live through it.   It will change.

I couldn't go to Aggie's funeral.

It took me a long time to take it on board: Aggie had had a brain haemorrhage and had died. No. Surely not ? She was dead before the ambulance arrived. She was dead before she hit the ground. That's what I was told.

Unlike when Richie died I was totally silent. I stared quietly at the receiver after her husband's phone call, as though there must be something wrong with the telephone to give me such horrid news.

It is an odd word, dead. Often, when something goes wrong, we instinctively cast about in our brains for how to rectify it. But with a word like dead there is no rectification to be made. The very word is dead by definition. That in itself takes a while to take on board. You can't change this, your brain says, you cannot make it better.

Debbie's disappearance and Aggie's death got fused in my mind. I felt there was something totally off-centre with my world, with the whole world. I was unaccustomed to being unable to sort things out. I always found a solution. But there was no solution here. None. Everything seemed to me to be coloured yellow.

A letter arrived from Aggie in the post a few days later. That confused me even more. It must have been one of the last things she did.

My dear! I do so hope you are feeling strong and cheerful and that you are not letting this get you down. Keep smiling. It will work out well, I am sure of it. Debbie will come prancing back in to the house any day, asking what the fuss is about.
Love my dear from your friend and ally and sex-mad object -
Ooooooodles of kisses,
Aggie.

I cried a bit when I read the letter, but apart from that I didn't cry at all till we went home to England months later, and it hit me that my old friend was no longer there. Then I cried a great deal.

All my enquiries drew a blank – I contacted the water and electricity boards, the telephone people, the post office, the social security office … they had nobody on their lists by the name of Manolo Costa. This meant that either he was not living in or near Arabor or that he was living with somebody else – or even under a different name.

The phone number I had scribbled down in the car by MacDonalds was no longer available; it was a mobile number, so impossible to know whether or not the call had been made in Paris. I had heard several other voices in the background and guessed that the call had been made in a bar, quite possibly on somebody else's phone.

She did, however, phone again a few days later, very briefly, again saying she was about to be cut off.

It was clear to us that there was no reasoning with her and, as she started to phone more and more frequently, we were able to open up lines of communication with her and even finally managed to get the new mobile number she used – the phone belonged to Manolo, of course.

She invariably wanted me to phone her back because, it goes without saying, Manolo couldn't afford the calls.

"For goodness' sake give me your number, Debbie, if you think you're about to get cut off."

"All right, but you must swear to me that you will never ever phone this number unless I ask you to."

"Yes, all right, I promise"

"Ready? 06 20 99 84."

I scribbled this down quickly and felt a sense of achievement. One step at a time, I told myself, first things first.

As Euan was out at work it was usually me who answered the phone. Debbie was cross and surprised that we hadn't given in to her demands and I deliberately kept my voice calm and bordering on bored. I realized she had no real aim in the way she treated us, and she was doubtless egged on by whoever she was with.

286

She seemed to be living in a house shared with several others, one of whom was a young female and two of whom I worked out to be older men, plus Manolo. She referred to the place as "our flat" but I strongly suspected it was more like a squat. I sighed slightly and asked her how she was, was she eating properly, did she need clean clothes … for if she was trying to make me cry I was not going to do so in front of her, and if she was trying to make me scream I would do so only in the silence of my heart.

We pretended to not mind too much.

We didn't want to drive her away by being angry or by threatening her, yet we needed to keep an easy medium between keeping him at arm's length and pretending to her that it was all OK. We allowed her to think that we would perhaps one day provide them with a flat if things went well. We pussy-footed in agony through our telephone conversations. Her quickest course back to the shelter of our wings was by us holding our wings open, to include him – God forbid – if necessary.

287

"She won't stay long with him," said Gran, "after all he has got nothing, he *is* nothing. She'll soon get fed up with it."

With the help of the police we were able to track down where she was. She was still pretending to be in Paris, but she was barely ten minutes' drive from her home. It was obvious to us she had been there all along, even though she had talked about her journey to Paris.

"Typical!" spat Euan, "she can't even run away properly! Where does she go, our girl?! Monte Carlo? Las Vegas? Paris? No! Arabor! Bloody Arabor!"

Ironically, although we were pleased to discover she was close by, I shared Euan's disappointment that she had ventured no further. It was a pity. I mean, if you're going to go you might as well GO.

We finally met at the police station. The police somehow managed to persuade Manolo that his only option was to come out in to the open, which he agreed to do – doubtless still thinking he had got a minor pregnant – on condition that we promised, in front of the police, to not lodge a complaint against him. We promised. We'd have promised anything, anything at all.

Manolo sat outside on the pavement and I pretended not to see him. Debbie waited for us inside with a police woman. She had had her hair cut off. All her long auburn curls had gone, but she had a pretty bob cut and had coloured her hair a kind of snazzy orange which looked great. Euan hated it. Men like long hair. We hugged her. I looked in to her darling face and there, in those pale eyes that I loved so much, I could see fear and uncertainty; I could see a little girl who was trying to be a grown-up, and a child who badly just wanted to go home. I squeezed her arm lightly. Then I went in to a separate room with the police, leaving Euan with Debbie.

My father took Bernie to a café opposite the police station where – he later told me – they got through umpteen cokes and ice creams. Debbie was defiant. We kept up our casual and unruffled act.

"You realize this man Costa has got a prison record?" the policeman said to me in private.

"Yes, I know."

"He attacked his wife. He threatened her with a shotgun and then beat her up."

I didn't reply but stared miserably at the floor fighting back my tears.

"Are you sure you don't want to lodge a file against him, Madame?"

"Yes. I do not want to estrange my daughter any further. She thinks she is in love with him. She would never forgive me."

"But Costa could suddenly turn against her," the policeman raised a finger as though I was in a classroom. I smiled.

"Not for now he won't," I replied, "he needs her. He needs our money to feed them and he is hoping we might – if things go well – give him a flat and a car. It is what I will tell him."

"He is not a stupid man, *Madame*."

"No, but I am far more clever than he is."

"What have you got in mind, Madame …?"

"I don't know at this stage … but I will think of something …"

The policeman smiled. He was young and had just had his first child. I had given him a tiny pair of socks with Union Jacks on them for the baby. He drew his hand through his thick dark hair and winked slightly at me.

"Ah, *Madame* – you are sly – sly as a fox!"

Debbie agreed to return to school, and that was the first step forward. She wanted to remain living with Manolo at week-ends but conceded that she would catch the bus to school every

291

Monday morning (if I would pay for it of course) and I was to fetch her on a Friday evening. This last was my idea.

"You'll be exhausted after a week at school," I told her, "you can't possibly get the bus back."

She agreed willingly enough. The police wrote it down and Manolo, who was hauled in unceremoniously from the pavement, had to sign. The police pointed out to him that Euan and I would not lodge a complaint against him we retained our right to do so if he broke his side of the agreement. The *gendarme* told him that he was very lucky, particularly in view of his criminal record. Debbie had the grace to recognize this, though the point seemed to be totally lost on him. You wait, I thought as I watched him sign our "agreement", you wait. I am the panther, the cheetah, I am the mother beast protecting her young. I am the fox, waiting for the right moment. I can wait. I will wait. You wait too. You wait and see.

Whatever else happened I didn't want Debbie to know that I was lying in wait, ready to pounce.

No, the snaring and trapping of this man had to be seen to be via somebody else, something else. At that stage I had no idea how I would work it, but work it out I would. Not for anything was I going to allow my child to be caught up with this man; not for anything was I going to allow the seedy decay of which he reeked to infect my girl, no matter how naughty she had been. She was still my girl. I bided my time. I waited.

Debbie stole food from our house every Friday evening, after I'd brought her home and she'd had a shower and picked up clean clothes. She thought I didn't notice but in fact I always made sure there was enough for her to take. Then, my heart like a blood-soaked sponge, I drove her in to Arabor and dropped her off – first at the *place de Chasseloup*, then, as her confidence in me grew, at the house where she stayed: 18 Avenue Gambetta. She didn't seem to think there was anything unusual or abnormal in all this. Finally I managed to get indoors.

"I'll help you carry that lot," I told her one evening as I dropped her off.

The double oak front door, thick with flaking navy paint and street dust, opened on to what had once been a fine entrance hall with unusual Eastern floor tiles in a faded red and gold, and a dado running along the wall and all the way up the stairs which must have been installed in the days of Napoleon III. The wallpaper had long been ripped off and painted and re-painted in dark yellow gloss, but at the far end of the hall a fine stained glass window survived, and in the centre of the ceiling, surrounded by exquisite, if very dirty, ceiling moulds, a wonderful example of an art deco glass lamp shade, echoed in the wall light fittings on either side. A traditional Charentais staircase, littered with empty fag packs and empty beer cans and emitting a strong stench of urine, led up to a first floor that had been divided and sub-divided so that nothing remained of the original landing where once – a long time ago – children had played and maids had swept. Now cheap hardboard doors led through to three little bedsits, seedy and smokey and reeking. Our girl shared one of these bedsits with a couple of old men and Manolo.

A Call From France

"There you go!" I said cheerfully as I dumped her boxes on the floor. I raised a hand in salute towards Manolo who was lying on the bed and who tried to leap to his feet when I entered. An old man leant against the far wall, nursing a cut lip.

He was wearing an ancient pair of baggy trousers, almost black along the thigh fronts, and old shoes through which protruded sockless toes.

"Stay!" cried Manolo grasping my hand.

I remembered his warm handshake from when I'd seen him outside the café earlier that summer. You can tell a lot about a person by their handshake, but with this man you could tell nothing. It was a firm grip, the accompanying eyes and smile were sincere. He was very good-looking. I seized the opportunity.

"I'd love to stay, Manolo, but I can't right now. I can come back later, however. Deborah's *papa* wants to get you to taste English beer!"

A Call From France

"Ah bon! Oui, oui, d'accord ...!"

He was really pleased. I said I didn't know quite what time we'd be round and left it at that. They had no money, they couldn't go out anywhere.

Euan was tired and dirty when he got in around eight that evening.

"I don't understand what you think we will achieve," he said, "it makes me sick to the stomach to even think about it."

But he came with me, of course, bringing some beer with him. I wasn't quite sure what we were looking for, but I knew there would be something. I wanted first of all to ascertain whether or not Debbie was in any danger. I also wanted to find something – anything – which I could use to lever her away from him, or persuade him to leave her. I also wanted to bribe him.

" Offer him 10 000f," I said, "that's over £1000. Tell him to take it, to go away, to never come back."

Even as I said it I knew that wouldn't work. My main aim was to not damage my relationship with Debbie any further – and, Lord knows, it was pretty badly damaged. Also, of course, there was nothing to say that Costa wouldn't simply come back for more money. However, Euan and I discussed it seriously for a while before rejecting it as a possibility.

"The beauty of it would be that Debbie would see he has exchanged her for money," I said.

"Hmmm …. Perhaps," Euan was cautious, "but I think the risk is too strong. He'll either take her too or come back for more of either if not both …"

Another old man had joined the seedy little group in the bedsit when we arrived. Costa was still lying on the bed and Debbie was leaning out of the window, smoking.

"Ah, monsieur! Bonsoir!" Manolo leapt up again and shook Euan's hand vigorously.

Euan had difficulty pretending to be happy to be there and I squeezed his arm gently as he sat down on the edge of the bed and opened the beer. I could sense rather than see him taking in the surroundings, the worn bedspread and the strong smell of unwashed bodies and lavatories and dog ends.

(Debbie, Debbie! What are you doing here ? If I grab you by the arm and haul you down to the car and take you home – will you kick and scream, will you come happily? Will you hold it against us if we insist on your return or will it be a relief to you ………?Will you simply run off again ……….?)

The two old men, upon closer inspection, were only in their sixties, but both were ill, thin, hungry and very very poor. Neither spoke though one of them smiled at me and proffered the solitary chair for me to sit on. There was also a small Formica table littered with old full ashtrays and empty packets of one sort or another. On the floor torn and very dirty blue and red linoleum covered boards which smelt slightly of rot. An old calendar dated 1986 hung on the wall with a picture of a well-endowed blonde on the front. Apart from the bed and a stool by the bed, there was no other furniture. A curtain hid the kitchen area where, pretending to be interested, I poked my nose, smiling:

"Ah! So this is where you eat!"

"Don't nose around, mummy!"

Manolo asked her to speak in French.

Dirty dishes and pans of every shape and size covered every inch, including some on the floor. A solitary tub of salt sat on the draining board, but there was no sign of any other food except, tucked away under a small bench, the cardboard box that Debbie had brought and which I knew contained some pasta and some packets of soup. There were several empty money-back bottles of wine under the table.

Sitting back on my chair I conversationally asked one of the older men if he lived in the same building. He nodded yes. I noticed him look over at Costa before he spoke.

"Oui, Madame,"

 Looking squarely at him I now saw that he had a black eye, till now hidden from me as he stood against the window with his back to the light. I felt a slight tremor run through me. I looked over at Debbie who seemed remarkably casual and at ease with our presence there, even pleased to see us. Perhaps it didn't dawn on her that there was anything seedy about this, or that she was still behaving atrociously, or that we, her parents, felt anything in the way of hurt or confusion. I remembered then that after the meeting at the police station, now over two months ago, she had told me she had felt relieved to see us there.

"I was really pleased to see you guys," she had said, and had meant it. It gave me strength.

We left as promptly as we could. We didn't need to lie when we said that we were tired after a day at work. I wasn't sure what our visit to "the flat" had achieved, except that lines of communication were now almost fully open, we had seen where they spent their time, we had convinced Manolo we were friendly. I remembered what the *gendarme* had said – Costa is not a stupid man, he had said. No, perhaps he is not stupid, but he is not wise either, I thought.

On the Monday morning Debbie took the bus in to school as usual, and I phoned her in the evening. Unknown to her I was in regular touch with the matron and the Head teacher. Debbie was always a great chatterbox and chatted happily enough with me whenever I phoned. I tried to do things as I had always done, and phoning her in the dorm was one of them. She had decided to go in for Law and I was very pleased about this, knowing that a bright girl like her wouldn't stay long with a man like Costa.

But she did. The weeks limped by and she doggedly went to him every week-end. I wanted to ask her if he was threatening her in any way, or if she felt trapped. I studied her closely for signs of fear or testaments to violence, but there were none. She changed. The pretty sixteen year-old had gone and was replaced by ... by what? She looked old, so old. She had had her hair re-cut in a nasty, fringeless style and it made her look in her thirties. Her eyesight seemed to have deteriorated suddenly and she wore her glasses all the time, hitherto worn only for reading. She was no longer pretty. Her looks had gone.

After school one Friday I suggested we buy some new clothes. To my surprise she didn't seem very interested, but nonetheless chose a new pair of jeans and a horrid maroon cardigan, the sort of thing an old lady would wear. When she put it on she looked positively ugly.

"What about this?" I asked her, holding up a snazzy disco-dancing type of outfit. I chose it on purpose, knowing she would realize that with

Costa there was no chance of ever wearing it. But no, she didn't want it.

"I hardly recognize her," said Eaun. It broke his heart.

Then one day I had the break I had been waiting for. Debbie had an appointment at the dentist on the Monday morning which meant that I had to pick her up from the bedsit on the Sunday night.

"I can't fetch you on the Monday morning, Debbie," I said, astonished at her demanding manner and her lack of understanding of all the things I had to do generally - never mind all the things I did for her, "I've got appointments all day – tenants I have to see."

So I picked her up on the Sunday, arriving an hour earlier than expected. I took the steps two at a time as I went up to the bedsit in case I had been seen parking; I wanted to be quick. I stood panting slightly at the top of the stairs and sure enough, I could hear Costa's raised voice. But he was not being violent with Debbie. He was being violent with one of the old men. I listened for a while, then stole back down the staircase, banged the front door loudly, and went up again. Debbie was waiting for me.

"You're early!" she said crossly.

"Yes – I wanted to stop for petrol, but of course it is closed."

Costa appeared at the doorway. It was obvious they didn't want to let me in.

"I'm not ready!" exclaimed Debbie.

"Oh – okay – I'll come back later, shall I?" She didn't detect the sarcasm in my voice. Parents are just part of the service somehow. I was nevertheless glad to get away, and I trotted back down the stairs calling out that I was going to visit a friend and that I'd be back in half an hour.

Back in my car I phoned Euan.

"I'm pretty certain Costa is beating up one of those old men," I said, "this could be it. We must get Debbie away first."

If Costa and Debbie were surprised to see that Euan was with me when we went back half an hour later, they didn't show it. Euan shouldered his way past Costa declaring to Debbie as he did so that he would carry her school kit.

"What has happened to you?" I heard him ask one of the men within.

I followed him in and before the old man could answer, Manolo said:

"He fell down the stairs." He turned to Debbie and in a voice that made my blood run cold, said to her in French:

"That's right, isn't it? He fell down the stairs?"

The old man nodded. His forehead had been stitched between his eyes, where there was a large gash.

A Call From France

"Oh dear," I said sympathetically.

"We took him to hospital," said Debbie, still in French.

"That was good of you," I replied, my lips thinning as I spoke. I saw that Euan was looking at Costa's hand around which a rough bandage was wrapped. Seeing us look Debbie said:

"Poor Mano hurt his hand while helping."

"Oh dear," I repeated.

You are not a stupid child, Debbie. Why do you think we believe you? It is almost as though you want us to know the truth. What do you see in this man?. He has poisoned you.

As soon as I had dropped Debbie off at school, as always cheerful and pretending that everything was fine, I picked up Euan and we drove straight round to the bedsit. Euan knocked on the door while I waited round the corner. Costa was there. Everything went according to plan for within a few moments I saw Euan and Costa reappear and saunter slowly off to the Café de Paris.

"I'll keep him as long as I can," Euan had said, "but for Chrissake be careful!"

The man who opened the door of the bedsit to me was not the one with the cut face. He stood awkwardly to one side and told me that Costa had gone out. Peering through in to the room I could see that the other man was in there.

"I want to talk to you," I said. I tried to sound reassuring.

They allowed me in very reluctantly and eyed me with suspicion. One of them smelt of shit.

"I see you are also hurt," I said to the second man, pointing to an arm he was holding gingerly.

"I fell on the stairs," he replied dully.

"Dear, dear, there seems to be a lot of falling on the stairs!" I said.

Neither replied. I was slightly frightened but the mother in me was strong.

"What really happened?" I asked gently, "can I help you in any way?"

"I fell on the stairs," the man repeated.

I took a deep breath.

"No you didn't, Costa beat you up," I said, finally taking the bull by the horns.

They both looked at me, blinking stupidly. One of them sat down suddenly on the side of the bed. Silence.

"You are not going to tell me, are you, that you LIKE Costa?"

"No … we hate him …"

Good. This was what I wanted. Slowly, painfully, the story came out. Costa had had nowhere to live and had simply followed one of them home one night, a total stranger, and told him that he would kill him if he didn't allow him to stay the night. The two men had till then shared the bedsit for several years, taking it in turns to sleep in the bed, the other on the floor. Now Costa (and Debbie) had the bed and they both slept permanently on the floor. Their social security money was immediately taken off them by Costa and if they tried to resist, as they had done that week-end, he would beat them. Costa contributed nothing whatsoever in the way of rent or payment for the water and electricity. They depended on Debbie bringing in food and even then Costa had the lion's share.

The man's arm was clearly broken. Both men were afraid. But, using my advantage to the full, I took charge of the situation. That part of France was old-fashioned and the lady from the Chateau, to these men, seemed like somebody important.

"Come with me," I said, "I will take you to hospital."

I was terribly frightened as we reached the front door. My heart was pounding viciously and my legs felt weak. Both men followed me willingly enough but I knew I could not rely on them in any way whatsoever if Costa reappeared unexpectedly. I knew Euan would not allow Costa to return alone to the building, but what I needed was these men's evidence against Costa. If he threatened them they'd give in to him with no protest. I needed to get them out of his reach quickly. They walked stunningly slowly. I tried to hurry them along towards my car. They were like sheep. They got in to the car meekly and, as I revved the engine, I saw Euan and Costa appear at the far end of the street and start to make their way back to the building. I drove quickly. I wished the first man's cut had not already been tended to, but it would have to do as evidence. I hoped to God they would cooperate when the time came.

The hospital phoned the police who came very quickly and took statements off both men. I was terrified they would retract their statements, but they didn't. The police, however, had to guarantee that Costa would be arrested that same day.

"Otherwise we're dead," said the men. And it was doubtless true.

Costa was condemned to three years in prison of which he served one. Debbie, defiant and tearful, declared she would love him forever. Despite long questionings by the police and despite an explanation of who she had been with, and full descriptions of what he could do, and of what he would one day do to her, she remained stolidly faithful. Nothing would move her.

Now, however, the influence of the man had been removed and we forbade her to attempt to write to him. We arranged with the school for all post and all phone calls to be intercepted. Under no circumstance whatsoever was Debbie allowed any visitors at school. At home at the week-ends she was not allowed to answer the phone or pick up the post. I wrote to the prison authorities and they agreed that, although they could not forbid Costa to write to Debbie, they would point out to him that Debbie was still under eighteen and that we, as her parents, retained the right to lodge a further complaint against him. I moved Heaven and earth. Not for anything was I going to allow this man any contact with my little girl, and not for anything was I going to allow my little girl to moon over that man a second longer than she had to.

We pulled out all stops. We got her to invite friends over, we got Max to get friends over, we arranged a party, I took her shopping and tried to get her to wear the pretty kind of thing that used to suit her.

"I have to get away from this hell-hole!" she wailed at me.

I took her with me to Brighton and we looked round a few flats and around the college, all thoughts of Poitiers University, her first choice, having been dropped. I doggedly avoided Costa's name and she doggedly continued to talk about him. The weeks drifted by and

Christmas was approaching. She sat down with me and together we made lists of what we should get for the family for Christmas. We laughed together at silly suggestions and funny ideas, and she composed long lists of possibilities.

But always the presence of Manolo Costa hung in the air.

She would not forget about him.

We went skiing over Christmas and New Year.

"We need to be gone two weeks," said Euan, "for two weeks will give her a proper break. It'll put other thoughts and other ideas in to her head."

He drummed his fingers thoughtfully on the table.

"That'll cost a fortune," he added carefully, "even one week skiing is enough for five of us."

"We'll manage. Two weeks is a long time in the life of a teenager. She might even meet a new boyfriend."

"You're right. Precisely. She won't while she's here – there is nobody here – and the few that know her also know about how awful she was. It's difficult for her to live it down."

We'd have preferred to return to the UK for the end of year celebrations but we realized that Debbie was emotionally still terribly fragile and that she was miserably aware (or was she?) of the worry she had caused to the entire family. But she was just a child after all – we wanted to protect her from any further hurt in any form whatever. I relied heavily on our Christmas sojourns in England, when I could catch up with my sisters and my old friends, and sit in my parents' living room, daddy in the corner by the lamp, mummy by the fireplace …

We chose a self-catering apartment in Val d'Isere and, like idiots, took the train. Men of six foot five inches can't sleep on trains. Families with three children can't sleep on trains. I thought it would save the drive but in fact it was a nightmare of

314

negotiating platforms riddled with bags, and trying to find seats and bunks which, no matter how "booked" they were seemed to be totally unavailable. Bernie was still at that age where I needed to clutch on to his hand, and for some reason not one member of the family seemed capable of remembering which bags they were in charge of, or where they had put them or even how to carry them. The trip was culminated by a coach ride from Grenoble station up to the ski resort during which both Bernie and Max were copiously sick (Max managed to get outside but Bernie was sick largely in to my lap) which made them even less able to cope with the bags.

Our solution is always the same. As soon as we reached our apartment and sorted out our skis, we headed for the bar.

"This is what it's all about!" I exclaimed, quoting my father.

Hot sugared red wine is just the job on a mountain, and as the five of us sat around in the bar, huddled warmly by a roaring fire, it started to snow again, covering the already white and frozen earth with soft, spongey white magic. It was so beautiful. I looked at my darlings, all dressed in a funny assortment of woolly things, and was filled with a huge sense of well-being. Euan saw me looking and reached over to me, putting his hand over mine.

"Okay, my honey?"

"Okay."

When we watched Debbie whizzing down the *pistes*, all her cares forgotten, we knew we had made the right decision. She skied well, with an instinctive elegance. She was cautious but fun-loving, and both she and Max braved the black pistes with no bother, invariably meeting us at the bottom. We rapidly gave names, as I daresay most families do, to the meeting points.

"We'll meet for hot chocolate at Grizzly Bear café" one of us would announce, or perhaps "when we get to the end of Red Apple piste (named after Bernie 's cheeks) we'll go for lunch."

Two weeks tripped by on the snowy slopes. We were both extremely conscious of Debbie and we

316

did everything we could to make sure she really enjoyed it. Max had to pretend to be over sixteen (easy enough when you're tall) in order to get in to the disco with Debs every night. We didn't dare count how much we were spending, but they returned in the small wee hours full of fun, and Max told me there was nothing of any note to report. Debbie danced a lot, he told me, she chatted a lot.

"She can be SO EMBARRASSING!" he declared.

Girls are, I replied.

Ironically the café we skied past on our way to the first lift had to be called …. wait for it – Costa. It couldn't possibly have been "The Coffee Shop" or "*Café des Pistes*" or something like that. No, it had to be called Costa. I don't know if Debbie noticed – I certainly didn't draw her attention to it.

A couple of times during day time Debbie and Max met friends they had made at the disco, but of course most people were there only the one week.

"Does Debs show any interest in the other boys?" I asked Max .

A Call From France

"Yes – in all of them!"

"Does she dance with them? Is she having fun?"

"Oh yes! She dances a lot. She's quite good at it. She dances with all the boys. She's having a great time."

"And you, Max ?" I asked, looking up at his young face with just the first hints of a bit of hair on his chin, "are you having a nice time too?"

"Brilliant!" he grinned at me.

"I know what you're thinking," he said, "but Debs has forgotten about Costa. She's looking forward to going to college in Brighton next year. She told me so."

Sometimes he was so wise for his tender years. He was certainly reassuring. I looked at him. Dressed almost entirely in black he still had the figure of a boy and I suspected he was extremely pleased at being able to go to the disco because of Debbie.

318

"I'm dying to tell Matthieu about this!" he declared, "and Jeremy and Julien! They will hardly believe it – disco every night and skiing every day!"

At the top *pic,* above Les Deux Alpes, there are some extraordinary ice caves, well worth seeing. We got the cable car part of the way up, squashed together with our skis and our sticks in the bubble that swayed rapidly up the cliff face, and the ski lifts and drag buttons the rest of the way up. We frequently went up as far as a certain piste, then had to ski down again to the next lift that would take us further up. That was half the fun of it, of course. It was very cold and the sun was making only the most half-hearted efforts to emerge. The last button lift, barely half a mile long, was an agony of survival, clinging desperately on to the uprights and concentrating only on keeping our skis parallel while an icy wind whipped around our faces, seeping in through the collars of our ski-suits and making our hands and feet go numb. The exit was covered in ice and many people slipped and slid as they let go of their buttons, hindering the exit of others.

Inside the cave it was relatively warm, away from the biting wind. Extraordinary statues, some huge, had been carved out of the ice, ranging from fantasy figurines to polar bears; little corridors and passage ways had been cut out to allow tourists to look around. Everything was white and blue-white and frozen in time, making you feel as though you should whisper, as if in church. Near where we lived at Les Cypres there was a walled citadel town called Brouage, and there we had been to see, only a few weeks earlier, a display of old "fridges" including a Roman cellar, where ice was packed. Much of that ice had been cut out of this very cave and transported down the mountain side, then taken by horse and cart many hundreds of miles all over France. Apparently the ice, if there was enough of it and if it was properly stored, could last all year till the next batch arrived, keeping food fresh with no problem. We tried to explain the significance of this to the children, but of course they weren't interested – children never are – though one of them did comment on what a lot of trouble life was in general in the olden days.

The wind hit us again as soon as we emerged. Debbie and I stayed with Bernie who had started to cry, darling little thing frozen beyond words, looking to me as his mum for a solution to his icy predicament. Euan and Max set off ahead of us to set up hot chocolate at the Grizzly Bear. I watched their figures disappear off in to the white haze as I wrapped Bernie 's scarf over his hat.

"There's no point in standing there crying," I said to him, trying to hug him through all our clothes and wiping the tears from his face before they froze too. "There is only one way down this mountain."

"You'll soon warm up when you get going," Debbie told him.

In a way I suppose I knew it was going to be our last family holiday. We stuck together and skied every day. Debbie and I fell over regularly even though we were the better skiers, letting ourselves go and being silly in the white fluffy world of an unused *piste* covered in fresh snow. I relished the sight of my children, all wrapped up against the cold, and was very aware of the years flying by.

I would not recommend skiing before February. My father later told me the sun doesn't really come out till February and the cold on that holiday was quite something. Our apartment was tiny – as ski apartments always are – and Euan, Bernie and I usually ate in the restaurant, leaving Debbie and Max to get pizzas and join their friends. They seemed to make friends with everybody. I encouraged it. Debbie no longer spoke about Manolo, her thoughts all engrossed in the mountains and the snow and disco-dancing at night. I kept a careful watch in case she tried to post a letter but if she did I didn't see it. I felt like a criminal snooping through her pockets when she was in the shower and quickly, hands shaking, picking through her belongings in case there was something I needed to know. We put everything in to her, making sure she was having a good time, keeping up a chatty, happy banter to make her feel absolutely we held nothing against her. She was joining in happily and whole-heartedly and, with a sigh of relief, Euan and I both felt that we could put it all behind us.

But no.

"I know you think I've forgotten all about Mano," said Debbie to me one day while we were in a ski lift, "but I haven't. I shall wait for him and marry him as soon as he's out of prison."

"Jolly good," I said.

I couldn't meet her eyes. I was afraid of slapping her. I stared out over the white landscape as we were borne higher in to the hills and pulled my sunglasses down over my eyes so that she couldn't see my expression or the tears that threatened there.

"You don't believe me, do you?" she asked after a few moments of silence.

She was deliberately taunting me.   I sighed heavily.

"Debbie, don't."

**

 The Charente Maritime is very flat, wonderful for cycling during the summer but grey and totally devoid of any interest during the winter. I was not happy to get back to Les Cypres. I'd have liked to have stayed in the mountains and forgotten my cares on the slopes of snow. But life goes on and work awaited.

Euan's   work   now   consisted   mainly   of renovating our own properties. We bought these very cheaply with a loan from the bank – it was so cheap in those days and the banks were all but throwing the money at us.   Euan converted them in to flats.

 My job consisted mostly of finding appropriate tenants. We worked hard but enjoyed it, and Euan particularly liked doing building work for himself rather than for other people. He had a brilliant team of men who respected him and who had by now been with him for several years. Big Michel was always there, of course, and took a huge pride in what he did and sort-of hero-worshipped Euan. He could not be left responsible for anything, however, and this role fell to another Michel whose careful and deliberate manner made him a good manager. Max referred to this second Michel as Michel-de-luxe because, compared to big Michel, who was coarse in the extreme, the second Michel was a total gentleman. Rene was our carpenter, again a man who had worked for Euan for a long time. He lived alone near Tulips; he was only 48 that year, I remember, but he looked 65 or so, a quiet gentle teddy of a man. He was one of the best men we'd ever had. A few years later he fell from a roof and was severely injured and barely able to work again. It was terrible to see this man, who had been so clever with his hands, hobble carefully between sticks, carrying a saw or a chisel under his chin, trying to continue even though we all knew he couldn't. And then there was Bruno who was my favourite and Euan's least favourite. Bruno hung around on the brink of being sacked for several years, and held on to his job really only because I always intervened for him.

The French system seemed to us to be designed to make life as hard as possible for those who wanted to work. Because Bruno had left school very early he had not attained the required certificate that allowed him to call himself a painter and decorator. This meant that it was impossible for him to get a job as such, even though he was (under supervision) perfectly capable. His only alternative was to work for himself and, because the self-employed are positively punished for being self-employed, with crippling social contributions and taxes, topped up generously with mind-blasting quantities of papers to complete, being self-employed was impossible for Bruno.

Very many of the men we took on over the years seemed to expect to be employed *au noir*. This created a considerable problem for us because, having teetered constantly (and utterly accidentally) on the brink of being illegal for several years, we didn't want to do anything that might compromise our legality in France.

Our local *notaire* told us to employ at least one of the men as a "gardener" under a system called *Emploi-Service* (employment in service).

"You know," said the *notaire*, "that he is not a gardener but a labourer, but the authorities don't know that."

This was a simple solution even if it was borderline, for the bank issues you (the employer) with a kind of *"emploi-service"* cheque book, designed specifically for home helps, cleaners and gardeners: you write the cheque and simply send the stub in to the appropriate place and all the paperwork is done for you.

"Michel, " I said, "you are a gardener, okay?"

"Okay," he said – *"d'accord.* Anyway," he added, " I was your gardener, wasn't I? Wasn't I your gardener? Back at the old house, I was your gardener, wasn't I? So I don't have to

327

hide it, see, I don't have to hide it, because I am your gardener."

The other solution was for each man to set himself up as a Mini Business – in fact called *mini-entreprise*, a system which was introduced in to the employment zone some five or six years after we'd been in France. The aim of the system was not so much to reduce the numbers claiming unemployment benefit – and the numbers were huge – but to reduce the numbers of people who found themselves obliged to work on the black or not at all. A Mini Business was not allowed to earn more than 100 000f (approx £10 000) a year, was not liable for VAT which at that time at 18.6% was prohibitive for most small businesses, and benefited from considerable tax concessions as well as social contribution reductions. More importantly, the paperwork was less of a nightmare because one of the multiple factors that discouraged workers from declaring their activities was the exorbitant cost in the form of bureaucracy. Nothing was straight-forward, the whole system reeked of ink and rubber stamps.

A Call From France

I accompanied Bruno to the *Chambre de Commerce* in Rochefort, our first port of call in the Legalizing of Bruno the Painter. He presented himself promptly at our back door, hair sleeked back with Brilliantine left over from his father's courting days, and sporting a nylon suit of dark blue-grey. He explained he had borrowed it from a neighbour and that he had taken the trouser hem up a bit, using cellotape. Around his neck was a red tie, inexpertly knotted too tightly and on his feet a pair of white trainers. Seeing me look at his feet he explained that they too belonged to a friend (a different friend, *Madame*, not the same friend as the suit, a different one) and was the best he could do as nobody he knew had got shoes suitable for wearing with a suit.

"You look great," I told him.

Inside I felt angry. Poor Bruno! He was so willing to work, and indeed was a hard worker, but he found himself in a system that not only made the paperwork difficult for him for he could barely read and write, but also made him terrified of presenting himself at the chamber of commerce.   All dressed up in Sunday best, he sat next to me in the car, nervously twisting his hands round and round. He all but bowed to the receptionist.

All our men ended up working under this system, calling themselves mini-businesses and relying on me to help them with paperwork. Of course, they carried on working on the black too, but at least – and it was a huge relief to us all – they were under the guise of being legal.

My cleaning lady, Josie, was also paid with the *cheque emploi-service.*   Although aged around sixty she had a kinky sex life which, at the drop of a hat and without so much as a by-your-leave, she would relate to me at every possibility, accompanied by descriptions of her underwear. It was hilarious.

Diary.   Twelve years later.   Goodness – Josie has slowed down so much I cannot keep her any longer.   I have told her she MUST wear her glasses when cleaning.   She's going to be gutted.   Do you know, she still wears kinky underwear. She tells me her present boyfriend is a lapin chaud. Or was it a chaud lapin ? I repeated this to Max who responded with "ugh! Yuk!" I can see his point!

By the end of that summer we had amassed quite a dossier of properties. Max called it The Empire. We owned flats or cottages in most of the villages near us – five flats and a cottage in La Tremblade, four flats in Bourcefranc, three cottages in Arabor, two cottages in St Sylvain , five flats in Corme Royal, two cottages in Trizay, two cottages in Cadeuil and eight flats in Saintes. Of course, we also had the chateau, and all the barns ripe for conversion.

We had arrived in France ten years earlier utterly broke, out of work and with the haziest of horizons. With three small children on tow, and Euan speaking no French, we turned it around. We made a success out of a disaster. Now we had over a million pounds of equity in our properties and had gone from being fairly naïve straight-forward working people to astute

331

and knowledgeable business people.

My years of running my little estate agency stood me in good stead with the houses we bought. I knew exactly what a property was or was not worth, and no estate agent could pull wool over my eyes. I knew how to negotiate, where and when to negotiate, how to get the price down and to then show it to the bank in the best light. I was sharp and energetic. My French had become very fluent and my vocabulary in the banking and conveyancing world surprised even me.

More importantly, I found that I enjoyed it. The taste of success. We were most certainly not rich – in fact we never seemed to have any cash on us! – but we lived comfortably enough; we had a big house and a big car and we went on holiday. The children were well dressed and we were able to pay for the things the family needed. Despite the inherent dishonesty of many of the tenants I dealt with I nonetheless enjoyed my role as a landlady. I became totally adept at drawing up appropriate contracts with the appropriate clauses and there were large elements of my working life that were very satisfying.

Euan and I both enjoyed watching a project come to fruition. A derelict old house would in no time at all be transformed in to acceptable flats or bedsits; our men had a huge admiration for Euan, though I think they were terrified of me ! It was me that brought their wages round on a Friday and they tended to associate me with that, though after a while I'd give it to Michel-de-luxe to hand out. I had an odd role with the men for they looked to Euan as The Boss, and rightly so, but were confusedly aware that The Little Wife played a vital role in the running of the show ... but they couldn't work out quite how or when. Oddly enough none of them would ever take an instruction from me, with the exception perhaps of Bruno, and would always refer everything back to Euan. That was okay – I had very few instructions to give when on site for that was not where I played out my role.

The local people treated us, if not with amiability, at least with respect and most certainly thought we were very rich. We became well known in the area and we found that we rarely had to give our name when ordering or reserving something – people knew who we were, and if they didn't they knew within minutes. The Charentais world is very small and we frequently ran in to people whose daughter/son/brother/friend was renting one of our properties, and we likewise frequently discovered that the cook in the restaurant where we were, or the mechanic seeing to our car, or the girl behind the desk - or whatever - was one of our tenants.

It was the ideal job. I got out of bed when I felt like it – admittedly during term time I was out of the house with Bernie by eight – but knowing that I could go back to bed for a while if I wanted to, changed my whole attitude. I never did go back to bed, of course, but I loved knowing that I could. I was completely my own boss and no longer had clients I had to pander to. No more did I have to do the endless driving looking at properties in the hope I might sell them one day, and the endless listening to clients while they used up all my time and energy, in the hope they might buy something.

It had half killed me.

Being the owners of thirty-two residences, however, brought its own problems. There was a constant and never-ending stream of complaints from tenants who invariably did not have to fork anything out of their own pockets because the rent was paid by the State, but who nonetheless felt free to complain about every little niggle which could range from a cracked window pane to a leak in the roof. Under French law, as landlords, we were responsible for *le gros*, ie the roof and walls, the water heater, the plumbing, the electrics and so on. The tenant was supposedly responsible for all the normal little things that crop up in a household – broken window panes, a tap that drips, a squeaky tread on a stair. Yet few would ever see to these things themselves and would periodically speak to me as though I was the worst landlady in the world, and all because of some small niggle that they should have seen to themselves. Despite enjoying the work, there was the odd occasion when I was reduced to tears.

Where it did affect me the most was that there was no peace. All tenants knew we lived at the chateau and, if they'd been unable to get me on the phone, they'd turn up at the chateau gates, invariably brought along by car with friends, plus the friends' wives and a dog or two. If this happened during the day it was one thing, but if it happened at night when I was trying to enjoy a film or chat on the phone to my friends, it would drive me to a frenzy. Not that they were necessarily coming round to complain about anything. Sometimes they came round to pay their rent.

"Thank you, Monsieur Biteau, here is your receipt. Next month could you put your rent on to my account, as agreed?"

"Oh no, *Madame*, I don't like to do that, seeing as its cash you see."

"But Monsieur Biteau, whether its cash or not doesn't matter – you just put it on my account. That'll save you coming round here **at night**, won't it?"

336

"I don't mind, Madame, it's only right I should come round to pay my rent …"

One of the buildings we had bought was a small block of flats in the centre of Saintes. It was on the *rive gauche* and in a perfect position. We kept the garden flat empty for ourselves so that we would have somewhere to go when the chateau was let – and the chateau, now far too big for us, was let as much as possible. I loved the flat in Saintes. It represented a kind of Safe Haven for me. Perhaps I had never really recovered from the fear of unwittingly doing things illegally, for the need to "hide" was very strong in me. I liked knowing that nobody knew I was there – except Euan and the children, of course. For a while even Michel-de-luxe wasn't aware of its existence.

I took to going to the supermarkets in Saintes and doing all other shopping there too. I set up a little makeshift office and, although it was half an hour's drive from Les Cypres, I liked to use it as my base. It was wonderful to be able to stroll out to the shops or, while shopping, to have somewhere to dump my bags, have a cup of tea, got to the loo. Saintes is a lovely old town and in many ways I prefer it to La Rochelle. Dating back to the Roman era it boasts a magnificent amphitheatre as well as many other Roman artefacts; the river Charente runs through the town, and there is an excellent market. The main street, called the *Cour National* used to be lined with wonderful old round acacias, but an infestation of termites meant that they had to be cut down. New trees were planted. There is a wealth of shops and restaurants and old cathedrals; the town is big enough to warrant exploring but small enough to be homely.

"When we go home," I said to Euan, "I want a house in a town. I want to be able to walk to the shops. Imagine being able to stroll out to a pub! How lovely that would be!"

We furnished the Saintes flat with second hand bits and left-over bits. I made a huge bed-spread out of gold and purple patches.

"It looks Syrian," said my father when he saw it.

"The Assyrian came down like a wolf on the fold," I quoted, "and his cohorts were gleaming in purple and gold …"

The flat had two bedrooms, a small living room, a tiny kitchen, a spacious and airy verandah, a bathroom and a cellar. Big Harry seemed to take up all the space and I have to admit that if Euan and Max were there too, both well over six feet, the flat seemed indescribably small.

A weight-watchers group started in a nearby village. I was not overweight but I was hoping to get chummy with some other women – which I didn't – and anyway there is no harm in watching your weight.

They pronounced it Witwot-Chess. There are quite a lot of words like that in French. There are in English too, of course, though the difference is that when we use a French word in our language it denotes a kind of … finesse … or educative level, whereas English words in the French language are simply a sign of the times.

A Call From France

In our language we use words and expressions like "savoir faire" or "élite" or "risqué" or "pied-a-terre", and you have to have attained a general level of knowledge and competence to use these words and expressions correctly. It is something the more educated classes do. But in French anybody and everybody will use English words sometimes without even realizing they are English and with no sense of situation or style of input. A sweat-shirt in French is a "sweat", pronounced SWIT, and white spirit is "white", pronounced WHIT and so on. The young in particular use English words (*bye* being the most common one I heard) and of course the influence of songs and films on the French culture is – despite efforts to cull it – enormous.

Something we thought was so funny was that some of Euan's workmen seemed to have no idea that the song on the radio to which they were signing along was in English and had a meaning. We heard Rene signing along loudly *yoo ent nussing butta hownddogge* and he was staggered when I translated this. "You are only a hunting dog" was the best I could manage for him. He had thought it was just a sing-song like doo-wa-diddy-diddy-dum-diddy-doo. Of course, we are all guilty of the same things. We say things like … we're cranky, for example … or we like kinder chocolates … without realizing these are German words. I have a T-shirt with a Japanese motif on the front which, for all I know, might mean "I am a fat lazy cow". On the other hand English is the international language and one that is heard and used by all everywhere, yet the French use and comprehension of it often seemed to me to be very basic. I saw a woman with "I'm a good lay" on her T-shirt and agonized for a long time whether or not I should translate it for her, for her own sake. I didn't.

At one stage we had a labourer called Taleb, of Moroccan origin. He badly wanted to be a singer and musician and, despite now being well in to his forties without ever having touched the tiniest modicum of success, he strove on with his guitar. He recorded, rather to my consternation, a couple of tapes for me to listen to. My knowledge or understanding of music is virtually nil, but I nonetheless put the tapes on

341

while driving and at first enjoyed them. Taleb went systematically through all the old favourites.

"Yessaday," he sang in a deep and heavily-accented voice, "all mytrab Liz soffa away, now my song for yessaday, Suddaly! I don't havva man I yusoo be, for yessaday kemsa dennli…"

This was followed by "Pretty Woman" – pretty woma alla downna stree, pretty woma, the kinda lik tamit, I don't beelee you cabby-troo …" and afterwards "I'm Alive", then "Boy Lollipop" all in the same deep voice which gradually deteriorated so that, by the end of the tape it sounded as though he was on the verge of being sick.

"Brilliant," I said to Taleb when he asked me.

Taleb's job with Euan didn't last very long – perhaps a couple of weeks – for he just wasn't up to standard. When Euan let him go, however, his main concern was only that I should remember the tapes, not that he had lost his job. I ran in to Taleb about a year later and he was standing outside the supermarket wearing an entire musical system, pinned and strapped in the form of a variety of loudspeakers and drums and everything in between all over his head and shoulders. He hailed me as a long-lost friend and asked about his tapes which were still in my glove-box thickly covered with dust.

Taleb had lost interest in them, however, and proceeded to show me the contraption he was wearing which, he assured me, would make him rich one day.

We all have our dreams, I said, Lord knows, we all have our dreams … as I turned away I noticed the caption on his T-shirt:

"Tread lightly on the earth, my brother" it read.

Debbie no longer had many friends. She never seemed to want to invite anybody round and was never invited elsewhere. It might be that, having spent some time with an

343

older man, she had somehow spoiled herself for young people of her own age. We watched her closely, for we had learnt the hard way we couldn't trust her. I felt that I was on a tight rope ... or more precisely that she was on a tight-rope and that I was underneath, frantic in case she should fall.

"Would you like to go riding?" I asked her.

"Nope."

"You used to be so keen on horses ..."

"That was when I was twelve, mummy!"

"Oh ... I see ... how about parachuting?"

"*What?!*"

"Seriously – why not? I wouldn't mind a go myself. There's a place just along the road that does it."

"Don't you *know* that I hate heights?!"

"Oh, Debbie – I don't expect you really hate them. Don't you fancy it, then ?"

"No."

"What would you like, then?" (apart from a slapped face, I thought)

"A motorbike."

"Goodness, Debbie … I'm not going to buy you a motorbike."

"I just want to go. Go to Brighton. Get away from this dump. I hate Royan. I hate this house."

"September will be round soon enough. Just concentrate on your *bac.*"

"I wish I could do "A" levels instead."

"You can if you want to – I'll help you."

To my amazement she seemed very keen on this. I got straight on to the phone and organized what I could with Brighton College. Within a few days, in a remarkably efficient system, the college had sent me all the appropriate papers for "A" level French and English by correspondence. It cost £500 for the two courses, which I considered money very well spent.

I had always loved books and had vast quantities of them. Wading through them I picked out several that were suitable for both languages at "A" level. I handed Debbie a copy of Nevil Shute's "A Town Like Alice", in English, and also a copy of Zola's "La Terre", in French. Debbie's first assignment was to read each book and then to write two essays, both in English, saying what she thought of the books. A chip off the old block, her fingers flew over the keyboard with speed and, although she had done almost all her reading and writing in French since she was nine years old, she rapidly produced two essays that were perfectly acceptable. We posted them off and they were marked and returned to us very promptly. She got a B+ of one and an A for the other with the comments "excellent work, Deborah. You are clearly an "A" level candidate." I was so pleased. Debbie was so pleased.

Nonetheless she remained in her room. She wouldn't speak to me or to Euan unless it was essential. She wasn't rude … she was just sullen. She no longer chatted on the phone with her friends or played any music apart from an Italian called Eros Ramazzotti which she played over and over again.

In an attempt at trying to get her to mix with other young people and do the kind of things young girls do, we arranged to take Debbie to a disco in Saintes with Claire's older daughter, Angeline. Debbie at this stage was not yet seventeen and Angeline was twenty-three – still, we felt that was better than nothing.

"She didn't even get past the bloody door," said Euan later, "not even past the bloody door. The first man she clapped eyes on, the damned **doorman** for Chissake – and she had to have him!"

Debbie met Hussein at the door of the disco.

347

A Call From France

During the day he worked in a factory staining wooden doors (he is a carpenter, said Debbie) and two nights a week he worked at the door of the disco (he is a bouncer, said Debbie). He was Algerian (he is Arabian, said Debbie).

A pleasant enough young man, Hussein was twenty-eight, clean-cut and serious. He was not at all what we had had in mind for Debbie but it didn't matter – she had plenty of time and unsuitable boyfriends are all part of growing up. Feeling she needed space we gave a full rein – within reason – at the week-ends, though during the week she continued to board at school.

A peaceful few weeks went by, during which time I felt a bit of normality was returning to our household. The top floor of the house was full every night with teenager friends of Max's, playing music and having a good time. Sometimes I'd find a crowd of them in the kitchen making tea and I had to lay down a few firm rules about bringing dead teapots and cups back down again. Max taught them all to drink tea the English way. I regularly found empty beer bottles hidden behind the sofa, but I turned a blind eye. It seemed harmless enough. If Euan and I went out we provided vast quantities of pasta and pasta sauce and a crowd of them would cook their supper and sit, chatting and listening to music, around the kitchen table till we got in. I loved to see Max with his friends, and had a genuine fondness for several of them – Matthieu, Fred, Julien, Benoit. There were several girls in the crowd too – the famous little Pamela, as pretty as a picture, and a few others whose names escape me right now.

I realize now that I was a very easy-going mother. Mat, when he wrote to Debbie, told her she should appreciate having such "cool" parents. Perhaps I was too cool. I had always liked teenagers, and our house was soon to be full of them, vast quantities of them in every shape and size, filling the top floor where Max hung out, accompanied by a formidable array of drums and guitars and loud-speakers, not to mention potted plants which Max insisted were geraniums.

"You don't pull leaves off geraniums and smoke them," I pointed out.

"Look, *maman*, for your own sake, they are geraniums. Okay?"

"Okay."

I was later to water these geraniums with bleach while Max was away Exploring the World, but that is a different story.

I've often wondered if other mothers are more careful about who their daughters go out with. Do they insist that their daughters come in at a certain time or wear (or not wear, more to the point) certain clothes ? Should I have forbidden Debs to see Hussein more than twice a week? Or perhaps I should have made her see him more so that she'd have got sick of him ? It seemed a bit pointless insisting she be in by midnight after where she'd been only a few months earlier. I certainly didn't want to be so small-minded as to object to her going out with an Arab – Heavens – when I remember some of the boys I went out with, give me an Arab any day! As for her clothes – well, she was relatively old-fashioned and sober in her mode of dress and what little she had in the way of trendy or colourful clothes, I had chosen for her.

Should I have insisted she study for her *bac* every Friday and Saturday evening before going out ? Should I have whisked her off to Brighton with no more ado ? Who would watch over her in Brighton ? Should I have sat down with her and her books and shown more interest ? Or did I show too much interest ? Is that the bit I did wrong?

The child had run away, had lived in the most seedy conditions with the worst kind of man, had been party to nigh-on criminal activities. She could have gone to prison. She could have ended up in juvenile court. There seemed no point in trying to lay down rules that she had long ago broken. We nonetheless tried to keep a bit of a rein on her.

"Try to be back at a half-way decent hour," Euan said as she kissed him goodnight, "if only because it's worrying for us. No later than one, okay?"

"Okay, fine daddy!"

I could see my daughter melting out of the family circle, before my very eyes. At times I felt I had managed to clutch on to her, but just as my grip tightened and I opened my mouth to impart some valuable advice to her, she'd melt away again, like an ethereal creature in the mist, almost intangible. Part of the trouble was that she always seemed so sincere and then, unexpectedly, a turn of the head, a flick of her hair, a look in her eye ... and I'd know she hadn't really been listening at all.

"Debbie," I said to her one day, "I know you think I'm an old-fuddy-duddy ..."

"No, I don't, mummy!"

"Good ... well, anyway, this is important. Debbie, you are the person in charge of you ..."

"Well, obviously!"

"No, it's not obvious ... you allowed Manolo to be in charge of you ..."

"Don't bring him up!" the blue eyes flashed and the lips tightened momentarily.

"Sorry – I didn't mean to – I'm just trying to illustrate what I mean, Debs. You never HAVE to do anything – within reason – because you are the person in charge of you. You make your own destiny to a large extent – you decide where you are going and who you are going with."

"I don't see what you're getting at." The tone slightly impatient now.

"Respect yourself," I ploughed on, "consider yourself an important person and you are the person in charge of that important person. Take care of the important person."

I rapidly lost the thread of what I was trying to convey and was frightened of saying totally the wrong thing.

I badly wanted her to enjoy life and see what goodies life has to offer. Some of the best days of my life were when I was dating Gilbert Noles; for two wonderful and exciting years, when I was seventeen to nineteen, Gilbert would pick me up in his car and take me out somewhere lovely. It was great to be young and beautiful and to have a boyfriend with a car. I even managed to convince myself I was in love. I wanted Debbie to enjoy these same things so that she would totally forget Manolo and his like forever. I thought it would help her to set her sights high, aim for something better in life, determine to never again be broke and hungry and crawling.

I had never had any nice clothes when I was young, (not only was I one of seven but we lived frequently in back-of-beyond places in Africa) so I bought Debbie a new outfit for disco-dancing and took her on a shoe-hunt – never easy for her size nine feet. When Hussein came to pick her up, always clean and smart and polite, I made a point of flinging the door open wide and welcoming him in.

"Salut, Hussein! Debbie arrive!"

The looks she had lost so totally were recovering rapidly. She was very slender and looked fantastic in tight jeans and a skinny-ribbed top. Her face made-up and her earrings flashing under the short *gamine* haircut, she looked great, hopping gracefully down the stone staircase, leaning slightly over the banister in to the hallway, as she came. She crossed the large tiled floor in a few easy strides, somehow managing to kiss me goodnight and steer Hussein back out to his car in one light movement, chattering animatedly as she went. I could see Hussein was thunder-struck by her.

She flung herself at him. He simpered behind her. The school phoned me one evening to say that this chap Hussein kept coming by the school to see Deborah and would I please explain to both of them that they couldn't allow visits like this, it was against school regulations.

"I have never seen a young girl so determined to see her boyfriend," the Head of the boarding house told me, " Deborah will act as though it is a matter of life and death. I allowed this Hussein to sit outside with her last evening, just for half an hour, and I asked Deborah if you, *Madame*, were aware that he comes to the school. She said you had said it was fine."

"No, I had no idea," I sighed, "I don't know what to do with her. He drives all the way over from Saintes, you know, to see her. He is besotted."

355

A Call From France

When Debbie came home that week-end I told her that the school had phoned. She was furious.

"Why don't they mind their own business?!" she spat.

"You are their business," I replied, "they are only concerned for your welfare."

"Humph! I can soon change that!"

"What is that supposed to mean?"

"I hate school anyway. Hussein says it is like a prison!"

"Oh, Debbie!" I was so weary of tiptoeing around her. When is she going to grow up, I thought, be sensible, have a thought for something other than herself? Aloud I said: "I doubt Hussein has the remotest idea whether it is like a prison or not, or even what a prison is like …"

"Yes, he does!" she cut in, "he saw prisons when he had to arrest people when he was doing his *service militaire* in Algeria!"

"You are doing well at school, " I said, ignoring her, "so don't jeopardize it.   The school doesn't want Hussein turning up at the school gates, so that's that."

I was surprised at her even mentioning the word prison in view of what had happened … I counted … that was barely fours months ago. Four months is a long time in the life of a child …

**

It was extraordinary when Debbie moved out.

"Hussein has asked me to go and live with him," she told me.

We were standing on the top floor, by Max 's room. I can even remember what I was wearing. Hussein stood defiantly next to her, ready for a fight.

Whatever else may happen, Hussein, I thought, I will never give you the benefit of a fight.

"What about school?" I asked weakly.

"I'll still go," she assured me, "but I'll be a day pupil."

"I thought Hussein lived with an aunt?"

"It's a kind of aunt – and uncle – Abdullah – but he's found a flat for us. We can move in tonight."

She had got it all worked out and this had clearly been planned for weeks. There was no point in being upset or angry.

"I want you to finish your education, do your *bac*, Debbie. It's important."

She translated this in to French for Hussein who kept nudging her and muttering that we should speak in French.

"A *bac* isn't everything!" exclaimed Hussein.

"Well, of course it isn't everything," I replied patiently, "but it is a good thing to have. Debbie will be able to get on in life far better with a proper education."

"It's more important to be happy," said Hussein, preening himself.

I nearly replied that one could be happy with a *bac*, but didn't. A huge weariness overcame me.

"And Brighton?" I asked. I wanted to grip her by the collar of her shirt and shake her. "What about your plans to go to college in Brighton?"

"Oh, *that!* "

"Yes, that, Debbie."

"Well, I'm hardly going to leave Hussein!" she exclaimed as though it were painfully obvious.

She translated this in to French for him and he smiled down at her.

"No, I suppose not," I concurred weakly, wanting in truth to remind her we'd heard all this before, "but I do want us to be clear about this Debbie ....."

"*Parlez en francais* !" Hussein snapped.

"*Deux minutes*," I said, holding up my hand; there was no point in antagonizing him. "Debbie, daddy and I specifically want you to finish your education. Listen to me. I am not going to harp on at you – though I could – about past mistakes........... Shall we apply for a place at Poitiers University?"

"Possibly."

"Debbie," I said, trying to be calm but firm, "I repeat that daddy and I do SPECIFICALLY want you to finish your education."

I could see there was no point in going on at her. I wanted to tell her that her dad and I had invested a lot of money in her education, that she's put us through a lot of heartache, but didn't. Kids don't see it that way.

It was almost as though she was running for her life, as though she was trying to sneak away quickly from an impossible situation. As she and Hussein loaded her things in to his car, I noticed that she scuttled by through the back lobby, almost as though she was afraid I would stop her. They took everything. Her unspoken statement was that she was leaving totally and for good. Why? I was worn out by her and an element of me breathed a huge sigh of relief when they drove away. Let Hussein put up with her attention-demanding for a few months, I thought. Yet I was cut to the quick.

Tears streamed down my face as I mounted the silent staircase to her room. I stood by the door for a long time looking at the disorder they had left there ... old clothes, masses of books, vast quantities of file paper, general paper, dried-up old felt-tips, magazines ... broken beads, a few ornaments, the picture of the ballet dancer that had hung in my room when I was a girl ... the chest I had decorated with flowers for her ... the tiny dolly chairs Euan had made for her. Her whole little life was contained in those left-overs and my heart felt utterly broken.

Well, she's gone, I thought. She'll be back in a few months' time and it'll give me a respite. I felt all used-up by her; I felt empty. It'll do me good not to have to deal with her for a while and it'll do her good too perhaps.

I dejectedly started to pick up a few things, mortified by her obvious desire to go as quickly as she could. I knew it was his influence; it was odd the way she was so easily taken-in.

I piled the things she had left in to three big piles. The first I mentally labelled "jumble", the second "bin" and the third "keep". It struck me, as I cleared up, how she took things for granted. All the things I had bought for her, all the presents she had received from the family – they were all carelessly flung about, and she had taken with her only the stuff she used or wanted. She seemed to have no respect for anything and, worse, I thought as I packed away little treasures I wanted to keep for her, she seemed to have no sense of sentimental value. It was as though her childhood meant nothing to her.

A Call From France

I had to drive over to Corme Royal to see some tenants that afternoon. Debbie, keen to build-up her driving hours, had usually come with me in recent weeks, and I could see she had a sharp grasp of the letting business and could not only remember names of people and places but also how much they owned me and what I had or had not said to them the previous time. I had been proud to introduce her as my daughter to my tenants. They had respectfully shaken her outstretched hand.

"Bonjour, Mademoiselle."

Well, I thought, that didn't last long. I wondered how she imagined she'd finish her driving course and rather doubted Hussein's car had anything other than third party insurance which would not, of course, cover her. That's her problem, I told myself firmly. I missed her enormously as I spoke to the tenants. She had been a kind-of back-up system for me. The very fact that somebody else was there to witness the trouble I had to go to in order to pick up the odd 200f here and there, money which was absolutely due to me, in itself gave me a strength.

"Is it worth all this bother for 200f ?" Debbie had asked, but before I could reply had answered her own question. "Of course, it's 200f every month. Plus all the other odd bits of money from all the other tenants. It soon tots up."

"I pick up about 3000f (£300) in cash every month, going round all the flats like this," I explained. "Most of them are incapable of putting the money on to my account. But more importantly, they somehow just don't *do* it … it is almost as though they think the money isn't really going anywhere if they put it onto an account."

"A lot of local people don't have bank accounts," she confirmed, "they can't cope."

When Euan got in I didn't mention Debbie. We had supper and I did the ironing. He didn't ask where she was till quite late, and he didn't react at all when I told him. Perhaps he realized I couldn't take his reaction, whatever it was, good or bad. I just didn't want to know.

Debbie phoned the following morning.

"Hello, mummy, it's me!" she said cheerfully.

Debbie continued to go to school every day, taking the train in from Saintes to Royan first thing in the morning and last thing in the afternoon. I felt this showed a sense of responsibility on Hussein's part and a level of intelligence on hers. We paid her train fares, of course – there was no question of objecting to that, and for a while we even thought perhaps Hussein would be a good influence on her.

"Let her spend her silly years with him," my father said.

"She's out of your hair for a bit," said Gran.

And that was the way we saw it. Hussein was clean, he had a job, he was serious. He didn't take drugs, he didn't touch alcohol. He was a sensible driver.

"Just imagine if she were out all night on the back of a motorbike!" said Gran.

A Call From France

All the fraught worrying in bed late at night, wondering when she would come in, was spared us. She wasn't with us. Out of sight, out of mind ... almost. She worked well at school and was still talking about going in to law. She obtained a provisional place at Poitiers University, though had now completely rejected any plans of continuing her education in Brighton and wouldn't even discuss it.

We pulled out all stops to be "cool". We visited them in their flat, had a meal there once or twice, took them with us to see Titanic (dreadful film, I thought – the old black and white version was infinitely better) and they regularly accompanied us to walk Big Harry or out to a restaurant. Euan put his head down against the wind ... Hussein was absolutely not at all the kind of young man he wanted to see his daughter with, but he accepted that it could have been worse – it could have been Manolo – and better the devil you know and all that. Hussein had plenty of humour which was a big plus and, always a joker myself, I found that although I certainly didn't particularly enjoy his company, I didn't mind it too much either. He was

A Call From France

nonetheless exhausting. There was something about him that demanded our attention; we had to think-out what we were saying all the time, fearful of putting a foot wrong and fearful of estranging Debbie. The sense of exhaustion that hit us after a visit by Hussein and Debbie was so strong that, when they phoned to say they were coming round, although on the one hand I felt a sensation of triumph and pleasure, our hearts also sank as we saw our peaceful Sunday evaporate in to a session of pussy-footing around these two young people.

"He knackers me," said Euan.

For my part, I noticed that my relationship with Debbie underwent a change. I spoke to her, and she spoke to me, as a friend. We chatted amiably and frequently went out shopping together, usually only to the supermarket but shopping nonetheless. Those were precious times. I felt that, despite Hussein, my relationship with her was recovering and I found new common ground with her as we chatted about food and cleaning aids and electricity bills. A part of her was much older than her

367

seventeen years. I loved her little grin. I loved her hands. I loved those times with her.

Debbie had since childhood been very baby-orientated. Much as I loved my own babies I had never been a particularly mumsy type and when I spotted the maternal longings, building up like a volcano in Debbie, I was quick to quash them.

"There is nothing romantic about having a baby," I told her. "Believe me. In fact it can be utterly disgusting."

"Oh, I know …"

"All new mothers think they will handle their baby like no mother ever did before. Their baby won't cry all night. But they do. They scream so much you want to throw them out of the window."

"Oh … I know …"

"Debbie, listen to me. PLEASE listen to me !"

"Yes, yes, I know mummy … don't worry so much!"

That September Max returned to England. He had a place at college in Somerset and his departure left a terrible and frightening void in my life. He was sixteen. The French system could at that time be very narrow-minded and we felt it best that he continue his education in England where lots of options remain open. It's a very hard thing for a mother, watching her child set off on his own, even if he is a mature sixteen and over six feet tall. I accompanied him to Bath and sorted out digs for him. He accompanied me back to Gatwick and put me on the return flight. He was far more competent than I. I was not worried about him for he had inherited Euan's savoir-faire and Euan's ability to rise above whatever situation was put in front of him. Max was a confident young man, with smouldering good looks and a kind of charisma all of his own. But I missed him dreadfully and missed the string of teenagers tramping through our hall way and up and down our stairs. Max had been a good ally for me during all the troubles we'd had with Debbie and I'd found –

369

and in time I developed this same relationship with Bernie – that I could confide in Max in a way that made me feel totally understood and comforted. I bought him a mobile phone while in England – at that time still quite unusual for young people – and I phoned him every day. If I'd been unable to get hold of him I'd stay by the phone till late at night in case he phoned.

"I need to go to the Grand Canyon," declared Bernie as he came out of school one afternoon.

Well, you do, don't you? When your kids come out of school declaring that they need to go to the Grand Canyon, you take them to the Grand Canyon, don't you?

We timed it to coincide with Max 's half term and met him at Heathrow airport. That was one of the best moments of my life as my boy appeared from the other side of the crowded lounge, bag over his shoulder, long legs in black jeans –

370

"Maman!"

"Max!"

Euan and I have since decided that we're not really very good at aeroplanes. Euan is just too tall and I …. well, I am just too impatient. Bernie , with all the bravado that one has at eleven years old, was excited and thrilled with the whole thing, and Max was too. Bernie was a brilliant kid. Never any trouble.

Debbie was furious.

"That," she said, "is typical! Totally typical! You never took me anywhere like the Grand Canyon!"

"But Debbie, darling, you can come too, of course you can!"

"How can I?!" she spat, "you know quite well that I can't! Hussein would never let me!"

A Call From France

"Debbie, that is your choice. You cannot seriously expect us to pay for Hussein too."

"No – of course not!"

"Well, there you are then. We'd be thrilled if you came too. But Hussein must stay behind."

"I'd be so unkind to leave him behind …" she faltered.

Hussein, sitting in the background as we spoke, muttered to her – as he always did - that she should speak in French. I could quite understand, it would annoy me too. He was a brilliant mimmick and often joked when speaking to me. He'd say:

"Hello mummy, it's me!" imitating Debbie to perfection.

Looking at her now, sitting at the edge of the sofa with Hussein determinedly grasping on to her hand, I felt terribly sorry for her. She'd have been so thrilled with Las Vegas – you *have* to go to Las Vegas, if only to see how ghastly it is! I could see her vacillating before my eyes, but Hussein won.

"My dear," I repeated, running my finger down the side of her cheek, "you can come if you want to. If you change your mind."

Have you ever been to the Grand Canyon? It is so striking it makes you realize how tiny your own personal world is. Have you ever been to Las Vegas? It is so utterly horrendous that it is fantastic. It is so blatant and so garish and never in my life before or since have I seen so many enormously fat people. We hired a car in Los Angeles and, after visiting Universal Studios (wonderful!) and Hollywood for a few days, drove out over the Nevada desert. We bought a Country and Western tape and listened to it as we sped along the neat, straight highways that cut across the flat landscape. Here and there were rocky outcrops and small shrubs, cacti straight out of cowboy films, even dust bowls whipping up in spirals in to the bright blue sky.

"Hey! Cool! A tornado!"

A Call From France

Las Vegas appeared after dark, on the horizon, many hours later. Like a great glittering Dame, the town rose up off the horizon ahead of us, a twinkling, sparkling mass of lights, gradually increasing, spreading out like a spill of liquid gold, as the car tore forwards through the flat blackness. As we neared this glittering Dame, the noise began – the sound of a thousand tunes, a million songs, the sound of people having fun, of fruit machines and money machines, car horns, glasses chinking. It was wonderful, hideous.

Max and Bernie were mesmerised by the huge brilliance of it all. In stark contrast to our little village of St Sylvain, Las Vegas thrilled them. Only in films had they seen anything like it. We remained ten days or so and visited the Hoover dam.

"I so wish we'd moved to the States instead of France," I said.

"They wouldn't have had us!" laughed Euan.

It was true that there seemed to be – or is it only when you're on holiday that you feel this? – a kind of zest to everything, an efficient and friendly aura that permeated life in general, something that we found totally missing in the simple rural world of France.

At the Grand Canyon we stayed in a log cabin-style hotel which I loved, but the boys hated .

"This is a dump!" declared Max .

I did a couple of sketches of Navajo Indians. Tall pine trees loomed skywards all around us, and I loved the smell of them and of the clean mountain air. The leaves on the trees were lemon-yellow, ready to fall. There was hardly anybody about. It started to snow. A huge roaring log fire was lit in the hotel sitting room. I'd have stayed all winter had we been able to. I want to go back some day.

Our next plan was to convert the barns into holiday gites. There were enough barns to make seven cottages. This is what almost all the British do when they go to France, it seems. It

375

had taken us by now eight years to get round to this way of thinking, for it seemed like a mug's game.

"It's the obvious thing to do," said my father, "it'll put the barns to good use and provide you with an income to the end of your days."

It was, of course, easier said than done. The barns came under an agricultural zone and it was not, it seemed, possible to get planning permission to convert them in to holiday accommodation. The idea was shelved.

"The laws might change," said Euan, "the horse may talk."

Old king Fred Bloggs sat on his throne one day and a man was brought before him, accused of stealing his horse.

"You know," said the king, "that the penalty for stealing the king's horse is death?"

"Yes," said the accused.

376

"So, you are condemned to die," said the king, "you will be executed at dawn."

"Sire," said the man, "may I make a suggestion to you?"

"Well what is it?" asked the king.

"Sire, you will not execute me if I teach your horse to talk."

"Proposterous! What a stupid idea!"

"Sire, please, give me this chance. If I teach your horse to talk within one year you will let me go a free man. If, when the year is up, I have not taught your horse to talk, you will have me executed as planned."

"Very well, then. It is agreed," said the king. "But tell me, why do you suggest it? You know quite well that you will not be able to teach my horse to talk."

"But sire – in a year a lot can happen – the law might change, or you might be merciful, or I might escape, or ... the horse may talk!"

Telling each other that the horse might talk was something we frequently did. Sometimes the horse did talk. Sometimes not.

We both enjoyed being busy. Josie came in three times a week and Euan had his team of men, now all French, having one by one sacked almost all the English who worked for him, out on the sites.

"Whatever is that?!" I jumped out of my skin one afternoon.

"It sounded like a gunshot," said Debbie.

We ran outside and there was Michel shooting cheerfully at the grass.

"Michel!"

"Qu'est-ce que tu fais?!" Bernie called out.

"I'm shooting moles!" he called back.

Big and sweaty he came sauntering over to us, shotgun in hand. He waved it in the air as he spoke. At the top of his voice, as was his way, he explained to me that moles appear out of the ground at the same time every day and that he had been waiting all week to shoot them.

"They are a pest, *Madame!*" he roared.

"Well, I am sure they are, Michel, but I don't really see why they have to be shot."

"It's cruel!" wailed Bernie , *"c'est horrible!"*

"How else am I to kill them?!" Michel was flabbergasted, "look at my lawn! Look at the mess they are making!"

He always referred to our land as "his", and it was likewise his ladder, his wheelbarrow, his roses, his weeds.

It was true that the local moles had a remarkable ability to create their mounds of earth all over the lawn, never in flower beds, never in the fields, never over in some corner by the pigeon house or by the sheds where it wouldn't matter, but always in the lawn. Michel was devastated. Although the lawn was a fairly mediocre version of one – a keen gardener wouldn't even call it a lawn – Michel had worked very hard on it.

"Wouldn't it be better to get rid of them some other way?" I asked.

"You mean put razor blades down in the holes?" asked Michel, impressed that I knew a different way of slaughtering moles.

"No! Of course not! That is as horrible as shooting them!"

"There is nothing horrible about shooting moles, *Madame,* nothing at all. It's nature."

I couldn't quite see the relevance of this, and it didn't seem to be nature or anything like it.

"Whatever. We can't have you wandering around with a shotgun, Michel," I said., "I'll ask *Monsieur* to buy something suitable."

Disgruntled, and swinging his gun up over his shoulder, Michel went over to his car. He declared sullenly that he needed a beer, which Bernie went to fetch for him, and things went back to normal.

Michel and Josie were both totally trustworthy and honest. Thick as two short planks, but trustworthy and honest. They both had keys to the house and both confided their problems to me.

"I've bought myself some new underwear, *Madame* ," said Josie one day, "in case I'm ill."

Oh dear, I thought, surely she's not about to talk about her underwear again?

"Er … I see … well, that's nice, Josie" I said.

"I'll show you!" she said with a conspiratorial look at me, and without so much as a by-your-leave she lifted her skirt to reveal a pair of very lacey pink knickers with a little row of pink fluff all round the edges.

"The bra matches," she added and, dropping her skirt, proceeded to hoist her jumper up and showed me a minute pair of breasts completely lost in a lacey pink bra which also had a little fluffy decoration on it.

"Very pretty," I said, vigorously rubbing the polish in to the table and hoping she would follow suit.

"Because you never know, do you?!" she said as she took the hint and picked up her rag, "never know what might happen."

"Quite, quite."

"I've been feeling poorly lately, *Madame,* see. I've reached The Age Of A Woman's Fatigue, see."

"Quite, quite."

"And so I bought some new underwear."

"Good idea. To cheer yourself up."

"Oooh, no! Not to cheer myself up! Nothing will cheer me up, not never. No, no, I bought it in case I get rushed in to hospital, see. Got to have some decent underwear on if I get rushed in to hospital!"

**

It wasn't as though I could say:

"Stop it immediately!"

There was no point in forbidding it, it was already done. It was typical of her to tell me on the phone, not having the courage to face me … yet in some ways it was better that way, for she couldn't see me drop my face into my hands or hear the rush of tears that engulfed me the moment we had rung off. Instead I chose my words slowly and carefully:

"Are you sure?"

"Yes."

"No offence Debs ... but we've heard all this before, haven't we?"

"Yes, yes, I know – I **knew** you'd go and say something like that !! – I've been to the doctor and it's certain!"

Could I detect a note of triumph ? Was she trying to somehow get at me by ruining her own life? Why had she done this to herself ... how had I managed to raise such a totally daft child?

"How has Hussein reacted?" I asked.

"Oh, he's pleased, really pleased!"

"Did you not ... did you not take precautions?"

"No. We decided if it happens, it happens. Fate. *I'nch-Allah.*"

"Pardon?"

"It's Arabic. It means "if God be willing". I'm learning Arabic. It's really interesting."

Knowing her as I did I knew she's pick it up pretty quickly. I bet she's reading the Koran too, I thought.

"I'm reading the Koran," she said, almost as if I'd asked the question out loud, "it's great. Really interesting."

"Good. That's fine, then."

I struggled for something to say and battled against slamming the phone down on her. Her voice was … defiant, triumphant.

"Debbie …" I almost whispered, "you're only seventeen …"

"Oh! That's nothing! Plenty of Arab women have babies when they're a lot younger!"

"But you're not Arab, Debbie," I tried, "you're English ..."

"Nope! From now on I'm an Arab, I'm a Muslim!"

"Oh ... oh, I see. Jolly good ... well, when is the baby due?"

"End of July – the twenty-ninth. So I'll be eighteen by then, you see."

She said "you see" as though it somehow solved all the problems. I calculated quickly. She was barely six weeks pregnant.

That evening my mother phoned to say that my Auntie Dulcie had died. Aged 92, she was the sort of person I'd somehow thought would go on forever and my childhood memories were richly powdered with memories of Auntie Dulcie. But when they're 92 you realize they're going to go one day soon, of course ... even though you thought they'd go on forever. I sat for a long time in the darkening hall, my fingers drumming lightly on the telephone receiver, looking blankly in to the gathering darkness and noting abstractedly the sag in the curtain over the round window and the chip in the floor tile by the piano. Giving the piano a good layer of rich polish seemed to become of extreme importance and I made a mental note to tell Josie accordingly in the morning. Euan came downstairs.

"Honey!" he exclaimed, seeing me sitting there, "are you all right?!"

I so loved this man. Big, tall, strong, smelling of warmth and comfort, I rose and fell in to his arms and he rocked me gently, quietly, waiting for the tears to subside.

"Auntie Dulcie has died," I sobbed.

"Oh my honey, I'm so sorry …"

"And Debbie is pregnant!"

"Oh my honey, our stupid daughter …"

"And I feel upset!" I blurted suddenly, red face spluttering stupidly as I looked up at him, "really REALLY upset!"

He kissed my face.   He didn't need to say anything for he knew we both felt the same way. We stood for a long time in the big stone hallway and the light in the room quietly changed, darkening imperceptibly; we held our arms round each other, rocking silently as the same thoughts went through our minds.

I didn't go to Auntie Dulcie's funeral.

But I used it as an excuse and I knew that my old auntie would willingly forgive me for doing so.

"I can't go by myself!" I exclaimed tearfully to Debbie, "Bernie and Max are in school, daddy is working and the only person who can come with me is you!"

"Hussein says no," she replied, a slight tremor of hesitation in her voice.

"Whatever has he got to do with it?" I asked innocently, trying to look totally perplexed.

There was a moment of silence, so I added, equally innocently:

"He can come too if he wants. Could he take the time off work? The flights are about £200 each, tell him."

"No," Debbie replied, "he can't afford that. But I'll persuade him I've got to be with you …"

I'm not quite sure what I was hoping for. Of course, first and foremost I was hoping she'd ask for an abortion. Once away from Hussein it was likely she would feel totally differently. On the whole I was against abortion – certainly in cases like hers – but when it's the future of your own child that is at stake it is different, and your values change. I tried to broach the subject a couple of times, without actually saying the word "abortion" – but it fell on deaf ears, so that on the last day in England I said to her:

A Call From France

"Debbie, you don't HAVE to go back to France or to Hussein if you don't want to. You are in charge of you ..."

It sounded so weak. I was trying to give her a chance to change her destiny. I was trying to hold doors open for her, when they were slamming shut all around. Also I was hoping that seeing her cousins and her grandparents – the people who loved her the best – would help her to change her values, re-evaluate her situation and re-think her course of action. But girls of seventeen rarely have a course of action.

While in England I encouraged her to spend time with the family. Gran – who at this stage knew nothing about the pregnancy – took us out for a meal. Debbie was very animated. If she suffered from the waves of nausea she claimed to be having (one could never tell with her), she hid it very well. I tried to avoid the subject while not ignoring it. I battled constantly against blurting out to her that she was a total idiot. I wanted to tell her how disappointed in her Gran was going to be, I wanted to tell her how disappointed I was. When I told my father his mouth fell open in astonishment.

"Grief!" he searched my face for signs of tears, "you certainly are having a time of it with that girl!"

I nodded dumbly.

"We must keep it in proportion," I said ... had I not said that before? ... "it could be worse. Hussein is with her. She's well. She's not imagining she's going to move in with us with a yelling baby on tow ... it could be worse."

"I thought she was getting over The Silly Years," he said, "I thought you'd seen the worst of it."

"So had we. Perhaps this is just the start. I wonder what I did wrong?"

"Nothing, my dear," my father put an arm around me, "you are a wonderful mother. You've got a difficult daughter, that is all."

We returned to France; I felt a sensation of defeat. Euan told his mother. As predicted she was shattered too.

"She's almost eighteen," said Gran, "it could be worse."

It could be worse seemed to be becoming our family phrase. Hussein picked Debbie up and took her straight back to their flat. Knowing I couldn't change anything I smiled cheerfully at them and told Debbie to phone me so that I knew how she was getting on. I couldn't, with the best will in the world, pretend to take an interest in her pregnancy or the coming baby. I was interested in so far as Debbie was my daughter and mothers are always concerned for their daughters, but talking about morning sickness or swelling breasts just totally disgusted me.

The Psychiatrist:- That's normal. You are not ready to be a grandmother. You still have a little boy and a teenager at home. You are no where near ready for this, and just as Deborah is too young to be a mother you are too young to be a grandmother. You cannot feel love and devotion for a grandchild you not only did not want but had not foreseen in any way. Deborah has caused you a lot of anguish and your instinct is to protect yourself and your husband from further anguish. Your intelligence tells you that Deborah's relationship with this man Hussein will not last long, so this in turn means you will have further problems with her to deal with. This time with a small child in to the bargain. Conversely, if the relationship does last a few years this in itself causes problems of a different nature. Your feelings of disappointment and hurt are totally normal. Try to not think about it or even analyse it. Just go on with your day to day life, include your daughter as you always do. Don't predict.

My mother: it can't possibly last. It's perhaps better if it doesn't. Dear oh dear – still, you never know, it may work out well.

A Call From France

*<u>Max</u>: so I'm going to be an uncle? How weird!
I don't want children till I'm about thirty.*

Debbie was enjoying buying things for the baby. I
felt I had let her down somewhere along the line,
that because of some foolish thing I'd done or said –
(I should never have left her with a child minder
when she was a baby?   I should have stayed with
her when she had her tonsils out ?   I was too vain ?
I asked too much of her ? I didn't ask enough ? I
drank too much, I'd worked too much, I was not a
good mother) – she had chosen a destiny that she
would not normally have chosen.   Whatever else
happens now, I thought, I will not let her down.
She must know that I am there for her, no matter
what.

Occasionally I sensed that Hussein resented the
things that I bought, knowing he couldn't do so
himself. On the other hand he willingly accepted
most of it – and regularly accepted it graciously and
with genuine pleasure. And it was not a lot to give
… this and that … my old tumble drier (it was
about time I had a new one), my old freezer
(bought that when Debs was a tiny baby), the cot,

some furniture, lamp shades and curtains, things to make Debbie's new home as comfortable and pleasant as possible. I tried to be casual about it and periodically asked Debbie if Hussein disliked it.

"No, of course not!" she exclaimed.

I turned baby clothes in to a joke between him and me, regularly presenting him with a packet of nappies or a teeny pair of frilly baby pants. He'd laugh and tell me I could do the nappies. I tried hard to pay less attention to work and more to Debbie. I had not enjoyed Debbie's teenage years and I wanted to try to enjoy this for both our sakes.

I was so concerned about salvaging what I could out of my frayed relationship with my daughter that I tiptoed around the situation in a dread of putting a foot wrong, even making a point of counting four or five days without phoning her so that I didn't come over as "pushy" in any way. I would then allow myself to phone her almost as though it was a kind of treat. I had a phone installed for her, although Hussein objected.

"I've got my mobile," he said, holding up a scarlet

mobile that he used at work.

"What if she goes in to labour?" I asked him, "what if she needs help?"

He seemed irritated. I had learnt that if I wanted to say something private to Debbie I had to either see her while he was out at the gym, which he didn't approve of, or I had to speak to her in English, which he didn't like.

"Is there some reason he doesn't want you to have a phone?"

"No – I don't think so …"

"Because I don't want to tread on his toes. It just seems mad to not have one."

Debbie had a couple of spells in hospital and, although she was a big girl with what in the old days would have been called "child-bearing hips", she seemed to be carrying the pregnancy badly, with spells of light bleeding and one infection after another.

"We'll go to choose a buggy next week if you like," I told her. "Hussein – you'd better come too, eh? In case you think it's the wrong type?"

I pandered to his male pride. He wasn't even slightly interested in choosing a buggy. Debbie was looking forward to it. I phoned a few days later. It was unusual for there to be no reply because Debbie was constantly – eternally! – in the flat. I thought nothing of it and tried again a little later. Still no reply. When there was still no reply late in the evening, when an exhausted Debbie would normally be lying on the sofa in front of the TV, I became concerned. I phoned both local hospitals in case she'd been admitted.

"Non Madame," I was told, "she is not here."

When there was still no reply in the morning I became really quite worried. With a sinking fear it slowly dawned on me that I didn't know anything about Hussein or his family; I didn't know any of his friends and – to my consternation – I realized I wasn't quite certain of his surname.

"It's something like Hessena or Hoossanu," I told

Euan.

I had a busy day dealing with tenants and the endless paperwork, but the feeling of fear persisted and I was conscious of the throat-tightening fright that had gripped me during her disappearance not even a year ago. I phoned again and again.

"Honey," Euan reassured me, "she could be anywhere – perhaps they've gone off for a few days? Perhaps the line is out of order?"

I drove down to Royan the following morning. I parked outside and looked up at their balcony. The shutters were closed.

"It's not the line out of order," I reported back to Euan, "they're not there."

Fear is infectious and Euan now became concerned.

"They can't have gone off for a few days, they have no money," I said.

"I always thought it very odd that Hussein didn't want us to meet his parents," Euan volunteered.

"He is secretive."

I switched on the Minitel and waded through every surname in area which remotely resembled Hannachi or Hennessa or anything like it. Neither of us spoke our fear aloud – that Hussein had taken Debbie back to Algeria. I couldn't sleep. Where Euan had coped badly with Debbie's disappearance a year earlier, I coped badly now.
I tried to think carefully and logically. Was there seriously any real danger that he had taken her to Algeria ? Would she be willing to go with him ? Was he sufficiently aggressive to insist she go with him ? I had no answers but Hussein had often spoken about Algeria the way you and I might speak about the Mull of Kintyre and Debbie, in her innocence, thought it would be a great place to go. However, I knew she was very keen on the baby's room and all the baby things and that she wouldn't want to disappear just like that. So, while on the one hand I recognized that she was daft enough to think that Algeria would be a nice place to live, on the other hand I was certain she'd want to stay where she was.

"Comment va Deborah?" asked Michel when he

came in for his beer.

"Humph!" he said when I told him that I hadn't been able to contact her for several days, "he'll have whisked her off to Algeria I expect! That's what they do, these Arab types."

Fear was like a cold wet cloth around my neck. I couldn't believe I had been so stupid as to let her move in with him in the first place. I phoned the Casino where he worked and was told that he was on his "off" (they used the English word to indicate time off).
On the sixth day the phone rang.

"Hello, it's me!" came Debbie's cheerful voice.

"Debbie! Where are you?!"

"At the flat ..."

"I've been trying to get you for days ..."

"Oh – sorry. We went to see some friends in La Rochelle."

"Come and see us, Debbie, we need to see you."

"Oh? All right … is something the matter?"

"You should have told me you were going away!" I thundered.

There was a moment of silence and I heard her translate this for Hussein. Her voice was cold when she came back on the line.

"Hussein points out that we don't have to report to you about anything."

"I realize – but there is such a thing as good manners. I was frightened."

"Whatever about?"

"That you'd had a miscarriage," I lied, "that you'd fallen down the stairs, that you'd broken a leg – oh, I don't know! I was frightened for you, Debbie."

Again I heard her translate all this for Hussein. His voice then came on the line.

"I am looking after Deborah now, not you. If she has a broken leg I will take her to hospital. It is clear to me you don't trust me."

"Hussein – I'm sorry – I didn't mean it the way it came out. All mothers are concerned for their children. It's only natural."

"It is because I am an Arab," he said, hitting the nail absolutely on the head.

"No – no, of course its not! Whatever has that got to do with it? I am sorry if I sound as though I'm interfering – but Debbie treated us very badly not long ago and the scars have not healed …"

He had clearly put the phone on to loud speaker for I then heard Debbie shriek:

"Typical! Of course you have to bring that up!"

"You are holding a grudge against her because of that," continued Hussein.

"Oh for pity's sake!" I snapped, losing my temper

with him, "grudges have nothing to do with it! I was frightened for her, that is all. Am I not allowed to be concerned for my own child?"

"No," he said, his voice crisp in its dryness, "she is none of your business."

I heard a little click and the line went dead.

I sat for some time – yet again - by the silent phone and looked around the huge quiet hall. I've sat here so often, I thought, feeling shocked after one phone call or another. A part of me was furious with Hussein for putting the phone down on me – how could he be so rude ? Another part of me was furious with myself.

"I handled that really badly," I said to my father when he phoned the next evening.

"It's not your fault," he said.

"Yes, it is. I should have been able to cope and I didn't."

"Well, I daresay you over-reacted when you thought Debs had disappeared again, but it's perfectly understandable under the circumstances."

"The trouble is Debbie and Hussein don't see it that way. I don't think Debbie really has the remotest idea what she put us through."

"Probably not. Young people are like that. Try to forget about it. Leave it a day or two and then phone them as if nothing has happened."

"Okay, daddy. Cheerio, then."

"Bye for now, my dear, God bless."

I followed my father's advice and phoned Debbie a few days later. It rang for a long time and, after several attempts during the course of the day, it was clear to me that they had unplugged the phone. I wrote her a letter.

Debbie darling,

Truly, I am sorry I upset Hussein and hope he is no longer cross. I was terribly frightened when I couldn't find you, that's all. Sorry. You would be frightened too if you couldn't find your child.

The letter was weak and didn't convey what I was trying to express. I posted it all the same. But when I tried phoning again later that same week a voice told me that the number was not in use. I was shattered. How could they be so cross that they'd actually change the number?! Heavens, I thought, it was barely a row at all!

"The trouble is you've probably offended his male pride," said Nicky.

"He seems to have a bee in his bonnet about being an Arab," said Euan.

"He is a childish and ignorant MOON FACED APE!" I roared.

The days tripped by and I tried to forget about it. My father came out to stay with us for a few

405

weeks and was disappointed to not see Debbie. Short of driving to Royan and banging on her door I could not get hold of her.

"Well, let's knock on her door," said my father, "it's not as though we're asking anything unreasonable. It is quite normal that I should want to see my grandchild."

Our reception was very frosty, though something I learned early on was that Debbie was far more amenable in every way if Hussein was not there. I watched her closely for signs of fear, but there were none. It seemed almost as if her personality changed if Hussein was in the room. He had a way of flexing his muscles (metaphorically speaking) when there was absolutely no need to flex them. He felt threatened when there was nothing threatening there and, as Euan had pointed-out, was sensitive to the point of being ridiculous about his Arab blood. My father and I sat uncomfortably at the edge of her settee, sipping mint tea (made the Arab way, said Debbie). We left soon.

"I'm sorry about that," I said to my father

afterwards.

"It was all quite unpleasant," he agreed.

I looked at him. He had aged. Although as fit as a fiddle, and always ready for a party or a night out on the tiles, he was an old man – eighty-three that year. Physically he had slowed down a lot. I noticed it particularly because I had changed my car that year from a Volvo (740 GL fuel injection – apparently a Really Nice Car) for a new Chrysler Grand Voyager (also a Really Nice Car) which was much higher up and my father had to haul himself up in to it. Completely illogically I had bought the Grand Voyager partly because Max was returning to France after his year at college in England and I needed something for carting him and his pals around in. My father was a small man, which made me regret buying the car. He reached out and took my hand so that I could help him in. His skin was so familiar to me – every year a bit older – soft, ageing skin with flesh loose over the bones, and a lovely comforting feel and smell to it.

I swung the car round down towards the seafront

and parked facing the huge ocean. It was June and tourists were just starting to reappear in the town; there were people on the beach and in the shops, and the town was like a great awakening creature, flexing and stretching as it starts its day.

"Did you ask why they had had the phone removed?" he asked then.

"Yes – Hussein said they didn't need it. He is so rude. I bought the thing so the very least they should do is give it back to me if they don't want it."

"Well, there it is, my dear. You managed to hide your antagonism very well, I thought."

"I tried. Actually – I don't really feel antagonistic towards Hussein, really I don't. Mostly I feel tired and bored with constantly limping around their sensitivities - the pair of them. He is rude and childish, but he can also be quite charming and very funny. He is not at all the kind of man we wanted for Debbie – but not because he's an Arab. Arab men have a reputation – rightly or wrongly – for dominating their women folk and keeping them indoors. If he were an Eskimo I would worry because Eskimos have a reputation for living in igloos. The chances of him making Debbie unhappy are greater than the chances of him making her happy."

My father knew all this, of course, and I was just thinking aloud.

"Well, she's stuck with him for a few years at any rate."

<u>Diary. Five years later.</u>   I feel bad that I am infinitely more interested in my sister's new baby than I ever was in Debbie's. Well, my sister is 44 and her baby has been longed for for many years, whereas Debbie was only seventeen and a baby was the last thing I wanted for her. That's where the difference is. Also, of course, Euan and I were totally cut-out of the whole thing, rejected like rubbish, so we were unable to forge a bond with Jasmina. She was a stranger to us through no fault of our own.

That baby was ten days old before Debbie phoned
to say she had had it. She might just as well
have raised her fist to me or slapped me hard
across the face. She might just as well have
kicked us in the shins or spat at us. Our hurt and
bewilderment was total.

"Surely," said Nicky, "Debbie must feel sad? I
mean, had she let us know we'd have sent flowers
and presents and cards. What a pity. Half the
pleasure of having a baby must surely be all the
flowers and presents and cards!"

"I don't want to see her," said Euan.

"Turn the other cheek," said my father.

So we went to the hospital where Debbie lay
post-Caesarean in a small side room. Hussein sat
belligerently in an arm chair. In a plastic cradle
lay a tiny black-haired baby. I would have liked
to have felt a gush of love for the little scrap; I'd
have liked to scoop her up and be thrilled to bits.
But I felt nothing. Blank. Bernie sat at the side
of Debbie's bed and I placed the baby carefully in

his arms. Well, I thought, hopefully Bernie will bond with his little niece. Hussein growled at me from the other side of the room.

"Don't pick her up!" he hissed.

Euan bent over and kissed Debbie's cheek, asked how she was, shook hands with Hussein, peered at the baby. I tried to say the right things. I think that was the greatest hurt of my life – and I have had many hurts, many ups and downs, many difficult moments – that was the worst.

That winter was very mild and I left my geraniums out and they were fine in the spring.   Several times there was a feeling of spring in the air, even as early as January, and we looked forward to life on the beach and the advantages in general of living in a climate where when they say it's summer it really and truly is summer. I watched the trees for signs of green, scanning them every day far too early, and was inordinately surprised each time we got a sudden cold patch.

"I love it when the trees suddenly burst into green," I said to Bernie as I drove him to school in the morning. The road was long and straight, with poplars on either side, just like an Impressionist painting, and the landscape was totally flat, dotted here and there by a small sparse tree or a stalks nest high up on a purpose-built platform. STORK'S

This drive in the mornings was very beautiful during the winter for frequently a thick early-morning mist pervaded everything at ground level, and you could see only a grey-white cotton bud veil over the fields, with a church spire sticking out on the horizon, or a few black and leafless trees.

"If this were a picture on a calendar," I said to Bernie , "we'd think it a bit corny."

In the evening the sun was setting. Bernie 's school finished at 4.45, and during the winter months the sun was just starting to dip as I headed west back out of Clion, a brilliant ball of fire, making me screw up my eyes and spreading

412

a mantle of scarlet over the mud where the mist had been that morning.

Euan was working on a property in La Tremblade, a big old town house that he was converting in to five flats. His vision, his ability to see what could be done, was the thing that always made him such a success, coupled with an unstinting devotion from his employees and a lot of blood, sweat and tears. I had more time on my hands now but was still kept pretty busy dealing with the nine lettings we had by this time built up, for there was always something that needed seeing to.

I learnt early on that you can't tell much about a tenant by his papers. The French system – and I was guided by this – asked all tenants to produce three wage slips, a reference from their previous lodgings, a full-time and permanent work contract and umpteen other documents that half the working population of the Charente Maritime would be unable to produce. And even if they did produce these things it did not necessarily mean they were good tenants. An early example that springs to mind was Gipsy

Lee (as we called her because of her dark, if ageing, beauty) who was a retired school teacher with a private income. Certainly, she paid her rent promptly and in full but she stayed only three months. Then there was an architect who stayed only two months. It was better to have tenants who needed to be reminded to pay their rent but who stayed a long time.

It was a positive and energetic patch. We built our empire up rapidly and soon became known as property owners in the area. We found a niche in the market for most letting agencies would not take on any tenant who was not working and there were no where near enough council flats to go round. Our flats, then, went almost entirely to "social cases" whose rent was paid by the state system directly onto our accounts. Although there was the odd one who was a genuine case, most were out for what they could get, and all the hard work Euan and I put in to make the properties nice for them was utterly wasted.

"If we make it nice, they will keep it nice," we said.

A Call From France

I put little net curtains up on the windows in the communal areas, a couple of tubs of geraniums out in the communal yards, a few inexpensive pictures on the walls in the communal corridors. But within no time at all, and despite notices and talkings-to and items in contracts, the communal areas were full not only with bikes and buggies, but cat litter trays, dustbins, rubbish, washing and a stench of urine, whether indoors or out.

It was exasperating. For a while I paid Josie to go round the communal areas to sweep and clean but I soon became totally discouraged by the tenants complete lack of any effort. Sometimes I would go round myself with a broom and a bucket, banging on doors and telling the tenants in no uncertain terms what I thought of the state of the place.

"Mais, Madame ..." it was never their fault – of course – it was always the other tenant, up there, over there ...

415

Between us Euan and I have cleaned up every kind of disgusting mess from human faeces to used nappies, from used sanitary towels to rotting food – and everything in between.

All tenants had to pay two months' deposit against damaging the property; this was forked out by the state system, of course, and also paid straight onto our account. Very few tenants ever got their deposits back needless to say. Several got evicted – in itself a long nail-biting system which favours the tenant at every turn. I appeared in court four times because of tenants but rapidly learnt how the system worked and played it to my advantage. I always defended myself and I never lost a case.

Sometimes we took the law in to our own hands. Many of these tenants had the *gendarmes* hot on their heels. As is the case in the UK, and probably almost everywhere in Europe, the tenant is At Home in his rented property, even if he hasn't paid his rent. As landlords we were not allowed to cut off the water or electricity, let alone boot them out. We were not even allowed to "harass" them for the rent. Tenants who did

not pay had to be sent a letter recorded delivery
– *avec accusé de reception,* as the French say –
to prove that we, as landlords had indeed tried to
recover the rent a minimum of three times. It
was daft because the recorded delivery proves
that you have received an envelope, it doesn't
prove the contents of that envelope and – more
importantly – because in the French system
anything even moderately officious is sent
recorded delivery, the tenant would simply not
go to pick it up from the post office. I would
frequently go back and forth between home and
various tenants, banging on doors and asking
neighbours when he or she was most likely to be
in. I found an effective way was to ask for the
rent in front of other people – usually terribly
embarrassing for the tenant.

What grieved me so much was that I was always
so pleasant about everything. These people
often had very little to call their own and, simply
out of kindness I would regularly donate a bit of
furniture that had been in our barn (we had a
constant stream of bits of furniture in our barn),
or perhaps a few tools to help them with
whatever they were doing, or logs for the

fireplace, or – very frequently – I would give them their first week or two rent free if they were moving in towards the end of a calendar month.

"If I'm decent with them, they'll be decent with me," I thought.

Conversations with tenants would frequently go like this:

"I've come for the rent, *Monsieur*."

"Yeh – well – I'll give it to you tomorrow."

"You said that yesterday."

"I don't see why I should pay my rent, the windows don't fit properly. How'm I going to heat this place in the winter?"

"You will recall, *Monsieur*, that when we did your contract, I supplied you with two oil stoves and also we wrote down that the window is a bad fit. I explained that that was precisely why the rent is not very high. You agreed to put insulation tape around the edge. I said I would give you the money for the insulation tape AFTER it is done."

"Yeh, well I'm not paying no rent till it's done."

"The window has nothing to do with your rent …"

…….. and so on. I had endless conversations like this with various tenants. I had one shove me violently on the shoulder and ask me what I was going to do about it if he didn't pay his rent, I had another threaten me with a gun and yet another with a dog.

One tenant died, poor old man. In fact he wasn't old – perhaps not even seventy, but like so many weather-beaten people in that area he looked a million years old. His rent was always paid but I went round to his little flat where he lived alone on the ground floor of a building in Bourcefranc-le-Chapus where we had four flats for something else – I think he had asked for a letter box, or something similar. I knocked but there was no answer, nor was there an answer the following day. One of the other tenants

419

informed me that he hadn't been seen for several days. Standing there thinking about it, I realized there was a bad smell coming from under the door. The *pompiers* went in for me – there was no way I would go in till after the whole place had been cleaned out. The poor old man had died in there all alone and nobody had known. There was nobody at his burial, but I stood silently by the coffin for a moment or two and whispered *au revoir Bernard Guilleau* under my breath. Within a few hours I was busy at something else and had forgotten him. I have often since thought that the saddest part of all was not that nobody knew he had died, nor that he had neither friends nor family at his burial, but that I – the one person who was there – forgot him so quickly afterwards.

The tenants we kicked out were always young men. We went along with a couple of our men and the van and trailer and simply removed their belongings, changed the locks and re-let the place. One man went to the police about it but I was able to prove that he was not the tenant (therefore had no reason to say I had invaded his home or touched his property or done anything to him whatsoever) for the place had been let to his lady friend and not to him, and she had long since written to me to say she had left. I still had to appear in court over it, however, but like so many of the things that happened to me in France, it was water off a duck's back for I had learnt to just grit my teeth and get on with it. I didn't worry about things. Perhaps because I had worried so much in our early days in France – had virtually been bludgeoned with worry – I had sort-of used it all up. The worrying mode in me had ended.

Sometimes there was such a sad and silly element to these evictions, for it invariably involved some young twit who simply couldn't get it together. I used to bend over backwards to be helpful

"I realize you can't find the rent for both the months you owe me straight away, so I suggest you pay me the month before last in full plus a little bit for last month. Then at the end of this month you give me this month's rent plus a little bit. Okay? That way it won't be too difficult, will it?"

A Call From France

"Oui, d'accord, merci Madame."

Then a couple of months later I would find myself with Bruno or one of the other men, and Euan and Max piling the tenants belongings on to the trailer. Depending on the situation we sometimes stored the things for a while in one of our barns (and subsequently listen to the tenant complain that we had allowed the damp to get to it!), but it was always after inordinate efforts to get the rent out of them, and many many warnings. Clearing out these places we invariably found cannabis plants or cannabis leaves, sometimes syringes and once a couple of hand grenades and a gun. The young *gendarme* who called in the bomb squad and removed the firearm was thrilled to bits and doubtless regaled all and sundry with the story for years.

I frequently kept small items long long after I had asked the tenant to come and fetch his stuff (they virtually never came to collect their things); these were things that looked as though they might have sentimental value in case one day the tenant asked for them. This happened only once when the tenant's grandmother phoned me and asked if I had by any chance found any snake skins when I had cleared out her grandson's flat.

"SNAKE SKINS?!" I asked, aghast.

"Oui Madame," she said and explained that her late husband had been an explorer in the 1920s in central Africa.

I rummaged through the boxes I had stored and sure enough found three huge snake skins. They were probably worth quite a lot of money. There was also an African jungle hat and a few African artefacts that looked quite old. I took these round to her where she lived in Rochefort. The grandson was sitting belligerently in the corner of the living room. The old lady was very pleased with the African things.

"Where's the rest of my stuff?" growled the tenant.

"In my barn.   Come and get it if you want it. I've asked you several times to come and fetch it."

"You had no right!"

"All you had to do was pay your rent.   Do you imagine I enjoy tramping over here with these snake skins, that I enjoy storing your stuff for free ?""

He never came round for his things, perhaps frightened that the police would be there. Bit by bit his belongings were dispersed, much of it to the dump and few bits more of it to the old lady.

*

One of the problems we faced was that we had no outside input in to our lives. I love women and love to chat and natter with other women like me, but there were no other women like me and I was terribly lonely.   I tried hard to strike up a friendship with Evelyne, Ben's mother, but it didn't work out for one reason or another. Alain and Sylvaine were the only people we could call friends in any real sense of the word, though we knew dozen upon dozen of people, most of them part of the Charentais élite … the lawyers and doctors, the mayor and the dentist … and through them we attended a lot of functions varying from charity balls to Round Table functions. Euan had been with the Round Table in the UK and tried to join in France, but felt completely an outsider and was never able to break in through the very local feel to the *Tableurs* near us.

I wanted to go home more than anything in the world. Homesickness and loneliness became almost like a mental illness for me and I was constantly packing up boxes of things in my determination that we would one day be gone. All my best books sat in cardboard boxes for about four years. Seasons came and went while I packed and then unpacked clothes. For a time I had cardboard boxes all over our bedroom floor, piled high with packing … they remained like that for months till Euan tripped over them one night and I knew I had to unpack them and put them all away again. I cried.

"I want to go home," I said.

"We will my honey, we will, just as soon as we're in a position to buy a house there."

"We can rent a house there."

"Perhaps, perhaps ..."

"Done France," I said, "now take me home."

We joined in with whatever we could for a long time – jazz evenings, Spanish films at the local cinema (like me, Claire also spoke Spanish), yoga, keep fit, Thalasso ... but after a while we gave up. I think part of the trouble was that Euan's French made conversation with him an uphill grind for whoever we were with, and his Meniere's problems zoomed, like a great tidal wave, he said, in to his head, buzzing and drumming as soon as he was under any kind of stress, which included trying to speak in French.

.

A Call From France

Diary, five years later. Arrived back this afternoon. Got the 10.30 flight from La Rochelle. All well, Bernie pleased to see us. We had a great time, achieved lots as we always do. Euan did the gutters along gites 5 and 6 and paved the area around the Wendy house, plus loads other stuff. Had dinner with Henri and Edith almost every evening – he got us to sample almost every wine of the area, not to mention champagne. Also ate with Daniel and Marie-Claude a couple of times. Looked up Alain and Sylvaine, of course. A new roundabout has been built on the La Tremblade road – about time too after that dreadful accident. That girl has been dead and buried three years now. Meant to bring oysters back for the family but didn't get round to it. Max fine, still with Emily.

The possibility of converting the barns into holiday cottages re-emerged. Contrary to popular opinion, building regulations in France are quite strict and are generally perfectly sensible. The French authorities are very conscious of their heritage

427

and are keen to have buildings remain in keeping with the existing buildings and to not over-build in agricultural areas. Unfortunately for many areas – as indeed is the case in any country – a lot of these regulations didn't come into being till after several hundred monstrosities had already been built. The Charente Maritime, however, being a poor area, could only build small monstrosities which, given time, will be camouflaged by trees and hedges and what-have-you. Goes to show there are some advantages to not having any dosh.

Our barns, built of local stone, and in varying degrees of dereliction, ran diagonally along one side of the land, separating the chateau and its gardens from the fields and forming a kind of L-shape at its northernmost end. In one of these barns was the bread oven that had served the chateau, and in another huge wine vracs. Some boasted ancient stone windows, and huge stone troughs, called *timbres* in that area, and massive beams. The babes had played camps in the lofts and the stone was decorated with felt tip markers here and here and paper signs that read "death to all who enter" and other similarly welcoming things.

The zone was classified as "agricultural", so technically there was no possibility whatsoever of converting the barns in to living accommodation of any sort. However, the Mayor in any French town is a figure considerably more important and more influential than his British counterpart and, while the DDE *(direction départemental de l'équipement)* – the planning office – was prone to prevaricate endlessly over what we called Our Barns Issue, the Mayor stated in no uncertain terms that it would be fine for us to convert the whole lot in to seven holiday houses. Of course, this was a benefit for the village for a small daily tax per head is levied on all holiday makers and holiday-makers are a quintessential item of village life, if only in the summer. Mercifully, we got the Mayor to put his agreement in writing for, some months later, after we had spent thousands of pounds and laboured thousands of hours with our team of men, the DDE decided to not grant permission at all.

Suffice to say, that it was a highly charged situation, traumatic in the extreme, as we negotiated our way in and out of the law, and watched all our money and all our effort teeter and wobble and very nearly fall. How we managed to get that agreement through was proof that there is a God.

Considerably worse, however, was the trauma we went through with the bank. We had accounts with five banks in the area and very rapidly got a verbal agreement with the Caisse in Saintes (place Blair, alongside the river – only go in there if wearing full armour). In order to catch the letting season in time we needed to start work on the cottages immediately. The situation was such that we had to place advertisements immediately because people book their holidays at least six months ahead. This meant that we were taking quite a risk, and really putting our necks in the noose. We had under a year in which to renovate the porter's lodge and convert the almost totally derelict barns into smart holiday houses. If we left it any later it would be a further year before we would get any lettings. There could be no hanging around – we either had to go for it full steam or not do it at all. We explained this carefully to the Caisse for it involved using each and every resource we had on the assumption that the bank would pick up the finance of the project. We discussed it all at some length with the bank and poured over plans and estimates with them. We filled in a variety of forms and produced a variety of documents. All was well.

"The dossier will be sent off," said our bank manager, "it will be back in two weeks."

He was very confident that there would be no problem and even mooted that he would pop by within the next few days to see the site and what we had stared on already, which was re-roofing almost the entire thing.

STARTED

We carried on with the work while waiting the estimated two weeks. Then we waited two weeks more. We were concerned about investing any more time and money without a written approval of the project. Finally I faxed the bank:

"We intend to continue work full steam, but we must be sure of funds, as discussed. Please confirm."

And they faxed back:

"Use your own funds for now and you can reimburse yourselves out of the loan when it is through."

Although this was not ideal it was a start, and we embarked upon a £300,000 building project with great enthusiasm.

For me, my one and only aim was to generate enough money for us to go home. I didn't really care whether it was through letting holiday cottages, or letting social-case flats, or writing a book or flying to the moon. I just wanted to go home. It was nonetheless a very exciting programme and one which would make the value of Les Cypres leap up three-fold and more.

A Call From France

My father put up £30,000 so that we could
crack on. We made several more trips back and
forth to the Caisse in Saintes for they seemed to
constantly want more papers about this or that
and, after a few months, and despite the go-
ahead months earlier, still no money was forth-
coming. There was no question of stopping
work. We had a duty to our men to keep them
in employment, and we had to plough on as hard
and as fast as we could. We got further and
further overdrawn, not only at the Caisse but at
the other banks too. The French banking
mentality is not the same as the English one for
an obvious solution was for us to mortgage one
of our properties. But while many banks were
happy to loan us money to BUY a property they
would not give us a mortgage on one we already
owned – in fact couldn't seem to understand
what we wanted. Furthermore "equity" did not
have the same significance; we kept pointing out
the good equity we had in the chateau and the
impressive property folder we had, but it meant
nothing.

We had a good team of faithful men. We took
on others, all on a self-employed basis, and Max

433

also became a full-time worker. During the
winter months the men all trooped in to the
chateau kitchen at lunch-time, sitting either in
the main kitchen or the back-kitchen, depending
on their "status". It never ceased to amuse us.
Big old Michel always sat in the back-kitchen
and was positively embarrassed on the one or
two occasions when I asked him to come in to
the main kitchen with us. Rene and Bruno
tended to sit in the back too, but Michel-de-luxe
and Josie felt free to sit with us, and the others
sat wherever Max happened to sit – and that
varied each day. Big old Michel was such a
curious mixture, for on the one hand he would
always doff his cap at Euan yet on the other
hand he felt free to help himself to beer from the
fridge. He treated me with the utmost old-
fashioned respect, all but calling me "majesty",
but insisted on always planting the most
splattering kisses on both sides of my face.

Max fell between two stools, which he found
quite hard sometimes. He was the boss's son but
he was also a labourer. He found he couldn't
join in the general chatter with the men because
he was in a way "separate" from them – yet he

was absolutely one of them. If Euan left the work site to go and fetch materials the men instantly referred things to Max who, all of sixteen years old, had to cope as best he could. This was not because the men couldn't cope but because somebody has to carry the can. The last buck must stop somewhere.

There was a long patch, then, when I wasn't involved in the cottage work for it was all heavy outdoor labouring, often in cold and wet conditions. I was kept busy with the tenants and the rents and running our home.

Our relationship with Debbie and Hussein improved a little at a time. I felt Debbie loved us and wanted to be with us, at least to see us regularly, but that she was torn between what Hussein told her was right or wrong (and everything and its dog seemed to be wrong as far as he was concerned) and her need for contact with her family who loved her. We did everything we could to show her that we loved her and we also did everything we could do To accommodate Hussein.

He seemed to disapprove of so many things. As a Muslim he didn't eat pork or drink alcohol or even smoke. All drugs were forbidden, of course. Gambling, card games and betting (not that we any of us did these) were out of the question, to the point where he binned a pack of cards I bought for Debbie – yet he worked in a Casino. All that was all right – he had his religion and we respected it, but his disapproval extended itself to me and my kitchen – you shouldn't cook lamb like that, he'd say – and even the things I did for Debbie – you can't hang wallpaper like that, he said. It was stunningly irritating. We made an effort to chat happily with him however, and even enjoyed his humour in small doses. We were grateful that he was good to Debbie … and Debbie seemed happy enough.

"Are you happy, Debbie?" I asked.

"Oh yes! Of course! Why shouldn't I be?!"

"No reason at all – I'm just asking, that's all."

A Call From France

There was still no word from the bank. I phoned them. Oh yes, they said, no problem – *pas de probleme* – and would we please go in and sign some more papers. Pleased, we set off for Saintes, half an hour's drive or more in each direction only to find that the papers we were to sign were the same as some we'd signed now five months earlier.

"Oh, are they?" said the woman at the bank and scuttled off to see the manager.

We went round and round in circles for a further three weeks till eventually the letter arrived. I ripped it open.

"Letter from Caisse – at last!" I called out to Euan.

Monsieur, Madame (read the letter)

…… After careful consideration of your dossier ……… we regret that we are unable to agree the required finance ………

437

We stood staring at it stupidly for several moments. There was clearly some mistake. It had all been agreed months and MONTHS ago. We had discussed the ins and outs of it in a very positive way with the bank manager several times. He had even faxed us to say to go ahead ... But there was nothing to be done. It seemed to be for no better reason than somebody had suddenly decided against it somewhere down the line, the bank had closed the file. What was intolerable was that they wouldn't even discuss it. I went to see the little woman we'd seen several times.

"Ah," she said, and sighed, "you are not French, you see, so the risk is greater ..."

"But this bank has known for YEARS that we are not French!!" I all but shouted.

"This is discrimination," said Euan, flashing the fax in her face, "and we will take legal action!"

The blow to us was terrible. My father had put all his savings in, we owed money to the men and money to the suppliers and we were grossly overdrawn on every account.

"I bet we could get compensation," I said, "that fax is professionally disrepute ..."

But the truth of the matter was that we just couldn't bear it. We knew from long and bitter experience that any judiciary action of the sort we had in mind would take years – and we couldn't wait years. My nerves couldn't stand it and Euan couldn't cope. I declared that I was going to scoop up a bucket full of Big Harry's poop and shovel it through the bank's letter box.

There was nothing for it but to go round the other banks. Euan got on with the work and that team of men continued to work **with no pay** for several months. I, in the meantime, went round to our other banks with our dossier. It made me sick to the teeth for we'd have had the money in months and months earlier if only the Caisse had been decent and honest about it all; I went through scenes, mentally, of suing them and torturing them and wiping them off the face of the earth. Months dragged on. Because the loan

439

we wanted was enormous by local standards the dossier had to be referred to Headquarters Elsewhere.

I spent a lot of time dealing with paperwork and tenancies, bills, taxes and insurances. We had till then been insured with a village man and it had often struck me that he didn't appear to know what he was talking about. We had a lot of insurance for we owned a lot of property and it was important that we be properly covered. That was easier said than done for, although tenants were supposed to have their own insurance, very few of them did anything about it.

"I think I'll increase the insurance on the chateau," I said to Euan, "I like the look of that new chap on the *quai* in Saintes."

The new insurer advised me to increase the insurance by a vast sum, which I did. We had had a bad fire in the UK ten years earlier and I'd learnt that it is better to be over-insured than under-insured.

"Not that we have the slightest intention of having another fire!" I laughed. I was quite frightened of fire.

We returned to England for Christmas. We stayed at Gran's. It was the end of the Millenium and she had a big party planned. We went to my parents for Boxing Day and spent a lot of time chatting in their little living room, looking at old cine films of our childhoods in Africa and talking – endlessly! – about banks in France and Debbie.

On 29th December the phone rang at Gran's. It was Josie wanting to speak to me.

"*Madame*!" she wailed at me, "there is a terrible storm! I'm in the chateau and I can't close the windows!"

"What in the world are you talking about?" I couldn't think what she could mean.

"I opened the windows to pull the shutters in, and now I can't close them again!"

441

It was true the windows were tall, but they weren't that big, no matter how fierce the wind. It could get pretty windy in the winter, as does anywhere on the coast.

"*Madame!*" she wailed, " you don't understand! This is a BIG storm, a really very very big storm!"

We then phoned Michel (de luxe) who confirmed that trees were coming down everywhere and that in Bourcefranc, where he lived, the tide was so high that he had moved upstairs even though he lived half a mile or more off the beach. He said the electricity was out and that it was only a matter of time before the phones were out. We explained about Josie and he said she was not exaggerating.

"This is a very serious storm," he told us, "I've never seen anything like it. You had better come back."

It was quite late, so we spent an uneasy night and Euan was up and on the phone early in the morning. He phoned big old Michel who confirmed there was a lot of damage, several people killed, many roads impassable. Gran rushed about carving up cold turkey and ham and Christmas cake. Within minutes she had prepared a couple of huge picnics for us, which we were extremely grateful for as the day wore on and we were stuck hour after hour in traffic jams from Paris all the way to Tours and beyond.

We almost lost everything we owned.

The storm, the worst in recorded history, had ripped through the area like a tornado, killing thirty people, tossing boats up out of the water onto the roads, knocking over lorries, ripping roofs off and uprooting trees. Our beautiful *tilleul* at the back of the chateau was down and lay like a huge mortally wounded creature over the woodland floor. Our roof had almost gone, two chimneys had gone, one of which had come crashing down through the babes' bathroom. The windows, left to bang around wildly all night, had been ripped off or had their panes smashed. Most of the shutters were off. The wind had whipped round the inside of the house, ripping doors off their hinges and mattresses off beds. All my pictures lay smashed on the floor, and dozens of ornaments and flowers and curtains ... all in shreds. What was not smashed was soaked.

"We are ruined," said Euan.

"Yes," I replied quietly, "I'm afraid so."

Translation of a letter found in our letter box, two days after the storm.

Monsieur, Madame,

*I was so saddened when I saw the terrible damage you have suffered at the Chateau des Cypres. After all your hard work it must be very difficult for you to see your way forwards again. To us local people it has been a great joy to see the old chateau renovated and alive once more, after so many years of abandon and darkness. Although I realize that **les anglais** here in our country are sometimes a little resented because the property prices have been forced up, we French nonetheless recognize that*

444

it is thanks to people like you that half our old properties have been saved and are living again. On behalf of the village of St Sylvain, may I wish you the greatest courage in the face of this adversity. After such a terrible storm we all have a great deal of work ahead of us and those of us who did not lose loved ones must just be thankful and press on as best we can.

Good luck and courage to you and your young family.

The people of St Sylvain .

At the end of this there was an illegible signature. This heart-warming message gave us both the very courage the letter wished for us; we wondered who had written it. It was a woman's handwriting. We didn't puzzle long over it. It didn't matter. We had to face inordinate repairs or simply close the books.

The day after the storm a party of fourteen arrived to celebrate the millennium at our chateau. They had paid a lot of money for the use of the place and arrived to find a wreck. Phone lines were down and there had been no way of warning them. To our amazement they laughed, gasped, grinned, opened plenty of bottles of champagne, lit all the fires, bought hundreds of candles and, despite babies and toddlers in a cold dark house which had cardboard nailed over the windows, had a great time. They were the epitome of the British stiff upper lip.

"There has clearly been a disaster," one said to me, "don't worry about it."

He looked abstractedly out of the window at the thousands of slates that had blown off our roof and now lay like black confetti all over the grass. The trees, lying on their sides, somehow seemed worse. All our hard work on the barns was totally lost for we had been re-roofing and the tiles also lay, interspersed with the slates, everywhere. Just clearing up was going to be a major job.

They had followed the debris left by the storm for a hundred miles or so, so were expecting the worst when they arrived. And the worst it was! We had a generator, which would have run the central heating, but this had been stolen – we assumed by one of our men, for it had been taken neatly out of the place where it lived by somebody who knew it was there. Euan reckoned it was Bruno and I suppose it probably was. Candles and torches suddenly became like gold dust, though we already had plenty of both because the electricity would periodically go out during the winter months anyway. We also had two ancient oil lamps and, with the fireplaces ablaze, we were able to make the house tolerably cosy, given the conditions, for our guests.

We moved in to our flat in Saintes for that fortnight and drove the half hour to Les Cypres every day. The men were brilliant; they all turned up, having waterproofed their own houses where necessary, ready to work without having to be asked. They had still not been paid, and their loyalty and devotion to Euan was significant.

Euan and I were both totally shattered. We didn't know which way to turn. We had taken a dreadful blow to our business and it seemed that no amount of courage was going to put it right.

We had lost the roofs on almost all our other properties. Actually, only one house in La Tremblade was not affected. Cold, wet and distraught, tenants had moved out and gone to live with family elsewhere, all assuming that we would see to the repairs straight away. Just one family stayed put and camped in their flat with neither water nor electricity, nor even a roof to speak of. Everybody wanted their roof repaired first and there were no roofers available. With no tenant in the property, there was no rent coming in. So the banks didn't get paid. Everything was insured, of course, and the French government announced a national disaster so that insurance companies would not make life difficult for those needing to claim.

The problem was that we had to fork-out the money up-front, and we hadn't got any. We were already grossly overdrawn at the banks, and getting worse, and grossly over-credited at the suppliers. It was impossible to find roof tiles, roof felting or labourers. Our project on the barns had not only bled us dry but had made all creditors, now stretched beyond endurance by hundred upon hundred of households needing stock, feel they had gone as far as they could go.

It was a nightmare. Worse, the insurance company would only cover registered and qualified builders and roofers – no DIY was possible.

"It is extraordinary that you put the insurance up just a few days before," said my father on the phone.

It was indeed extraordinary. The insurance man told me some time later that had it not been a natural disaster he'd have assumed foul play. He agreed to an advance on the money for repairing the roof and confirmed that the insurance would cover 100% of all building and labouring costs. But we still had to find a roofer.

"Just use your own men," said my father.

I explained that Euan's team were not registered "roofers" and that they therefore didn't count.

"Ask your insurance man if he will cover a team of English roofers," suggested my father.

I did as he said and then phoned him back:

"Yes, that's OK – but where will they stay? There is nowhere to stay."

"I have decided to be a roofer, not a doctor," said my father casually, "and I've got a firm called ......The Roofing Doctor. How's that?"

"I see ... and the Roofing Doctor is going to take on Euan and his team of men ..."

"Precisely."

Necessity is the mother of invention. It worked a treat. The only problem arose when the insurance company made the cheque out to The Roofing Doctor, which meant that my father had to quickly open an account in that name.

Euan and his men, including Max , worked six days a week up on that roof, forty feet high, for ten weeks. Scaffolding surrounded the house for all that time. Because our house was a chateau we had slates and not the local tiles, so were able to get hold of the appropriate

450

equipment easily enough. Tarpaulins were put over the other properties. The French authorities mobilized the army and teams of electricians and telephone engineers came in from all over Europe to help. Army tents appeared in muddy fields and – you have to hand it to them – the French had the roads cleared and emergency services operational within hours of the storm abating. They were brilliant and worked day and night for over two months, getting France back into activity. The devastation was huge. Pavements and roads were up in almost all the seaside towns, caravans smashed beyond recognition, and almost all seaside business ruined. The tide came up waist-high in our favourite restaurant – indoors, that is. Overturned cars lay like dead mules by the roadsides and there was barely a building without a tarpaulin or scaffolding, or both. The air hummed and buzzed with the sound of chain saws.

I sat on the floor in the flat in Saintes and went through the figures. I didn't see how we could recover. Even allowing for the insurance paying for everything –which they did – we had lost almost all in-coming rents and, worse, the building of the gites would now suffer a terrible set-back. We had taken a lot of bookings already for the summer, totalling over £20,000 in rents already in – this would have to be all paid back to the holiday-makers if we couldn't build the cottages. Of course, the money was already spent on the building work. The insurance didn't cover loss of income. This was early January and our first holiday-makers were booked for mid-July. The attractive Maritime pines that had lined the edge of the property, thus hiding the sight and sound of the road, were all down, making the place less viable as a holiday site. A lot of the supplies we had bought were ruined – sacks of cement and sheets of plasterboard that had been stored in the barns were spoiled and now lay in many segments and many sections all over the field. And it wasn't just the cost of replacing all this, for before we could even begin we had to pay the men to clear away the hundreds of trees. Of course, the insurance doesn't pay for tree clearance. On top of all this we still hadn't got a go-ahead from a bank.

A Call From France

I was beside myself with fear and worry. I had put up with so much, we had both worked so hard. I felt we really just couldn't take any more. Euan, always calm and careful, also became very stressed. The nightmare sensation of cracking-up came back to me, filling my head and looming over my shoulders like a dark cloak. During the day I concentrated on clearing the debris and picking up the broken bits in my house.

"If we do close the books, as you put it," said Euan, "what do we do then? Where do we go? We have no choice but to plough on."

"We could run away," I said, "we could just sell what we can and go – just go."

"But go where, my honey? Where shall we go?"

"Back to South Africa, to New Caledonia – I don't know what we're doing here in France anyway!"

Euan took out a hankie and dabbed at my tear-splotched cheeks.

"And when we get there? What will we do?"

"I can teach …"

"Sure, you'd love that, wouldn't you?" He tried to make me laugh.

"I can't take it. Truly, I can't. This is the end, Euan. You don't realize. I've been through all the figures, I've added them up in every kind of way I can think of and it adds up to the same each time – we are ruined."

"All we need is to find a bank who will go with us …"

"Oh stop it! Get real!"

"Come on, honey, stop crying, we'll find a way. The horse will talk."

"No bank is going to go with us, Euan. Listen to me. You don't realize how serious this is. You don't deal with the banks and the books. This is Big time Serious."

"All we can do is plough on," he repeated.

And so we did.

*

Debbie always spoke in French. She always spoke in French to everybody – with perhaps smatterings of Arabic every now and then with Hussein– except when speaking to me or to Euan. She said it just came out in French, and that that seemed natural to her.

Language is a funny thing. The French love to say *"ah, c'est tres compliqué, le francais!"* but actually English is a vastly more complex language and with double the vocabulary to boot. In our language we have the Nordic influence as well as the Latin and the Teutonic, which is what gives us our huge vocabulary – more than any other language. We have at least two words for everything, sometimes several words; the French have no word at all for … blossom, for example, or snigger, ... there are dozens though I can't think of them right now.

Of course, the English are the worst possible at learning another language. I don't know why that should be. French is badly taught in our schools, but then English is badly taught in French schools ... and so on. I think the English have a terror of sounding foolish. Or perhaps other nations don't realize that perhaps they might sound foolish when trying to speak our language. Well, they <u>don't</u> sound foolish. Yet somehow an Englishman trying to speak in another tongue can be really terribly funny.

We put far too much emphasis on getting the accent right. I have often heard people say "he seems to have got the accent right", or "I can't do the accent" as though that is relevant. But it is not relevant. There are very few people who have no accent whatsoever – Max and Debbie, for example. My own French is pretty-much fluent, but within seconds of speaking the listener, if he is French, knows that I am not. That does, however, depend on the listener: some people just do not really listen and therefore don't hear an accent. Gran never seems to notice an accent. As soon as somebody speaks to me I have placed them, usually before they get to the end of their first sentence, in the relevant part of Europe, or the relevant part of the British Isles. Unless you are thinking of becoming a spy there is no point in struggling to get the "right" accent – simply because it is not possible.

Conversely, Euan, whose accent when speaking in French is very heavy, periodically found people decide they could not understand him no matter what. The moment they spotted a *foreigner* they would panic and claim to be unable to understand anything at all. Hilariously, we would often get people trying to speak to us in English and they would labour on in appalling English, even if we replied in French.

It seems the gap between being able and not being able to speak in a foreign language goes deeper than merely the memorizing of words and grammar. There is an entire unseen element of comprehension on the part of the listener and also on the part of the speaker, ie the speaker's ability to put over what he or she has to say in such a way that the listener feels he can understand, assimilate and react appropriately. Providing those elements are met, the accent is of no importance whatsoever. Even the grammar loses its value. Euan's French, throughout all our years in France, has remained very basic and very ungrammatical – yet everybody understands.

The ability to learn a foreign language is a gift, like being able to sing or draw. I daresay it is a gift that can be acquired, or at any rate enhanced through practice, even faked. I'd say my father "faked it" when speaking in French. It is akin to acting. Which takes us full circle to not worrying about sounding foolish.

Letter from my father.

Be grateful for small mercies – Hussein is not a fanatic, and Muslims can be fanatics in a way we're not accustomed to in the Western world. Having met him, I'd say he is quite moderate, and I daresay many a Muslim would say he's barely Muslim at all. It's important to understand that Islam is not a religion in the usual sense – it is more a political system in the name of God. It is based on poems and sayings set out by Mohammed in the Muslim year One – our 622 AD. Where we, as Christians – or westerners at any rate, regardless of our beliefs – can say a prayer or sing a hymn in almost any way we want to, and can in fact **believe** *(Roman Catholics and Protestants, for example) in any way we want to, Islam has only the one way.*

Furthermore, that one way has not changed at all since the 622 AD. It is stuck in that mode, for the Muslims believe that there NO OTHER way, that all and everything and every aspect of all things are covered by the Qu'ran (Koran) and that there is absolutely no need for any further ideas or inputs in any form. There exist only the prayers already in the Qu'ran, and not only do they have to be said in that tongue, all the intonations have to be the same too. Otherwise it is a corrupt prayer.

In our culture we don't mind which language we pray in – French, Spanish, German – the Our

Father is still a prayer. We can sing it or whisper it. Islam does not have this luxury. Some might argue – and probably correctly too – that that is why Muslim countries are so backward – precisely because of their inability to allow an intake of anything other than what they already accept. It must be quite galling for them to see (I'm thinking of Americans and the Gulf) "corrupt" people in their country.

Anyway, I wouldn't worry too much about Hussein. He is clearly very fond of Debbie and Jasmina, even if he does impose his Muslim ways of thinking on them. He has lived mostly in France, so I doubt he'd be willing to exchange the comforts of the western world for the unhygienic sluminess of Algeria. He seems to me to be pretty off-hand about his beliefs for on the one hand he forbids alcohol and card games, but on the other is a bouncer at a Casino.

Hussein had indeed a foot in each world. It explained some of his aggressive macho-ism towards me, for he felt that I was a mere woman, yet he lived in a world, recognized and accepted that world, where women play as important and worthwhile a role as men. He veered back and forth between Muslim principles and western ways, making a kind of wobbly ideology so that one never really knew where one stood with him.

My father came out to stay with us and was there when a bank finally gave us the loan. We opened champagne and leapt around in joy. At last! I had really given up hope and Euan and I were just going through the motions, doing what we could to fend off the crash, paying the men what we could where we could, and just ploughing on. It was March and our first guests in the cottages were due in twelve weeks' time. We have never moved so fast. The men, at last all paid, were fantastic and worked long arduous hours alongside us, frequently late in to the night and often six days a week. In that short space of time we created six holiday houses, to include building walls and laying floors, installing bathrooms and kitchens, plastering, rendering, insulating; everything had to be done from installing a staircase to fitting a socket.

We were full of energy and excitement. Like us, Max was not afraid of hard work.

Bernie and I made long lists of what we needed to buy to equip the cottages. I can't tell you how funny it is to go in to a shop and say you want sixty-three plates, sixty-three bowls, sixty-three cups ... and so on. We dashed with great speed in and out of shops, buying everything from beds to wardrobes, from shelves to cookers, kettles, place mats, cutlery, duvets, bed linen. We chose bright orange, bright yellow and bright green because the ancient cottages were dark with dark oak beams and quarry tiled floors. They looked fantastic. We were rightly very proud of ourselves.

Not least of the feats was the swimming pool, which was finished two days after the arrival of the first two families. All around us were the left-overs of building work, and we tried to clear up what we could before the first families arrived – but it just wasn't possible. The grass had not – of course! – grown in the cottage gardens and watering it to make it grow just made it muddy. There was sand and cement all over the kiddy play area where the concrete mixer had been, and great piles of planks and breeze-blocks and broken bits of plasterboard all piled up in three or four corners around the property. Bernie and I just went back and forth, back and forth between each pile of rubbish and the skip. The skip got taken away, emptied and returned to us twelve times, just dealing with the clearing. Particularly annoying was the unnecessary clearing – cigarette ends everywhere that had to be picked up, empty beer bottles the men had drunk, dead tea bags (me I expect) and constant bits of paper and plastic bags and even bits of clothing from men removing sweaty T-shirts during the day and then forgetting about them. Bernie and I planted geraniums everywhere, and begonias and lobelia and every colourful flower we could buy, and we put bright parasols in with the garden furniture and little palm trees, and did everything we could to make the place pretty.

During this time we saw very little of Debbie. She needed plenty of space. She needs to make her own home, we said, our help is perceived as interference, she knows where we are if she needs us.

The arrival of Jasmina brought about a change in Hussein. Or perhaps he had always been like that but just hadn't allowed it to show ?

The macho Arab side of him became all-prevailing. He made it utterly clear that I was not welcome in the flat on the very rare occasion I went round. He had started to speak to Debbie in a way I didn't like, and became very angry if I spoke in English. Because he worked nights he was usually around during the day. My visits became more and more difficult. Debbie looked worn out.

"It is only natural that I should help her with the baby…" I tried to reason with him.

"No," he replied, his tone unnecessarily aggressive, "Fatima, my mother, helps her. We don't need you. Jasmina has everything she needs."

A Call From France

"My concern is rather more for Debbie …….." I ventured.

"Do not be concerned for her. She is my concern. I buy her food and the things she needs."

In the background I saw Debbie make a tiny hand movement, indicating to me to not argue with him. She didn't intervene, but sat quietly on the sofa, the baby in her lap, her fingers twining round and round a corner of the baby's wrap.

This was horrible. I didn't want to have to beg to see my own daughter. I did not want to traipse over from Les Cypres to find this cold reception. I wanted to shout at her "what are you doing here, you daft kid ?! Why are you not at school ?!" But I said nothing. It would have achieved nothing.

I glanced back at Debbie. A look of slight impatience crossed her face. Impatient with me ? With him ?

"Are you all right?" I asked her.

"Come back at 6.00" she replied quickly.

Hussein thumped the door frame.

"Speak in French!!" he shouted.   He swung round at Debbie:

"What did you say ?!" he demanded.

She looked up at him.

"My mother asked if I am well and I replied that of course I am," she lied smoothly.

Hussein opened the front door wide, indicating that I should leave. He made a jerk of the head. I found that I was shaking.

I returned that evening soon after 5.30 and parked off to one side where my car couldn't be seen.   After a quarter of an hour or so (Lord, isn't fifteen minutes a long time when you are waiting?!) Hussein emerged and went to his car.

He sat there for some moments on his mobile, and then he drove off.

I climbed the stairs and knocked on Debbie's door.   I could hear the baby yelling.   After a few moments I heard her voice at the other side of the door:

"*Qui est la?*" she asked.

"It's me".

"I can't open the door, he has locked it."

"WHAT ?!!"

"It's because he is worried that I might get attacked."

"Who in the world is going to attack you?!"

"It's best that you go, mummy.   The neighbours are also Algerians.   They will tell him if they hear.   Thanks for coming though …."

Thanks for coming ?! Thanks for coming ?! I didn't know what to say. I wanted to kick the door down. Just as I turned away she spoke again:

"Can you come back tomorrow?"

"Yes, yes of course!"

"He goes to weight-lifting at about 11.00"

"I'll be here," I promised. As an after-thought I pulled a 50 Euro note out of my purse and slid it under the door.

The following day we had an hour together. Debbie was waiting and I stepped in to the flat quickly in case the neighbours should see me. I had expected her to throw herself in to my arms and cry, but she didn't.

"He really loves me," she explained. "We have a baby together. He doesn't want you to have anything to do with us."

Jasmina, now five weeks old, was asleep on the sofa. She looked vastly more like Hussein than Debbie, with dark hair and an olive skin.

"But why in the world not ? Surely Arab mothers take an interest in their daughters ?"

"That's just it, you're not Arab .... he wants everything to be Muslim. He doesn't approve of you ...."

"Surely things can be Muslim without him being so rude ? Without him locking you in to the flat ?"

She sighed.

"You don't understand," she said woodenly.

"Too right I don't understand! I'm sick to the back teeth of even trying to understand!!"

She didn't reply.

"Does he hit you?" I asked then.

"No!!"

"But you seem frightened of him ……..?"

"I don't get him … sometimes he can be so lovely. But he has this big macho deal going on all the time. It's since we had Jasmina. As though he thinks she will somehow be corrupted. But he gave me this, he can be really sweet …" she held out a small silver chain from which hung a cheap stone of some sort. I pretended to admire it.

She looked at me then.

"But I'd rather see you a lot more. I wish I could see daddy ….. and everybody …." her voice trailed off. Then:

"Thanks for the 50 Euros by the way. I've hidden it. He doesn't let me buy anything so it's good to have a bit of money of my own. His mother does all the supermarket shopping with his dad, and she gets everything for the baby .."

I looked at her closely.

"Do you love him?" I asked.

"Yes, of course I do!" she said, and I knew that she didn't.

As it was we were not going over to the flat very often, but now we made sure we kept a good distance so that Debbie could build her nest and work on the relationship she had chosen. Lord knows, we were so busy, fighting against all odds to get the gites ready on time. I think in some ways, being a man, Euan was better able to put Debbie out of his mind than I was. He was more logical. She's had a baby, she was living with this creature she claimed to love, there was nothing we could do to change it. Furthermore we were not welcome there.

"It's Hussein who is not welcoming," I said, "not Debbie."

"Oh I realize," replied Euan. "But she has made her bed. Good and proper. She has to lie in it."

"She likes it when we go over," I volunteered, "I think she's slightly frightened of Hussein."

"He's not hurting her," he reassured me. "He has an odd way of showing he cares, but he does care. He is looking after her in his own way, whether we agree with it or not."

"She's only just eighteen......!"

But Euan was right. She had indeed made her own bed.

I always timed my visits to coincide with when I knew Hussein would be out and, hopefully, the Algerians next door at work. I made a point of parking a way off and quickly scanning the car park for his car. Sometimes I got it wrong and Hussein was still in, generally cross and unpleasant. But usually I managed to arrive just as he was driving away. A few times Debbie and I went out for a walk, the baby in the buggy I had bought, always remarkably quiet. I'd have loved to treat Debbie to a few things – some new shoes, a nice hair cut – but I couldn't because then Hussein would know I had been there. Sometimes, however, he told her to ask me for money, grunting at her crossly as we stood awkwardly by the front door of the flat. I always gave it – more for her sake than his. It was never large amounts, and I knew he didn't drink or gamble it away. Giving the money was in a way a system of keeping the lines open, for as long as he needed a bit of money he would never totally forbid Debbie to see me.

I couldn't go back for well over a week because of deliveries at the gites. I could see she had been crying. Hussein was out – it was his weight-lifting time – and the flat was clean to perfection. I hugged my daughter and picked up the baby.

"Gosh, the flat is amazingly clean and tidy!" I commented.

"Cleanliness is part of the Muslim culture," she said.

"Do you need anything? Shall we risk the supermarket this time?"

"Mummy, you <u>know</u> Hussein doesn't like me to go out!"

"Does he know we've been out before?"

"I think we were seen. I don't know …. I daren't go out."

"Do you mean you are happy to stay in this flat all day every day?!" I remained standing, preferring to take her out than stay in.

"No!" slightly irritable now, "at week-ends we mostly go over to his parents. Fatima is showing me Arab cooking. It's really good."

"Daddy and I would love to meet them some time …….."

"That's out of the question. You are not Muslim. They don't want to know you."

It didn't seem to dawn on her that this last was perhaps hurtful, let alone ridiculous, but I let it go. Risking everything I said:

"I'm surprised they don't insist you get married, you and Hussein."

There was a silence. Minutes ticked by while she looked determinedly out of the window.

"He's already married," she said.

I sat down heavily. It was a thunderbolt, but I was nonetheless glad. Very glad. This meant that she could not be totally scooped up by him or his family. I could see why she had been crying, and I felt for her.

"I didn't know till a few days ago," she continued. "*Grand'mere* – his gran – told me. He has a son called Mohammed. Five years old."

"Ah …… and where do they live ?"

"In Algeria."

So, was this good news or bad? A thousand thoughts rushed through my mind. A thousand scenarios. But before I could say anything she said:

"They – Hussein's parents – are having a big family house built next door to the wife and son. They want to go back to Algeria. There's a lot of discrimination against Algerians in France."

"And Hussein ? Does he want to go back ?"

"Of course! Just like you want to go back to England. It's home!"

Fearful that Hussein might return by this time, Debbie suggested I leave. She asked me not to tell her dad about our conversation, but of course I did.

"Leave her to it," said Euan, "she's a big girl. She can sort herself out. She knows we'll always be here if – when - the need arises."

I saw her again a week later. She said time had dragged terribly, stuck in the flat and this time was desperate to go out for a walk. I watched her carry the buggy down the stairs, as I followed with the baby. She was dressed in brown, a long drab skirt, a long-sleeved old T-shirt, trainers. Euan was right – this was out of our control and out of our hands. Almost.

"Are you happy?" I asked her as we strolled along.

"Why do you keep asking me that ?!" cross now. "Why would I not be happy?!"

I ignored her.

"Debbie," I said, "Algeria is not a nice place to live. Don't go."

"Oh – I don't think it could be so bad." She calculated quickly. "You were there over twenty years ago, mummy, so you don't know anyway. Hussein says it is great. Anyway, they haven't got anywhere near enough money to finish building the house for years and years ….. And Hussein wouldn't make me go because of the wife and Mohammed …… it all depends …" her voice trailed off.

477

Back at the flat I kissed her goodbye. For years afterwards I wished I had kissed the baby.

"Algeria is not a nice place, okay Debbie? You would hate it. Please try to take in what I am telling you."

She said nothing, but looked at her feet.

"Well, I'm off. I'll see you in a few days. But always remember you can come home any time – any time at all, regardless of anything."

"No," she replied, and I saw that her eyes were filling up with tears. "No. He would never let me take the baby. He would kill me if I tried."

I didn't know it then, but I was not to see her again for almost four years.

*

A Call From France

<u>*Conversation ...*</u>

Hello daddy.

Hello, my dear.

I was just thinking about you.

Yes, I know you were.

I think about you a lot. Sometimes I can almost see you. Sometimes I can feel you touch my hand.

I know, my dear.

I miss you terribly.

It will pass.

Debbie has left us.

I know, my dear, but she'll be back.

Are you going? Why are you going? Why did you go?

A Call From France

We all have our time. It was my time.

No ...it wasn't ... we were not ready ...

One is never ready, my dear. I was not ready either.

I so long to see you.

You'll see me again. In dreams. For several years you will see me in dreams. And then that too will pass.

Bye-bye for now, daddy.

Bye-bye, my dear, God bless.

We buried my old daddy on a frozen hillside in Kent. We were brave. The wind whipped in off the valley and we huddled miserably in the mud, my mother, my brother Howard and me by the graveside, and the others on the tarmac for we had been told the ground was too soft to stand on. Everybody came to say good bye. Everybody had loved him. Somebody read out something from the Bible. I clutched the collar of my mother's coat around her neck and tried to protect her from the cold and tried to protect our bleeding hearts and our splintered world.

My father would have liked that hillside. It is very Kentish, at the edge of Tenterden where the land slopes away from the graveyard on the western side. Uncle Bob picked up a little mud and grass and threw it down on to the coffin, as we had thrown our flowers. Dust unto dust, he seemed to be saying. The ewe trees all around YEW stood darkly over the graves and we scuttled, frozen, in to the waiting cars, with the mud and our tears and all the words we wanted to say … and tried to say … and all the choked whisperings … goodbye, goodbye … Our world had changed for ever. Nothing would ever be the same again.

A Call From France

I went round to the flat three or four times before I realized they were gone. I knocked on the door and listened, my ear pressed up against the cold wood, in case I could hear something. It made me think of that poem ...... *is there anybody there? said the Traveller, knocking on the moonlit door ..*

Then one evening a door behind me opened and an Algerian woman came out, her head wrapped up in a grey scarf. She swung a broom back and forth.

"You looking for your daughter?" she barked at me.

It took me a few moments to understand what she was saying for her accent was very strong. She clearly knew who I was.

"Yes."

"Well, they've gone, *Madame*. Left a few weeks ago."

"Gone ? Gone where?"

She shrugged.

"How should I know?" she turned to go.

"Wait – do you mean gone away, left the flat, or do you mean gone on holiday?"

"*Eh bien, Madame*, they took all their furniture, so I hardly think they've gone on holiday!" she smiled, shrugged again and went back indoors.

I stood there for a few moments. I stared at the closed door. Suddenly I hit it hard with my fist *(suddenly he smote upon the door ………..)*

"Debbie!" I shouted, "Debbie!"

Was I angry or upset or both ? I don't know. In my heart I knew that Debbie would have let me know had she been able to. I detected the poison of fear creep in to me, and I shoved it ruthlessly out.

483

Outside it had started to rain, that thin drizzle that sometimes goes on for days in the winter months. It was cold. I looked around the car park for Hussein's car, knowing it wasn't there but looking all the same. A few people walked past me. I stopped one, a young woman who I knew had a small child.

"You know the English girl in Flat 33? The one with the baby?" I asked.

"Ah, non, Madame, desolée."

I drove home slowly and went straight to bed. Bernie came in and snuggled up to me, and I breathed the delicious boy smell of him and buried my face in his hair. No tears came for a very long time.

For months I kept looking out for her. I was constantly thinking I could see her – over there at the corner of the street, or surely that was her in the car that just went by ………. But I didn't start a search the way I had when she went with Manolo. This was different. She was a young adult now and she had made her choices.

"Hussein will take care of her," Euan reassured me. "Even if they have gone to Algeria, he will take care of her."

I put her largely to the back of my mind. I forced her back there, like a naughty child who keeps trying to leave the corner of the classroom. But when her birthday came round I bought her presents and wrapped them, and then stored them in the attic. I did the same at Christmas, and then on Jasmina's first birthday ...... and the birthday after that .... And the one after that ....

After she had been gone two years or so a man came to the Chateau door.

"I have a message for you from your daughter," he said.

My heart leapt.

"She has a son, born last week, she is well, she lives in Paris."

"You've seen her?"

"No, Madame, but I received this message via my sister whose friend lives next door to your daughter. I have no other information. I was asked to bring this message to you. I live in Arabor."

"Is she still with Hussein ? Do you know what she called the baby? Have you got her address ....?!"

"I have no other information," he repeated, "except that the baby is called Mustafa and she lives with a large Algerian family. Sorry."

"Thank you for bringing me this message," I clasped his hand in both mine, "it means a lot to me ...."

He made an awkward little bowing movement and left.

Apart from that we had no news of her at all ………….. Till one day, almost four years later, she phoned me from the Hotel Bois d'Amour.

**

Epilogue by Debbie.

Hussein became extremely possessive after the birth of Jasmina. In fact, he changed completely. He was totally devoted to Jasmina and, later, to Mus, but as time went by our relationship deteriorated. He became aggressive towards me and exceptionally protective of his children – to the point where he suggested I was bad for them.

He argued a great deal with his mother. She, his dad, and *Grand'mere* were all besotted by the children, but they didn't want me there. I was an irritating non-Muslim foreigner in their household. They wanted him to return to his wife and son in Algeria.   I, in turn, did everything I could to make things work and, had it not been for his family I think we'd have got a flat together and things may have worked out. I begged him to allow me this and I think a part of him would have preferred it too. But he remained absolutely adamant that I must break all contact with my own family.   They represented everything he and his family were not – educated, well-heeled, modern and not Muslim.

He said he would kill me if I tried to leave him. On several occasions he flashed a knife in my face. He had a gun. It was a pride thing. He didn't want me, but didn't want me to leave. He said that if he suspected any kind of contact with my family he'd set Les Cypres on fire, slash tyres, even injure my brothers. He was perfectly capable of it when in a bad mood.

As is often the way with a foreign language I could understand a great deal more Arabic than I could speak.   As the months drifted on I was more and more silent – they didn't want me to speak anyway – but I picked up Arabic.

And one day I therefore learnt that the house in Algeria was at last ready and that they would return as soon as possible. By now I was four years older and four years wiser and there was no question of my going to live there. As I listened, I learnt that they had no intention of taking me, but would take the children. When I discovered that Hussein had got passports for the children, naively hidden under our mattress – I left.

I live in the West County and am happy. Jasmina and Mus are now aged eleven and twelve and I think anybody would agree they are wholesome and contented children My parents, who now live partly in France and partly in England, are big features in our lives, as indeed are my two brothers.

And Hussein ? Well, I have no idea. Despite all his macho rantings, all his threats, and all his devotion to his children, neither he nor his family made any attempt at all to contact me. I suppose they all returned to Algeria. I never saw any of them again.

THE END

A Call From France

We asked the author 10 questions.

For many thousands of British people, moving to France to live is a dream. Yet you seemed to have been very unhappy there at first ?

Yes, I was. It was loneliness quite simply. I'm a girl's girl; I like the company of other women. But in France there does not appear to be that same "conspiracy of womanhood" that one finds with most women. My best friend here in France is from Mexico. Bear in mind I've been here over 20 years and am an easy-going chatty kind of person – yet I have never established a serious, chummy relationship with a French woman.

You have homes in Sussex and Belize as well as France. Which would you say is the better country to live in ?

I am essentially English and always will be, and England is my home. France is very comfortable and bang-up-to-date (though it certainly was not in 1989 when we first came here - in fact it was very backwards compared to the UK!) and Belize has the warm Caribbean sea ….. so I cannot say, I truly cannot, though I have come to love France and I think we will grow old here.

What advice would you give to the mothers of teenagers – sons or daughters ?

I wouldn't give any!   There is no recipe. All parents do what they think is the best thing at that particular moment. That is all any parent can do, even if it turns out to be totally the wrong thing.

You already spoke French when you arrived. That must have been a massive advantage ?

In many ways, yes. But it also meant that I had to deal with everything – if the phone rang, if somebody knocked on the door, helping with homework, talking to the bank – anything and everything fell on my shoulders.   It was exhausting.

Do you believe in God ?

Yes and no. I don't want to get in to a
theological discussion, but let's just say that I
believe in God but that I do not believe he is
necessarily in the image that Christians – or
Jews, Buddhists, whatever – have decided on. It
is beyond us.

When did you write your first book ?

When I was seven!   I have still got it. It is
called The Wood in Fairyland and my father
encouraged me to write it.

*Your book "French Sand" is based on a true
event in the South Pacific. Do your other books
have elements of true events in them ?*

I think most writers base their novels on
something they know about and have
experienced. My book "Saying Nothing" is set
in Spain, where I lived for three years, but that's
as far as the truth of it goes.

*Your book "The Man With Green Fingers" must
have demanded a great deal of research ?   And
have you also lived in Cyprus ?*

A Call From France

We went property-hunting in Cyprus, both north and south, several times, so I have spent quite a lot of time there but not actually lived there. Yes, the book did require a lot of research because the main character, Stella, is a very complex person with a psychiatric condition that needed careful handling.

What are your favourite things ?

Apart from my husband and children you mean ? I have loads of favourite things – snuggling in to bed at the end of the day, tea in the morning, red wine, Rupert Brooke, sunny days, the sound of rain on a tent, my friends, walking on the beach ….. I love to travel, I enjoy sketching, I like interior decorating and design. I am involved in several charities, and that is very satisfying too.

Have you any tips for new writers ?

If you are writing about somebody famous who you know well, it is vastly easier, or if you have a specialist subject, but otherwise writing is a stunningly difficult market to get in to. Writing the book is the easy part. Persuading an agent to read the first few chapters is almost impossible, let alone the whole manuscript ….. and that is before a publisher even begins to enter the equation. You have to be very tough, very resilient, prepared to take a lot of rejection …. And ready to persevere no matter what.

****

CPSIA information can be obtained at www.ICGtesting.com
Printed in the USA
LVOW081546110712

289684LV00011B/2/P